THE COMING

THE COMING

Michael Rigg & John Alexander

Majestic Books Ltd.

This edition published in Great Britain in 2003 by Majestic Books
Ltd., PO Box 3106, South Croydon, CR2 8WA

A catalogue record for this book is available from the British
Library.

ISBN: 0-9543445-0-2\

Fiction/Thriller – Any similarity to actual persons, living or dead,
is purely coincidental.

Front cover designed by a-creative-experience.com
Printed in Great Britain by Mackays of Chatham.

Contents

Prologue

PROLOGUE

Qumran Region, Dead Sea, Palestine
March 1947

Jum'a the goatherd boy climbed higher up the hill to find a place where he could survey all of his flock. The slope was rough, almost bare rock and dirt, dotted sparsely with tufts of weeds. Stones slid under his feet as he clambered up, sending up puffs of dust. Fifty feet up, he took a run against a tumbling scree of rocky gravel, his feet pedalling for a few moments before he finally made the ledge he'd spied from the ground. He sat down, breathing hard, leaning against the rock wall and closing his eyes against the sunlight. At this height there was a faint wind coming from the sea, which brought slight relief from the afternoon heat.

After a few minutes he sat up, shielded his eyes and gazed down. The land stretched a mile or so from the cliffs before reaching the Dead Sea. Left and right, as far as his eyes could see, there was only brown baked earth and rock, dotted with green squares where farmers irrigated their fields. Directly below he saw his younger brother Mohammed in the midst of the flock of goats, all sixty of which were spread for hundreds of yards, chasing patches of scrub. He could hear their bells and occasional bleats, rising and falling in the breeze. He memorised the distant positions of some of the stragglers who had strayed away further than the main group.

He sat down and rested, grateful to be out of sight of his tiresome brother.

As usual his mind wandered after a few minutes and he threw small pebbles to relieve the monotony.

There was a smallish hole in the hillside a little higher up, and after several attempts a pebble disappeared inside. He threw another in. This time, he heard a strange, distinct 'clunk'. He scrambled up higher, and stepped onto another small ledge, crouching down to look into the hole. There was a cave beyond the small entrance, but little light penetrated inside. He could barely make out some dim, small shapes. He tried to squeeze inside but his shoulders were too wide. He threw another stone. This time he heard two sharp noises. There was more than one object in here, definitely something other than rocks or stones.

He stood up, cupping his hands to his mouth to call to his younger brother.

"Mohammed! Mohammed! Come here quickly. I have found treasure!"

Minutes later Jum'a was pushing his little brother by the legs until he disappeared inside the hole.

"What can you see?" asked Jum'a impatiently.

Mohammed felt all around himself, his eyes slowly adjusting from being in the bright sunlight. As far as he could make out, the cave was about ten feet across. Cautiously touching the walls, he felt that they were rocky in some places, crumbly earth in others.

"There are some things on the floor of the cave," he shouted out to his brother, squinting his eyes to make out the form of various humps in the dust of the cave floor. He bent down; something small suddenly shot away from him to the back of the cave.

"Ah!" he cried out.

"What is it?" asked Jum'a.

Mohammed caught his breath. "Only a mouse."

"What are the things in there?" shouted Jum'a impatiently.

Cautiously once again, Mohammed touched the objects around him. Some were heavy and solid – rocks and smooth stones. Others felt hollow and light.

"They are pots! Pots and vases," shouted Mohammed.

"Look inside them!" called his brother.

Mohammed tentatively reached inside – he didn't want to discover a sleeping scorpion hiding within.

"It's just paper." He tried another earthenware pot. "Just old paper. It's useless."

Mohammed squeezed back out of the hole, covered in dust. He carried a small scrap of parchment in his hand.

Jum'a snatched it from him. It was covered in faded, black characters, and obviously torn across one corner. They meant nothing to him. The writing looked nothing like the words in the magazines that the village doctor would read to the boys from time to time.

"There's a cave in there. Lots more pots, but no treasure," said Mohammed, laughing mockingly at his brother.

"Get back to work!" shouted Jum'a. "I will tell father about this tonight."

3 Months Later

Qumran Region, Dead Sea, Palestine
June 1947

"Hello? O'Brien?" The older man shouted down from the ledge above to the slight figure below him.

Having climbed half way up the steep slope, Michael O'Brien felt a little dizzy, and had been immersed in the view down to the sea. He snapped to attention and looked upward.

"Oh, yes!" he replied. "Is it OK if I come all the way up?"

The man above gestured positively to him. "Of course! We've been expecting you!"

O'Brien clambered up to stand on the rock ledge. He stood, out of breath, sweating in his dark jacket, already half white with dust, and wiped his pale brow with a stained handkerchief.

The older man was Arabic looking, smiling through a deeply lined, heavily tanned face. He wore a boiler suit, also covered with dust. He transferred a small trowel from one hand to the other before offering to shake O'Brien's.

"I am Mazal Sharif. From the Museum of Cairo. Welcome. How was your journey?"

"Well, er, not so bad," O'Brien replied, and then smiled himself.

"It's not so easy to get into this area, is it?" Sharif said.

O'Brien shook his head. "That it is not. This is the British sector of Palestine, isn't it? I never thought there would be so many officials asking questions."

Sharif nodded knowingly. "The war has ended, but this is still a dangerous country. Nevertheless..." He let go of O'Brien's hand and waved around at the surrounding scenery. "It is safe around here at least! Nothing of what we are digging here is of the slightest interest to those damned politicians!"

O'Brien looked up, shielding his blue eyes from the fierce sunlight. It was much hotter here than he had imagined when, months ago, the Vatican's request for his mission had come to him from the Bishop in Dublin. He pictured many weeks exposed to this burning heat, without shade, and felt dizziness once more, making him sway on his feet.

"Easy, my friend," Sharif laid a steadying hand on his shoulder. "You are new here. You will get used to it. Come; the caves will wait. Let us go down to the camp. We will sit in some shade and have something cool to drink."

"These are what we have found so far." Sharif and O'Brien looked along the trestle table, which was sheltered under a long canvas awning. There were lines of parchments, carefully arranged like an incomplete jigsaw. Each was covered with written characters. Many were torn. A few yards away in the encampment, O'Brien could see further tent coverings, with earthenware pots and pottery shards laid on more tables. Another person much like Sharif, a quiet, bespectacled man called Mahal, sat at one of these, brushing and examining the remains. Out in the open several men, probably locals, crouched around cooking utensils and a tea urn, smoking and chatting quietly in Arabic. Apart from the occasional workings of Mahal, the porters' whispering, and the occasional gentle breeze flowing through the open tents, everything was silent.

O'Brien went to examine one of the papers more closely. Sharif laid a hand on his arm.

"As I have said Michael, you are welcome, but I am a little puzzled. I hear you are a very promising young archaeologist. But how do you come to be here? You are sent by the Vatican, is that not so?"

O'Brien shrugged his shoulders. "Apparently so, yes." He nodded. "But I'm afraid I can't give you much of an explanation. I've never even been to the Vatican. I received the summons from the Bishop at home. In Ireland, I mean."

Sharif furrowed his brows. "How can a man so young be a priest and an archaeologist at the same time? Are you looking to find your God amongst these relics?"

O'Brien felt suddenly stupid, like a boy trying to talk with sophistication in front of the school headmaster.

"Ah. Well..." said O'Brien, hesitantly. "I'm sorry – it must be confusing. I suppose I always wanted to be a priest when I was a boy and I followed my calling. But then I discovered archaeology, did some studies and – well here I am. I suppose the Catholic Church has more need of scientists than priests at the moment. That suits me, of course."

Sharif was nodding, still looking serious.

"Hmm. The Catholic Church," Sharif said, "I can see how they would have an interest here, of course. But there is another development that I do not understand – apparently my department has received a request to send all of these parchments directly to Rome for translation. They have made some arrangements without telling me. For money, I suppose. Do you know of this?"

O'Brien started to speak and then stopped, trying to phrase his words diplomatically. He blushed, and then held up his hands as if to reinforce his ignorance.

"Well, I promise you I haven't had any instructions like that. But…" He looked up at Sharif's accusing face once more. "Look, your people have looked over the first one or two of these documents, haven't they?"

Sharif was impassive for a few moments and then gave a grudging nod.

"Well," O'Brien continued, "you already know that the dialect suggests that these things are probably first century A.D. Also, the word 'Jesus' occurs several times in the text."

Sharif raised his eyebrows. "So?"

"Well, not to put too fine a point on it, these documents could well be older than the gospels."

The two men looked at each other in silence for a few seconds.

Sharif smiled. "What if these accounts say things you don't like? Perhaps they will contradict your precious Bible! It could be the end of your religion!"

O'Brien shrugged his shoulders. "So you can see why the Vatican is, let's say 'interested'. I've been told there is quite an urgency to resolve these matters."

"For good or bad, eh?" Sharif smiled again.

"Well, I'm afraid that's about all I know." O'Brien held up his palms. "Nobody has given me any more explanations. They just asked me to come here and, well, help out a bit. I have done some local digging work back at home." He saw Sharif's eyebrows rise again. "Oh – and of course I've studied the ancient Middle East. The standard works, anyway."

There was a nervous silence for a few moments. Then Sharif's face brightened again into a resigned smile. He placed a hand on O'Brien's narrow shoulders.

"Of course my friend. I am sorry. Tell me, how old are you?"

O'Brien blushed again. "Well, I…well twenty two actually. Next month."

Sharif nodded. "I am more than twice your age and yet even now I have no more understanding of the wheels of power than you do. I just like to do research. I get the feeling that you do, too. Perhaps we will work well together?"

O'Brien relaxed, and nodded with relief.

"Come, finish your lemonade. Let us find you something less expensive than an English – sorry, an Irish clergyman's clothes, and we will look into the caves! OK?"

**56 years later
Jackson County Hospital, Texas
January 4th 2003**

"Mister Wilson?" The nurse's voice was calm and low. "Doctor Kalowski will see you now."

Myron Wilson got to his feet, still somewhat annoyed at being kept waiting for three minutes.

"Thank you ma'am, I know the way."

This was his third visit in two months and the thought crossed his mind that it could quite possibly be his last. He walked to the end of the corridor. In this most expensive clinic, the walls were smooth and white. Tasteful art prints arranged perfectly showed a designer's touch. Thick carpet exaggerated the near-silence and fresh flowers in Tuscan pots glistened with recent water.

Wilson felt fine, apart from a slight cough. He paused briefly at the door marked Robert Kalowski and strode purposefully in without knocking.

The office resembled a comfortable living room, excepting the Doctor's desk and a discreet examination couch. Kalowski was dressed in an immaculate business suit. He had perfectly smooth black hair and a deep tan. Wilson thought he bore too much of a resemblance to an tax lawyer to be a medical man. He got to his feet and stretched out a hand to Wilson.

"Good to see you again Myron."

"And you Bob. How's business with you?"

Kalowski smiled as he shook hands.

"Fine, Myron. Very good. Now have a seat. Can I get you something? A coffee or a cold drink?"

Wilson shook his head. "No thank you. Let's get started shall we?"

Kalowski paused for a few moments, then opened the file in front of him and spread three x-rays on his desk.

"OK. We have your recent x-ray prints here and I'd like to take you through them."

Wilson leaned forward in his chair.

"Bob, you have known me for over twenty five years. Just cut the crap and tell me yes or no."

The doctor sighed and then smiled gently at Wilson.

"I guess you'll never change Myron! It's bad news my friend. The cancer is spreading through your body."

Wilson showed no sign of surprise, no emotion at all. Just a gentle nod. His whole life he'd been a man of power and to show anybody else exactly what he was feeling was a terrible weakness.

"Just how long do I have left Bob?"

Kalowski held up his hands and pursed his lips. "Myron, you know these things are never really easy to say. My opinion? Six months, eight at the most. But, well, some people who've been given such a short time have survived for several years.

But…whatever, I'm afraid it ain't going to go away, I'm very sorry…."

"Spare me the bullshit," Wilson interrupted. "I am not finished yet. I intend to fight this thing. What could you do with more surgery?"

Dr. Kalowski pinned the x-rays onto the brightly lit board and pointed to the lungs.

"This is what is left of your right lung. As you can see there is a secondary shadow appearing just here."

Wilson nodded again without emotion.

"Also, the tumour on your left lung is growing and spreading. We can't take this away Myron or you would stop breathing."

"Goddam useless body!" shouted Wilson. "Why is it doing this to me? Goddammit I gave up smoking five years ago!"

Kalowski smiled ruefully. "Yep and that probably kept you going for this long. But what can I say? How long did you smoke? Forty years? Some people smoke all their lives and never get sick. Others…well – there is no further clinical intervention that'll make a difference, I'm afraid. You have to try to accept this."

"So how do you usually advise your dying patients to do that?" said Wilson sarcastically.

"You want my advice?" Kalowski looked rather hopefully at Wilson. "Stop work. Enjoy some relaxation. Enjoy your family. Make peace with God – whatever. And enjoy your last days as well as you can."

Wilson's eyes flicked to the ceiling. "My family? Three wives, eight kids, all of 'em wasters, keep tellin' me how much money they need." He shook his head.

"Bob, after twenty five years you still don't know me, do you? I will fight this thing. If God is my last hope, then it's to God that I will turn."

Dr. Kalowski looked surprised.

"Well, good. I am glad to hear that Myron. Many people find comfort in the Church. Talk things through with the pastor."

"No you don't understand," Wilson smiled, for the first time. "I've been preparing for this day. I got bigger plans than you can imagine. I'm going to get closer to God than anybody has ever done. I'm going to touch me something that belonged to Jesus Christ himself. Maybe get hold of the Ark of the Covenant or maybe the Holy Grail. Perhaps God's power that is in these things will cure me. I'm gonna offer God something that he cannot refuse."

Kalowski looked open-mouthed. For several moments he was lost for words. He shook his head gently.

"Myron, I er, don't quite know what to say. You know more about these things than me. But I have to say that this sounds like, well, a fairly normal reaction. I understand you're angry, who wouldn't be? You need to go away and think about things for a while. Come see me in a couple of weeks. Keep your feet on the ground. I urge you Myron, don't run away with these impossible ideas. Make your peace with the world. Don't add any more stress at this time. It'll only hasten the inevitable."

Wilson got to his feet with a new confidence.

"You underestimate me, Doctor."

He took a deep breath, straightened his suit and opened the door to leave.

"I have contacts."

Dallas University Chapel
February 2nd 2003

Myron Wilson walked down the centre aisle of the deserted chapel, the clicks from his cowboy boots echoing around the tall arched ceiling. He had not been here for fifteen years, yet everything looked exactly as he recalled it. The high walls were 1900 brick; the windows' stained glass was bright and fresh. On his left stood the massive 1935 Vandervelt organ fascia, rank upon rank of pipes, a great crown of carving straddling the top of it like a proscenium theatre arch.

Wilson shook his head slightly and smiled to himself. One of his earliest business triumphs had been the toppling of Josiah Vandervelt's oil empire, back in the 1950s.

He looked up to the much newer ceiling, a magnificently crafted replacement to the chapel's crumbling original. It was rebuilt in steel, with shining white plaster, framed by gold-leaf beams on the inside; clean, new and pure, he thought. It had been a good move on his part, back in '86. He had donated $250,000 to the church restoration fund. It had greatly raised his standing in the Dallas community, got him on TV. Almost certainly it had swung the state government in his favour over a huge land deal in '87.

"Mister Wilson!" His reverie was interrupted by a shout from the far end of the aisle. He looked up to see a man standing by the altar, who then walked towards him energetically.

The man was about forty-five, grey haired, with a priest's tunic and dog collar. He wore a crumpled black suit and carried a battered briefcase. He took Wilson's hand and shook it vigorously. "It is indeed a pleasure to welcome you back here, sir."

Father Tom Gresham raised his head to the ceiling. "Great job wasn't it?" he said gushingly, "you're a true friend to this college. It seems so long since you visited."

Wilson smiled and nodded slightly at Gresham. "Seems you haven't done so badly yourself Tom. Head of Theology Faculty now, eh?"

The younger man lowered his eyes, a little embarrassed.

"Well, yes. What can I say? A lifetime's ambition. But without the grants you've given to the University, I don't know…"

Wilson waved away his praise.

"Ah, you know it was my pleasure. You were the best man for the job. But now," Wilson's face became much more serious, "to the reason I'm here. As you know I gave you a call last week. What have you got?"

The priest nodded and motioned them towards an office just off the nave. The room was starkly business-like in comparison to the chapel. They both sat down at the bare, functional desk and the priest opened his case and drew out a notebook.

"OK, where to begin?" he paused for a moment, scanned his writings. "You asked who were the people in charge of archaeology research at the Vatican? Well, I've been working on a cross-denomination committee with a Catholic Bishop from Albuquerque and he says that it's the 'antiquities committee'. The guy in charge is a man called Cardinal Carlo Vanutti.

"Vanutti," echoed Wilson. "OK."

"But this Bishop says to be careful of him," continued Gresham. "Apparently he's got quite a reputation with the Catholics. My friend described him in various ways…'bastard' was the kindest thing he said. Anyway, he told me there's another man there, Gianni Coppella. He said that he's a good man, really useful, although I am not sure of his exact role in the antiquities area."

Wilson took a sheet of the notepad from Gresham, folded it and tucked it into his jacket pocket.

"Good. Now, what about my other enquiries?" said Wilson quietly.

The priest looked quizzically at Wilson. "I must admit I'm a little surprised at your line of inquiry. It's somewhat of an unusual request."

Wilson remained impassive. "I have my reasons Tom. Tell me what you've got."

Gresham shook his head. "Well, I wish I knew more facts than I do. As you know, there are so many conspiracy theories, rumours and speculations surrounding the Vatican, it's difficult to come to any conclusions. If people want to believe in something real bad, then it becomes true, you know?"

Wilson held up his finger. "I know you, Tom. You're a level-headed guy. Now tell me. Be totally honest. What do you think is actually true?"

Gresham drew in a breath and thought for a while before responding.

"We've got some pretty good history guys in the faculty," he said at last. Also some great researchers. I've talked to pretty near all of them, as well as reaching my own conclusions. OK, here it is, top of the list are the things we are almost one hundred per cent on, then they get sketchier as you go down." He held up his left hand and counted on his fingers.

"One. The Dead Sea scrolls. Almost certainly there's more to those than is in the public domain.

Two. The Vatican has had an archaeology team working in the Middle East continuously since the

Second World War. Whatever they find, they keep it to themselves."

"Doesn't anyone else do archaeology there?" said Wilson, slightly incredulous.

"Absolutely. There have been hundreds of digs. The British, French, Israelis. Many US universities. Of course they've dug at hundreds of temples, Roman buildings, ancient towns and so on. But the artefacts identified in the scrolls? Nothing has been found. Ohio are probably the best biblical archaeology group in this country and even they have found precious little of any significance."

"Why?" asked Wilson.

"Well, that's number three," Gresham continued. "We think that the Vatican may have something that nobody else has."

Wilson raised his eyebrows in expectancy.

Gresham leaned closer. "Some of the missing parts of the scrolls. They say they were always lost, but somehow we don't quite trust them."

Wilson nodded, digesting the information. "Anything else?"

Gresham lowered his voice. "Yes. But remember that the further you go down this list, the less sure we are."

"OK Tom," Wilson held up his palms and nodded again, "I understand. What is it?"

"Well," Gresham continued. "Number four, we think there is something very important hidden in the Vatican. Hasn't been for long. Ten, twenty, thirty years? We don't know. But there have been rumours. Stories from Rome about a discovery. Staff who have asked too many questions – they've been moved a long way away, distant postings. Big security."

"What sort of thing is it?" whispered Wilson, his eyes wide.

"Ah. Now there's a question. We know the Ark of the Covenant actually existed. Then there's the vessel that took some of Christ's blood at his Crucifixion…that's a bit more symbolic, but there's no actual reason why it couldn't be real…"

"The Holy Grail?" said Wilson.

"Yes. Or a piece of the Cross. Or the real shroud. Christ had a lot of followers when he died. Anything could've been taken, kept and passed down the years. It's highly unlikely, but…well, you never know." Gresham looked up and smiled.

Wilson nodded, his eyes distant. "Thank you Tom," he came sharply back to focus. "That's what I needed."

Gresham looked puzzled. "OK. I'm delighted to be of any help. But I'm still not clear how I've done so?"

"I'm gonna try to find the truth. To find out what they've really got at the Vatican." Wilson said.

Gresham's eyes opened a little wider. "You're going there?"

"Yep," said Wilson, smiling and looking at his watch. "My private jet should be ready to take off in about four hours from now."

The priest didn't quite know what to say. "Well, I wish you luck. I'm afraid it sounds a very great challenge. Nobody's got anything new out of the Vatican for years, probably because of this Vanutti guy. Is this so very important to you?"

Wilson began striding away towards the two large oak doors. He turned as was leaving the church, speaking in a loud voice. "You could say that it's a matter of life and death." His voice echoed and reverberated around the high ceiling.

St. Mark's Vicarage, Godalming, Surrey
September 25th, 2003

The Reverend Graham Woodbridge gazed out of his study window. His pen rested idly in his hand. He was trying to finish writing his sermon for the coming Sunday service, but the afternoon sun was just sinking behind the vicarage, throwing brilliant light onto the gold and red of the leaves in his garden orchard, and the oak and plane trees that climbed away to the fields and hills beyond. He loved this time of year. Harvest festival had just passed. Christmas would be here all too quickly, and at least then the local people would flock into his usually empty church.

He turned his head to look at the photograph of his wife, Edith. This had been her favourite time of year too. He sighed as he looked back towards the trees and imagined her there with a basket picking up fallen apples. As usual his eyes began to fill with tears, even though it had been over six years since she'd died. He fought back his anger again. She had told him not to be bitter, but to celebrate the life they'd had, and to stay close to their son, help him cope. He wished he'd had her strength. For all his faith and knowledge he could not help but think how unfair it was. He'd given forty years of his life to the Church only to be rewarded by having her plucked away so suddenly.

He sighed and closed his eyes, listening to the rhythmic ticking of the clock in the corner of the room. Sometimes it seemed that this was all he had now. Old books, the faded wooden panelling, the slow passing of time. He sighed again and looked down at the notes he'd been making.

He jumped at the sound of his telephone ringing.

"Hello? Reverend Woodbridge speaking."

Upstairs, David was engrossed in two huge books that lay open on his bed. Handwritten notes were scattered seemingly at random all over the room.

He heard the phone ring downstairs. He smiled and shook his head gently. Only Dad would still have one of those old bell-ring dial phones. He listened to the sound of his father's voice. The caller was probably a parishioner inviting him round to tea.

He always had mixed feelings about coming home. He loved the atmosphere of his father's study, with its library shelves and map prints on the walls. Dad had kept many old textbooks from his youth, Greek translations, bible study texts, and many other reference works. Exploring these had fired him with enthusiasm for language and history. That was the start of the drift away from all of the other features of life here. As a young teenager, he'd been a committed Christian. His mother had dearly wanted him to go into the Church, but by the time he was seventeen, his faith was fading. He knew his future lay in another direction. He'd always worried about how he'd tell his mother, but she had died suddenly from breast cancer before he'd had to face that confrontation. When David won his place at Cambridge, his father didn't seem to mind; perhaps in his grief he preferred David out of the way?

At university he found a fantastic outlet for his passion for language. The huge library was a joy, with thousands of old scrolls and texts. Gradually he became more and more obsessed with Middle-Eastern history and the translation of obscure and fragmented documents. He had sailed through his degree and by the age of twenty four had just completed his PhD. The work he'd done on an aspect of the Dead Sea Scrolls had led to an offer of a paid research post in the college.

He looked up over his spectacles .at the clock on the wall. It was nearly time for afternoon tea. There was silence downstairs, so David closed his book and went in search of his father.

He opened the door and approached the grey haired man, silhouetted by the window, scribbling at his desk.

"Dad?"

His father turned around quickly.

"Oh David. I didn't know you were in. There was a telephone call for you. A very strange one."

"Who was it?" David replied.

"It was a University in America." His father smiled, with a mixture of surprise and pride. "They have heard about you, apparently!" He looked down at his desk and found a piece of notepaper. "Here I have written down the details. Apparently they want you to do some sort of project. I asked them what it was but they wouldn't tell me anything."

David took the note.

"State University, Columbus Ohio. Which department?"

His father shook his head. "He didn't say. You can see he left a telephone number. He said it was a direct line. Whoever it was seemed very insistent that I wrote it down carefully!"

"Can I call them Dad? It's long distance – I could wait until this evening?"

His father smiled and nodded. "Yes of course. Do it now. It certainly sounds important. You sit here, I'll go and make some tea."

The vicar left the room, the floorboards creaking as he walked away down the hall towards the kitchen. David sat down and carefully dialled the long number.

"Andrews," a flat, American voice said.

"Hello? This is David Woodbridge. Somebody just called me?"

"Oh hi David!" The voice suddenly jumped in enthusiasm. "This is Keith Andrews from Columbus. I'm professor of Antiquities here."

"Right. Well, I..." David stumbled with his words. "I know you by reputation of course. I've read many of your papers! Standard reading at Cambridge! I..."

Andrews interrupted.

"Well it's nice to know that someone appreciates me! But, let me tell you why I called. I have – let's say a project – that may be of interest to you. We would like you to come and work with us for a while. Something related to the Copper Scroll. You've studied that in detail, haven't you?"

David furrowed his brows. "Well, yes of course. But what is there to do? All the scroll fragments have been thoroughly investigated, haven't they? Unless someone's dug up another one!" David joked.

Andrews drew in a breath, hesitating. "Well...no, not exactly. Listen David, we really need to talk to you face to face. This project is absolutely secret. We need you over here."

"Me? Er, this is kind of a shock, Professor. Can I ask why you've chosen me in particular?"

"Well David, you have been recommended by your Professor McCloud at Cambridge. He says you're the best man. Didn't you alter the meaning of a whole passage of one of the Scrolls last year?"

"I did, yes," David replied. "More luck than judgement maybe!"

"Don't be modest," said Andrews. "I read your paper. It was good, very good. Now let me get to the point. We've got – how can I put this – a very substantial grant for this work. But we need to proceed with it urgently. So I need to put a team together quickly. I'd like you to fly out here tomorrow."

David was lost for words. "Tomorrow?! Well I…"

"Listen David," Andrews interrupted again, " I know this is a ridiculous sounding schedule, but I promise you'll see why when you get here. I can easily sort things out with Fred McCloud. You won't lose your post at Cambridge. What do you say?"

David sat in silence for a moment. He could hear his father pottering in the kitchen, and the distant voices of birds in the garden. But his mind was racing.

"Well, I don't know how I could arrange to get to you," he replied. "Is it possible to do things like this in such a short time?"

Andrews laughed. "I'm afraid I've already taken the liberty of reserving a plane ticket for you. Two thirty out of Heathrow; Club class, taxi pick-up from your home. Oh, and there's one other thing. You'll be acting as a special consultant to my department while you're here. We think it could be for about three months. So we'll get you an apartment here, and we'll pay you a fee of forty thousand dollars. More if you have to stay longer. How does that sound?"

"Did you say forty thou… what?" David was stunned. No university he knew would have anything like that amount of money available to pay research staff. Even if it did, it wouldn't pay it.

David stood with his mouth open for several moments before responding. "That's incredible.

Look, what is this all about? What do you have there?"

Andrews paused.

"David, I have one of the most important discoveries of the last two thousand years."

56 years earlier

Qumran Region, Dead Sea, Palestine
June 1947

Beyond the entrance to the cave, which had been opened out, there were three chambers, each about twelve feet across and connected by a hole large enough to climb through. These were natural caves, perhaps further hewn a little by those who had concealed all the pots here. There was no decoration or workmanship. The walls were rough rock and earth, dry and crumbly.

O'Brien and Sharif had continued to dig for two weeks, straining to see by the hurricane lamps that had been hung from the ceiling in each chamber and by electric torch light for close work. Grids of string stretched across the cave floors, marking the areas still to be worked on. Gradually they had removed layers of the earth floor until they had reached almost two feet down across most of the floor surface.

They had found two further buried pots since they'd started and that was in the first few days. Since then, nothing had been unearthed.

"Perhaps if we just finish digging all of the grids?" said O'Brien. "We should really go right to the edge of the caves."

They sat beside the entrance hole, glad for the sunlight after hours of painstaking work.

Sharif rubbed dust from his eyes and shook his head, holding his palms up.

"Michael, we have found everything. All of the pots were in the centre of the caves. It's clear how the Qumranis buried them. I think it's time to go home. Come on. Let's go down and make our plans for packing everything."

O'Brien sat in tired contemplation for a few moments, then half nodded in agreement.

There was a small noise behind them. One of the small mice that lived in the caves ran to the back of the chamber, disappearing into a tiny hole. O'Brien stared after it for a while, then got up to examine the back wall, poking around the mouse hole.

Sharif spoke half jokingly, half impatiently. "Come on my friend. Has this place driven you to madness? Perhaps you hope to find a small cache of nuts that the mouse has hidden?!"

O'Brien was stroking his hands across the surface of the rock formations at the rear of the entrance cave. There were several adjacent rocks, unusually smooth, each about two feet in height, at the base of the wall.

"I know, Mazal," the young priest said apologetically, "It's just something I thought…"

O'Brien bent down as low as he could. "I wonder?" he said, as he prodded around with his hand spade. "Hmm. Look, the earth between these two stones is softer, newer than the wall around it."

Earth began to fall away from the join between the slabs. He wedged one hand into the gap. It pushed right through into empty space.

"Holy Mother of…" he said loudly, and turned his hand to grip one of the rocks from behind. He pulled hard, and it fell towards him, thumping onto the ground, raising a small cloud of dust. In its place was a small entrance, just big enough to squeeze his head and shoulders into. Crouching down, he tried to look inside. Total blackness. Then he stood up and lunged back out into the open air. Sharif was crouching down excitedly.

"Allah take my tongue! What have you found? What's there?"

After moving the two smooth stones, O'Brien was able to squeeze through into a much smaller chamber.

"What is inside?" called Sharif.

"I'm not sure yet," O'Brien replied. "Perhaps it's a tomb? I'll have a feel around. Can you shine your torch in through the hole please?"

He felt around the walls in the darkness. The space was about six feet across. Clods of earth and stones fell from the roof as his hand brushed along it. Ovals of light played across the floor as Sharif waved his torch through the entrance. Suddenly there was a tiny glint from the earth floor.

"Hold it!" said O'Brien. "Back a bit with the light. No, where you were a second ago. There!"

The young man crouched down. He gently prodded the soft earth and felt a hard, curved shape. A small jagged edge protruded, sharp to the touch.

"What have you found?" called Sharif, stretching his neck down to peer into the entrance. "Another pot? What is that reflecting the light?"

O'Brien carefully scraped earth from around the object with his trowel.

"I just can't see yet," he said. "It's a small vase I think. But it's a very odd shape. Cylindrical. Made of metal. Just let me clear a little more of the dirt – damn!"

More clods of earth had started to fall from the roof. A stone the size of a fist thumped down onto the floor two feet away from him.

"Michael! The roof will fall! Come on!" called Sharif.

"Just one moment – I can get it!" shouted O'Brien. "Keep the light steady – ouch! – there!"

His hand emerged from the hole, holding the object for Sharif to take. Then his head and shoulders emerged, Sharif pulling him out by the arms.

Out in the sunshine the two men stared at the object on the table, as Mahal gently brushed dirt from it. He was shaking his head. "I have never seen anything like this. These people did not have metal pots of that shape."

"What is that? There. All down one side of it." Sharif pointed "A dark line. Perhaps some decoration?"

O'Brien ran along it with his finger. He looked up at the other two men, puzzled, then moved his head close up to the earth-encrusted cylinder. Very gently he pushed his fingernail into the line of dirt. "Well well. Will you look at that!"

"What?" said Sharif and Mahal, almost together, as they all pushed their heads close to squint at the object.

"This is an edge. This thing is like… a rolled up carpet. Here, if I'm careful I can unroll it a little."

O'Brien pushed two fingernails under the rolled edge as Mahal held the ends. He managed to pull the edge open, about an inch, before the stiffness of the metal stopped it. On the other side of him, Sharif's eyes opened wide, and he drew in breath.

"What? What did you see?" said O'Brien, as he let go of the edge, and the roll snapped shut again.

Sharif looked up at them. "It's full of writing. It's a scroll. A wonderful scroll."

A breeze wafted in from the sea, gently blowing the canvas roof, fluttering the papers on the tables. The three stood and smiled to each other in the silence.

Vatican City, Rome
July 1947

Father Michael O'Brien nervously approached the large, ornate wooden doors that led to the Cardinal's office. Since he'd arrived, he'd been astonished by the mazes of sumptuous corridors, galleries of treasures and the lavishly robed Catholic clerics roaming everywhere. He stopped to look up at the ceiling, probably twenty feet above. It was a latticework of carved decoration, gold leaf covered wood frames, interspersed with painted scenes.

There were a few minutes before his appointment so he walked over to a high window that looked out over one of the inner courts. He could see two bishops chatting within the stone cloisters. In the grassed court, a workman stooped over one of the many statues, trimming the growth around its base.

He looked around the upper levels of the encircling buildings. Everything seemed tranquil, undisturbed. It seemed that neither Mussolini nor the Germans had made any impact here.

He recalled the peasant farmers of his own hometown, some twenty miles from Dublin. What would they make of the splendours here? They lived in rough cottages, patched with mud and rags. Forever poor, the aftermath of the war had made their life even harder.

He looked at his watch. Nearly time.

His urgent summons to Italy had interrupted the final activities at the dig. But a meeting with one of the Vatican's senior officials had been ordered and O'Brien had had no choice in the matter.

He knocked hesitantly. "Enter," said a stern voice.

O'Brien walked into an old room full of antique furniture, rather dark, although the sun streamed in from one of the windows.

The Cardinal sat behind his desk, looking down at what he was writing. He did not look up as O'Brien entered.

"Please sit down."

O'Brien fidgeted in his seat for a while, looking around the rows of huge, dusty books on the Cardinal's shelves.

Cardinal Celliani, head of the Vatican antiquities committee, looked up and gazed intently at O'Brien from beneath grey bushy eyebrows.

"I hear that you have done very well?" he said.

"I am flattered, your Grace," said O'Brien, genuinely surprised. "Thank you, I…"

"What is the latest news from the dig?" interrupted the older man.

"Ah," said O'Brien, excitement in his voice. "We are continuing to discover some incredible finds. As you know, we have already pieced some of the scrolls together and sent them here for translation. There is an unusual one as well, have you heard? It's like a roll of metal, bronze or copper perhaps. I…well it was actually my discovery! I think it arrived here a few days ago. Has anybody been able to do any translation work on it yet? I don't…er, read the symbols very well but there are a couple of them that I did manage to…"

Celliani was holding up his hand. He was staring wide-eyed at the young priest, with an otherwise flat expression, like a teacher despairing of a rambling junior pupil. O'Brien stopped talking in mid sentence.

"First things first, Father. I understand your enthusiasm. You are young and you are doing your job well. But I wonder, have you heard what our scholars are saying about the meanings in the writings?"

O'Brien's eyes looked at the floor.

The Cardinal lowered his voice, as if he was concerned that somebody else might hear. "We have an interesting situation here. It seems that these scrolls date from around sixty years after the death of Christ. Have you considered what that means?"

"They may be older than the bible," the young priest replied.

"Exactly," said the Cardinal. "And did you know that there are hints in these texts of…how can I put it…other Messiahs, some said to be known before Christ's ministry in Palestine?"

O'Brien struggled for words. "Your Grace, I am just a scientist. I am not…qualified for theological debate and…"

"You are certainly not qualified, Father, but let me remind you that you are not *just* a scientist, or archaeologist, or whatever. You are a member of this Church and your continued career is in my gift."

O'Brien nodded his head in apology. "Yes, your Grace."

"What on earth do you think will happen if the scrolls suggest that Christ is some sort of fake or an impostor?" the Cardinal said sternly. "It will be the end of two thousand years' worth of history. The Catholic Church as we know it would be severely damaged. We cannot allow that to happen."

O'Brien sat open-mouthed, unable to reply.

Ceilliani sighed. "At the moment, you are the best we have. I would very much like you to continue some more archaeological work for us. But can I trust you?"

O'Brien nodded eagerly. "I am very dedicated, your Grace…I would like to do anything I can to help. I won't reveal any of these things."

The Cardinal was silent for a few moments and then smiled slightly.

"There is something I will tell you, a very important development. But I warn you."

The smile disappeared. He looked O'Brien directly in the eyes, threatening and cold. "You may like to gossip about your archaeological successes with others, talk with pride in university cloisters, or tell big stories to the newspapers. But concerning these scrolls, you will never do that. They will remain secret. Is that understood?"

O'Brien sat dumbfounded for a moment and then slowly nodded in agreement.

"Very well." The old Cardinal paused, in total stillness, before taking a deep breath. "Now. As to the copper scroll you have found. I have some of the news you were seeking."

O'Brien sat even more upright in his seat.

"We are beginning to translate this strange scroll. It is nothing like the others. It seems to hold clues, pointers to other hidden artefacts, to locations all over Palestine. Dozens of them. Perhaps more."

O'Brien sat with his mouth open.

"This is the reason I have called you here. From this day forward, you will have a new set of duties. This scroll will be your project," Celliani continued. "It may take months or years. But it is your calling. Your mission. Do you not agree?"

The young man could do nothing but continue to nod.

"Go back now to Palestine. Clean these caves and make sure nothing remains. Then consult with our experts here and continue your search for these hidden artefacts. Everything will be brought back here to me, and will be kept in the strictest secrecy. Will you swear to silence on this matter?"

"Yes your Grace, I will," said O'Brien.

"Very well." The Cardinal heaved himself out of his chair. "If these so called treasures are unearthed and found to be harmless or forgeries, you can then have your moment of fame with the newspapers."

O'Brien stood up. "Of course, your Grace."

"Now I have other business to attend to. You may go and make your arrangements."

O'Brien turned hurriedly, opened the heavy office door and disappeared into the Vatican corridors.

GENESIS

37 years later

Ruins of Khirbet Qumran
May 1984

"It's hot. Jesus, it's hot."

Ahmed untied his neckscarf, wiped his sweating forehead and threw it down into the dust. The footpath to the top had gradually been shrinking from a two-yard wide trail of packed earth, into a twisting, narrow vein of dust and small rocks. The hill was just seven hundred feet high, but the heat made the climbing exhausting. He looked around the flattened summit, a rough mixture of rocks and scrub bushes, brown and dry, then clambered up onto the nearest flat boulder and sat down, holding his head in his hands and breathing heavily. A crow that had been perched some ten feet away, gave fright and flew into the air with a squawk.

A little further down the slope, Father O'Brien plodded upwards, slowly and carefully. He chuckled to himself and shook his head. Ahmed always needed to demonstrate his youthful enthusiasm principally by running off everywhere at top speed, or digging frantically until he exhausted himself. But honour had been satisfied this time; the boy had reached the top first. Picking his way over the last few stones, O'Brien finally arrived at the summit. He gave a friendly but sarcastic look at the young man.

"I thought you did not believe in Jesus, Ahmed?"

O'Brien sat down beside the boy and Ahmed looked up at the old priest.

"How can you talk so easily Father," Ahmed said, still gasping a little, "after climbing up so far?"

O'Brien's lined face broke into a faint smile. "Do you mean at my great age? You do everything too fast. I have been climbing up and down hills like this for fifty years. I pace myself."

"Anyway, I do not believe in Jesus. I believe in science, Father. Just like you," Ahmed replied. "Except that all of our science has not found us any good relics this season. Nothing from God, Moses or King David."

"Well perhaps we need some luck, my boy. I had luck when I was young, just a little older than you are now. Perhaps you'll bring me some more."

This was the tallest hill in the group that stood south of the ruined town. O'Brien scanned the sky from left to right. It was clear, dazzling blue, dotted in the distance by the dark, wheeling specks of birds that glided above the ruins of the structure below. The air was completely still. Apart from Ahmed's wheezing there was no sound at this height.

They sat in silence for several minutes. Ahmed sat motionless, holding a pebble ready to throw at a tiny lizard that was basking on the next boulder. He threw it quickly, but not fast enough to catch the little reptile, who bolted away.

"So what are we going to do now, Father?"

The old man straightened his back and took a deep breath.

"Well, soon I must go back to the Vatican and make my report."

"But what is there to report? We have found nothing but mud and stones!"

O'Brien sighed and smiled again.

"Just because there is no news, does not mean that I don't have to tell them anything. They won't continue to pay for our efforts here for ever."

Down in the valley behind them, from Beth Shela village, a distant call to prayer floated up over the hill. As if suddenly inspired by it, O'Brien tipped his head to one side, his eyes momentarily vacant, turning thoughts over.

"But I think there is time for a little more investigation. I fancy we should have another look in the kitchen corridor."

Ahmed stood up, shaking his head.

"No! Please no! Father, we have spent days in that one tunnel. We've looked at every centimetre!

O'Brien laughed.

"Patience, my boy. That is the best lesson I could teach you if you want to be a scientist. Patience and persistence."

"Pah!" Ahmed threw another stone into the dust and got to his feet.

"Brilliant ideas usually come after lots of fruitless work, Ahmed, not before. Now come, we've rested enough. We climbed this tiresome hill so that we could survey the complex from a new vantage point. Let us do that."

Michael O'Brien found a sense of peace in working with Ahmed. The young man was keen, if a little headstrong and a bit too enthusiastic a digger when the archaeologists' gentle scrapings were required. He was bright and well educated for a native of Beth Shela. His schooling in the small Palestinian town had made him strong on opinions but had left him untouched by knowledge of any history prior to the twentieth century. Thus their work was free of argument over plans and theories. O'Brien was both the boy's employer and teacher and he found more happiness in that than almost anything else that had happened in the past twenty years or so. God now had very little consideration in Father O'Brien's daily life. There was a time when his spirit burned bright for the doing of God's work, serving the Church. But this had been ground away by the long and fruitless years of search and toil, the disappointments and more than anything else by the hypocrisy, ritual and greed of his masters. All that remained was O'Brien's self, his intellect and the seemingly unending effort to make discoveries, to satisfy his own ambition. If he thanked God for anything, it was that his mission in this dusty land kept him away from his sponsors in the Vatican for as much time as possible.

They moved to the north edge of the hill summit and gazed down at the outlines on the ground that the walls of the town had left on the earth. The complex had crumbled to ruins a thousand years or more since. The priest showed Ahmed the remains of the houses, the courtyards, the common refectory. Then at the centre, the holy places, the synagogues, with their assembly rooms and holy of holies. From this height it was a patchwork of squares and rectangles, a map that O'Brien knew every feature of. Yet still whenever he looked at it, he was turning in his mind the clues that had occupied most of his life, still hoping for some new insight, some crack in the code.

"Where is the place that you found the incense jar?" Ahmed interrupted the silence.

O'Brien pointed downwards and to his left. Both of them shielded their eyes from the sun.

"I believe it was, yes, just down there. Look, can you see the gatehouse? That smaller square to the edge of the complex? OK, come towards us two more little squares? There was a Roman water cistern just outside the wall and the jar was underneath it."

"But it was not put there when this place was built?" Ahmed asked.

"Correct Ahmed! That's well remembered!" O'Brien nodded, impressed by the boy's grasp of his teachings. "The people in these parts began building this community long before that. It was just that somebody simply decided that the cistern would be a good hiding place."

"In which part did you discover the scrolls?" Ahmed continued.

O'Brien smiled a little and drew in a breath.

"Ah, that is a little more complicated." The priest furrowed his brows. "The scrolls are why we are here; but they were not found quite here." He shook his head. "Hmm. I tell you what, let's walk down and I will think of the best way to explain. I have seen enough from this sun-blasted rock."

As usual, Ahmed dashed off to pick his way over the rock gully leading down the north side of the hill, then began to complain when he bruised his shins. But after ten minutes or so the path had become a much easier route of gravel and scrub, snaking down towards the temple compound, still four hundred feet below. The sun had just started to be obscured by the tip of the hill and they descended in cool shadow.

O'Brien spoke as they walked.

"The scrolls were found in this area, Qumran, a few miles from where we are now. There are high hills, similar to this one, just a little way from the shore of the Dead Sea and they have caves in them. I was sent to the area just after the scrolls were discovered in one of the caves."

"And you found the metal one?" Ahmed asked.

"Well, yes. All of the scrolls are parchment, which is like paper. They have writings and stories, like the Bible. But the thing I found was a very unusual one – a rolled up sheet of copper. It's known as the copper scroll. The words on it were very unusual too. They weren't religious stories, just directions to various concealed artefacts."

"Treasures?" said Ahmed.

"Well, not all treasures. The scroll says that some are gold and silver, some are just jars of incense and oils. But also, there were other things referred to that were not identified, just directions to them."

"But you haven't found all of them?"

O'Brien smiled ruefully. "No indeed not! I have looked for many years and so have many other people, but it is a very difficult job."

"Why Father?"

"Well, the writing is in the Qumran dialect. That isn't easy to understand. Also, some of the instructions refer only to relative locations."

Ahmed looked blank.

"Oh – let me explain." O'Brien closed his eyes for a moment, thinking of the best way to make it clear. "Hmm. Ah yes, there is one line on the scroll that reads: *'In the Second Enclosure, in the underground passage that looks east.'* You see? We don't know where the second enclosure is, what building it's in, or in what area."

Ahmed nodded this time. It looked like he just about understood, but he seemed to forget this tricky point and his face changed to a childlike look of triumph.

"But you found the incense jar!"

O'Brien gently nodded his head, smiling. He'd told Ahmed the story a few times, but neither of them seemed to tire of it.

"Sometimes, Ahmed, when I look back, so many years digging in the dust and rocks for nothing, then the only real happiness is the memory of that jar of ceremonial oil."

"But the jar was worth nothing, Father?"

"Not so, my boy. It was worth more than all the gold and silver I have ever seen. For twenty years after I found the copper scroll, nothing could be found. Many people tried to follow the clues and they found nothing. So it became accepted that the scroll was a fake, or a joke. But I kept trying. I chose one clue and followed it to all of the possible places it could refer to, and finally after years of travelling I found the jar. Do you see? The scroll was right. It proved that all the other clues in the scroll could also be real."

"And is the kitchen corridor another of these clues?" Ahmed asked. "What shall we find there? Gold coins?"

"Well, I don't know for sure. One of the most important clues in the scroll almost certainly points to that corridor in the ruins here. But perhaps," O'Brien looked around at Ahmed, seeing that he had the boy's undivided attention, "...it will lead us to something better than gold."

"What can be better?"

"I don't know," O'Brien continued, "but this clue is very interesting indeed. It says that this is the greatest treasure of all of them. It tells us fairly precisely where to look."

"Yes, I remember." Ahmed repeated it like a litany. *"One hundred and forty cubits along the passage. Behind the two key stones*. But we were digging there for days. That corridor is empty. Just stones and earth."

O'Brien didn't need to be reminded of their fruitless labours over the past weeks. He drew in a breath, as if to clear the weight of disappointment from his mind. Ahmed walked on ahead, kicking stones over a steep incline to the valley floor below.

"Perhaps the clue is the Qumrani's *'fath'an'*." The boy shouted back up the path.

"What is that?" asked O'Brien.

"It is a game we used to play as children, Father. When we didn't want the Israeli boys to know what we were doing. We made up a code. We called it fa'than in our language. When we were going to smoke cigarettes behind the factory, we would say that we were going to the shops for our mothers."

O'Brien stopped on the path. He thought for a minute. A code to disguise the clues? Codes upon codes. His mind sagged at the thought of any more complexity to his quest, yet at the same time he was fascinated by any addition to his tired lines of research.

He hurried to catch Ahmed on the path as they walked down to the valley floor.

One month later

Vatican City, Rome
June 24th 1984

"I don't know Father. You wish to keep on? I'm really not sure."

Cardinal Carlo Vanutti took a sip of his coffee. He rested his chin back onto his upturned palm, elbow on the carved wooden arm of his chair. He resembled a snake, deceptively relaxed, blank green eyes impossible to read. His sharp, black eyebrows framed them heavily, looking down at the sheaf of papers in his hand. His eyes flicked back and forth, between the words on the pages he held and glances he shot at O'Brien.

"I have been looking at your reports, going back over twenty years," Vanutti said with a sigh. "You had some great successes at the beginning. But so many years now with so little to show? I wonder, is there really anything else to find?"

O'Brien sat uncomfortably, facing the large, green leather-covered desk, looking away as Vanutti's eyes flicked up to stare at him again.

"Well, I haven't discovered any more of the treasures, not since the first few, the incense jar and some small decorated boxes."

"Treasures?" Vanutti raised his dark eyebrows. "I would view treasures almost as a miracle. If there had been anything at all – any scrap of new information in – what – ten years? – I would be pleased."

He took another sip of coffee. O'Brien had not been offered any. Vanutti raised his head and stared at him, then spoke.

"Well, what is it you propose, Father?"

The old priest looked up, like a chapel boy suddenly let off a punishment. Vanutti pondered how lucky it was that a church congregation had never been exposed to this man's ministry.

"Your Grace, just one more season. I feel so certain that we are close to something important. Just a few weeks ago, Ahmed and I were on the verge of a breakthrough in the east of the temple."

The Cardinal looked up sharply from the report he'd been gazing through.

"Ahmed? Who is Ahmed? You have an Arab involved in our work?"

"Oh…I'm sorry, don't worry," O'Brien gushed. "Ahmed is no threat in that way. Not at all. He's just a young man from the local town. He has no religious interests. He wishes to attend university, study archaeology. He helps me, for little money. If you will allow me I'll..."

"Father! Enough. I understand, thank you." Vanutti was shaking his head despairingly. "Now, let us think about what to do."

The priest waited silently, trying to maintain his calm, as Vanutti vacantly looked at the report once again, turning over the stapled pages one by one.

"Let me ask you two questions. Firstly, how old are you, Father?"

O'Brien looked down, furrowing his brows. For a moment he wasn't sure. It had been so long since he celebrated a birthday. And of course the Cardinal would know in any case, so there was no point in concealing the truth.

"I am sixty years of age, your Grace."

Vanutti frowned.

"Hmm. Can a man of your years cope with this work?"

"The work is not too taxing. As long as my mind is active."

"Very well. Now, the second question. Tell me, after all your years of study, what is your view on these treasures we have yet to find?"

"I try to keep a scientific detachment." O'Brien felt pleased with that statement, thinking that Vanutti would be impressed by his integrity. But the Cardinal flicked his eyes to the ceiling as if searching vainly for some divine guidance, before continuing.

"Yes, yes. But you have studied these scrolls for most of your life. All of the words in the copper scroll that anyone has managed to translate talk of concealed artefacts. Of gold talents, receptacles of oils and spice. Do you believe that's all they are?"

"Well, the few we have managed to locate have been nothing more, but I am sure that…"

Vanutti became more irritated.

"Father, I am growing impatient with constantly trying to justify the cost of these failures. We do not subsidise research for the sake of scientific truth! Why should I not stop your work immediately?"

O'Brien tried to respond, stammering a little. Vanutti raised his hand to calm him.

"Look Father, perhaps you have grown a little isolated. You must realise that there are many other mysteries in the world that require our investigation – stigmata, Virgin visions – these may all strengthen our Church's image and stimulate the hunger of people to join it."

The old priest suddenly found words.

"But your Grace – as I tried to say to you a few moments ago, I am certain that we are close to something important. Surely, with respect, the scrolls are authentic records, not just the hysteria of crazy people. Imagine if we found the Ark, or pieces of the Cross? These would be truly sensational discoveries."

Vanutti didn't react to O'Brien's enthusiasm. He simply raised his dark eyebrows and sat deep in thought, nodding almost imperceptibly to himself. Finally he took a deep breath before responding.

"Perhaps you are right Father. But I am still not sure. The world is changing. You have been too long away from the body of the Church, I think. Many Catholics today believe without needing any physical evidence. As you know, the disappointments of the Turin Shroud did not really affect our Church."

O'Brien began to hang his head.

"However, do not think that all is lost," Vanutti said. "I have not yet made a final decision. You know that in public we support the view that the promises of the scrolls are a fantasy. Privately – well, you know that things are different. But now, I must get on."

Vanutti discarded the sheets of paper and cleared a space in front of himself.

"That's all for now, Father. I will consider your report at length and talk to the Committee of Research."

One day later

Vatican City, Rome
June 25th 1984

O'Brien sat in thought. His desk was in a corner of the hall that was the main space for the Vatican Repository. This huge room was never on show to the public. The once-splendid gilded window frames were peeling. The frescoes adorning the ceiling were dirty and faded. Stacked in all directions were works of art and archaeological finds, either not important enough to display to the public, or in the midst of examination and cleaning. Dust cloths covered small statues that stood in rows along one wall. Beams of sunlight stabbed through dust, high in the ceiling space.

Normally, O'Brien felt at his calmest in this room. He would far rather have been many hundreds of miles away at a dig site of course. But at least this ragged space was somewhere that the Cardinals and other high officials never deigned to enter.

After his meeting with Vanutti however, he sat unable to concentrate and was thumbing through the abstracts of science journals. The list was sent monthly and contained hundreds of references to publications, mostly Italian, some worldwide, all supposedly of value. Much of it was mildly interesting, much not. Many were from journals that related only marginally to his field. But at the bottom of page 2, he suddenly stopped his rapid scanning of the text – something caught his eye.

'Blueprints of the ancients – linguistic analysis demonstrates that similar systems of codes were in use by Levant peoples between 300 B.C. and 500 A.D. Hebrew, Samaritan, Qumrani, Hashemite.
Paulo Baldovini, University of Rome.'

The priest said quietly to himself, "Qumran."

He sat for several minutes in silence, a hand idly clasping his mouth. Then he picked up the telephone.

"Yes, can you give me an outside line please?"

He waited a few moments, and then dialled.

"Hello? Operator? Can you give me the number for the University of Rome please?" A pause. "Which Department? Oh. I'm not sure. What do you have listed?"

He listened as the operator read off a long series of faculties.

"Ah! Yes, the Arts Faculty, I think that's the one. What's the number?"

He stared idly up at the faded ceiling, listening to the ring tone.

"Ah, hello! Arts Faculty? Yes, I'm trying to reach Paulo Baldovini. Bal – do – vi – ni," he said slowly. His Irish accent, still present after his many years away, still gave the Italians some problems. "Which department? Oh, I don't know. Can you check through for me? He is something to do with ancient languages."

"Hold on," said the receptionist brusquely at the other end, with obvious displeasure at having to search through a long list of names. O'Brien drummed his fingers, waiting what seemed at least ten minutes in silence.

"Hello?" said a man's voice.

"Ah hello," replied O'Brien. "I'm trying to reach a Doctor Baldovini please?"

"That is me. Paulo Baldovini. Who is calling please?"

"My name is Michael O'Brien. I work at the Vatican, in the – well, I'm one of the museum staff."

"I see," Baldovini said. "How can I be of help?"

"Well I just read an abstract of your article. I wonder if I could get a bit more information?"

"Article?" Paulo replied. "I have written many articles. Which one is it that you are referring to Mister Orb...Ob..."

"O'Brien. An Irish name. Best to call me Michael. Anyway, the article is about systems of codes used in Levant languages. It's..." O'Brien leaned over the papers and scanned the abstract again. "Ah yes, it's actually from 1982 originally."

"Oh yes. I know the one," Baldovini sounded more interested. "You can get the full article from the journal. The University Library would have a copy."

"Hmm, I'm afraid I know very little about your field. I am not sure that I would grasp the details,

O'Brien said. "Look, I know it is somewhat of a favour, but I wonder if we could meet?" O'Brien looked down at his hands as he was speaking. He had unconsciously crossed his fingers. "I confess that many people would not see my work as very important, but I have an urgent need to solve a little mystery we have here. I would be happy to come over to your campus, if you have a little time free?"

There was silence at the other end. Then, just audible, some papers rustling. O'Brien closed his eyes.

"Hmm. I have a suggestion, Michael," Paulo replied at last, sounding now much more enthusiastic. "I am going to see a relative of mine tomorrow, quite near the Vatican. Perhaps tomorrow afternoon? At about two thirty?"

O'Brien smiled and opened his eyes again.

"Ah, that would be excellent, Doctor Baldovini! Let me suggest where we could meet…"

One day later

Vatican City, Rome
June 26th 1984, 2 p.m.

Michael O'Brien walked out of one of the huge side-gates of the Vatican City and into the streets. He passed the 'Swiss Guard' sentry, who was dressed in the traditional renaissance costume that they'd worn for hundreds of years, as he stood to attention outside the guard hut. The Rome sun was at full strength at this time of the afternoon. The city outside the walls was as noisy as ever, hot and busy with tourists and traffic. A small flock of pigeons startled him as they flew into the air to his left, after a car sounded its horn close by.

He let his imagination run and wondered if he'd rather be in the cool, damp, fields of his home town in Ireland, or the baked desert, even hotter than here, of the Qumran dig site. He cast a wry smile to himself as he looked into the sky, shielding his eyes. This reverie was often what he fell into when he felt nervous about meeting new people. Perhaps his life of archaeology had equipped him better for puzzling over shapes in the ground than for dealing with people.

He looked across the busy junction and spotted Paulo, standing outside one of the many small tourist cafés outside the Vatican walls. This man was obviously an academic. He was about thirty years old, scruffy dark hair and beard, crumpled suit, holding a battered briefcase. O'Brien crossed the road, dodging cars, and walked up to him.

"Doctor Baldovini? I am Michael O'Brien."

"Ah, Michael – hello – Paulo Baldovini, yes. But perhaps I should call you Father?" O'Brien's uniform was obvious.

O'Brien was surprised at first, then glanced down at his tunic and smiled. "Oh, of course! Yes, or Michael, it's no matter. Thanks for coming at short notice. Shall we go in? I will buy you some coffee."

They sat by the window. There was a small group of tourists across the room, on the other side of the entrance. Otherwise the café was empty. O'Brien and Paulo were obviously locals; the waiter had just got them small espressos. Paulo lit a cigarette and idly stirred two lumps of sugar into his coffee whilst contemplating the man in front of him. The priest had light brown hair, greying at the temples and accentuated by his sun-browned, lined face. He certainly didn't look like a priest who spent all of his time inside a darkened room or church.

"So what is your position in the Vatican, Father?" he asked.

"I, er…I work within the museum. I am a sort of librarian, cataloguing the archaeological records. We have many ancient artefacts as you know, some of which are still mysteries to us. That is why your article was interesting to me. What is it you do at the University?"

Baldovini put down his coffee cup.

"I am a specialist in ancient languages. I have been studying documents from the classical and late Roman periods. The Bible, the scrolls of course; but also many other fragments. I am trying to draw conclusions about their day-to-day correspondence – about the prices of goods, architects' instructions for constructing buildings and so on. I'm afraid I am working on nothing of religious significance!"

O'Brien smiled, shook his head and pointed to his dog collar.

"Don't worry my friend. I confess I am more of a scientist than a priest, despite this uniform. Your work is very interesting to me. When I read your article…well, I'm reviewing an old and I'm afraid rather unimportant collection of documents from Qumran. Our linguistic experts have translated them, but they still make no sense. You mentioned 'codes' of some kind?"

Baldovini nodded. "Ah. Yes. Well, I have something here that may be of interest to you…"

Baldovini opened his case and pulled out some papers. They moved the coffee cups to the edge of the table and he spread them out. Paulo scanned across them for a few moments, studying the photocopies of parchments covered in symbols. O'Brien had seen this writing many times, on the scrolls. Then Paulo pointed to several symbols in one particular block on a page.

"Look here," he said. "This is one of the ancient texts – Qumrani script of course. We translated this many years ago. It's a typical day-to-day document. In fact it's an estimate, if you like, from a house builder. But comparing it with many other documents, I have found ambiguities. The builder says he will take sixty days to finish, but I think this really is saying 'thirty'."

O'Brien looked up at Paulo, nodding gently, but a bit blank.

"The point is," Paulo continued, "we've found a lot of things like this. People who have something in common – you know, like house builders, moneylenders, cloth makers – use expressions which mean something special to them. Slang, if you like. Just like we do today. The thing is, we didn't think it was common in ancient times, until we studied these documents."

"Hmm. I see." O'Brien responded, struggling in his mind to make a link.

"Of course, there are many different aspects of life that these colloquialisms refer to. We are still trying to identify many of them," Paul continued.

"Yes of course," said O'Brien, furrowing his eyebrows, and gazing for a while at the mass of mysterious shapes on the documents, his chin resting on his upturned palm.

"I wonder," he said at last. "Would there be any of these expressions for, say measuring – distances, directions, that sort of thing?" asked O'Brien.

Baldovini looked up, pleased that the priest seemed to understand.

"Why yes! There are. Wait a minute." Paulo shuffled through his papers.

"I don't know about distances. They were pretty much using Roman miles," Paulo said. "At least we haven't found anything different yet. But measurement – hmm, there was something. Ah yes, here."

Paulo put another document on top of the pile and pointed to another block of text. Do you recognise this symbol, or this one?"

He pointed to two of the angular marks. O'Brien had seen them many times, in the scrolls. He never tired of staring at them. He shook his head.

"I have seen the symbols of course, but I cannot read them, I'm afraid, I have always worked from translations."

"Well, you know that a standard measure in the ancient world was the cubit? It says here that the building will be twenty cubits high. But I have checked many other documents, and I think he is actually meaning 'stone blocks'."

O'Brien did not respond. He was suddenly motionless and silent.

"Yes. Do you see? The builder is measuring in blocks instead of cubits. I'm sorry, are you…"

"I have found it." O'Brien whispered.

Paulo looked puzzled. "What have you found? Will this be of any help in your research, Father?"

O'Brien's head jerked into motion again. He calmed himself.

"My friend I am sorry. My mind was wandering. You may have helped me to solve a small segment of our puzzle. I apologise, my thoughts wander. I get excited over the most trivial successes. If you would excuse me, I will get back to my studies while this is fresh in my mind."

"Well, OK. I will stay and finish my coffee. I must say I don't know what help I have been."

O'Brien got up, walked over to the bar, fumbling in his pockets for money, and paid the waiter. He left, smiling and nodding at Baldovini.

He crossed back over the road to the entrance to the Vatican, trying not to break into a run.

One day later

Vatican City, Rome
June 27th 1984, 5 p.m.

"Ah! Welcome my old friend. Come in and take a seat at the table."

Cardinal Vanutti strode to the door, where an old man stood, falteringly supported by one of the Vatican porters. Vanutti pushed the old, heavy door fully open. He took the old man's arm and dismissed the porter. He helped him totter towards the table, where several of the other men in attendance got up to help him sit. Vanutti closed the door, which clunked heavily into place. The old man was clearly half blind. Yet he smiled cheerfully as Vanutti guided him to sit at one of the gilded chairs around the table. He peered around at the six other men in the room, not helped by the gloom, caused by the heavy curtains blocking most of the sunlight. He lowered himself carefully into one of the red leather upholstered chairs. His spindly, gnarled fingers gripped the carved arms as he made himself comfortable.

When he'd settled, he exhaled with relief and looked up smiling and nodding at the seven men seated around the meeting table, a few strands of white hair bobbing under his braided cap.

Vanutti coughed lightly and the others came to attention.

"Can we begin please gentlemen? As you know I have called this meeting of the antiquities and research committee to reach a decision about where our efforts should be directed in future years."

The others all made agreeing nods. They were all Vatican clerics, some from the museum departments, and a representative from the finance office.

"I think you all know Cardinal Celliani?" Vanutti continued, "I have invited him to lend his wisdom to us, as he was the leader of this committee before myself."

There were smiles of recognition from the other members.

Celliani cleared his throat.

"You might say it was me who began this!" He shouted a little, obviously slightly deaf as well as partially sighted. "It was I who sent Father O'Brien in to capture the scrolls for us!"

"We owe you much respect, your Grace," said one of the younger men present, Father Thommasen. He stood up and turned to Vanutti. "I have to say that of the choices before us I must support the continuation of the work in the Holy Land. We cannot waste all of our resources on this crazy expedition to South America. What are these stories but peasants' ravings? Cardinal Celliani sent Father O'Brien to follow a true discovery, based on scientific..."

"This is not in dispute Father Thommasen!" said an older man, Bishop Grazzini. "But the fact of the matter is that nothing is coming out of the Holy Land and nothing else will, in my opinion. What we need in this day and age is..."

Vanutti was holding up his hands to quell the disagreement.

"Gentlemen, let us not argue. Let us consider the facts and weigh the possibilities here."

A few of the men who had been waiting to pitch in to the discussion relaxed in their seats and deferred to Vanutti's authority.

"We live in times that have changed. There are now many demands on our finances, eh Cragnotti?"

Vanutti smiled towards the finance office man, who nodded enthusiastically.

"So," Vanutti continued, "Father Cragnotti's accountants tell us that we must choose between two areas of research. O'Brien's continued work in the

Holy Land, plus any other archaeology we pursue in that region. Or, an expedition to examine the visions of the Holy Mother that we hear reports of in several villages in Ecuador. At present, we cannot do both. Now, what I suggest is that…"

There was a knock on the office door, just audible through the massive wooden panels. A middle-aged woman entered hesitantly. Vanutti looked around.

"Yes Clara, what is it? Just a minute gentlemen."

"I'm sorry your Grace," said the woman. "I'm afraid it's Father O'Brien. He insists that he must see you on a matter of the utmost urgency."

Several of the committee members chuckled quietly. "Perhaps he can't find the toilet now," whispered Grazzini to the man next to him.

Vanutti held his head in his hands for a moment, then sighed in resignation. "I'm sorry, this won't take a minute," he said, a scowl growing on his face. He rose and walked towards the door as O'Brien's head popped in around it, clearly a look of excitement on his face.

Vanutti's eyebrows were never more threatening. "This had better be an urgent matter, Father. I take it that Clara informed you that I am in the midst of an important meeting."

O'Brien entered, casting a nervous look at the men seated at the table, then back at Vanutti.

"I apologise your Grace," said O'Brien, "but I have found something very important. I think it may affect your decision concerning my work."

"I doubt it Father. But quickly, what is this amazing discovery?"

"Well," continued O'Brien, "it's rather complex but I will try to explain. You may recall a particular area of study in Khirbet Qumran, a location that is sometimes known as the 'kitchens corridor'?"

"Yes, yes of course Father," said Vanutti, growing ever more impatient. "It was an important clue but you found nothing there. Now…"

O'Brien held up a finger. "I…I have discovered that I was reading the clue wrongly. There is a new translation. I think I know now where the clue leads. Another place in the corridor entirely."

Vanutti stood silent, thinking for a few moments, gazing into space. He turned to the assembled group, some of whom were leaning forward with interest, others dismissive.

Finally Vanutti drew in a deep breath, and spoke. "I'm sorry gentlemen, this is new evidence that I think we cannot ignore, do you not agree?"

Once again, there was mixed agreement.

"I must postpone for a while, I am sorry. Clara, please can you show these gentlemen out and make arrangements for another meeting, perhaps tomorrow if we can make that?"

Clara nodded and busied herself with these arrangements while Vanutti rudely gestured O'Brien to go and sit by his desk.

"For your sake Father I do hope this is as important as you say. Go and sit down. I will come there momentarily."

The Cardinal straightened his tunic and said goodbye to the committee members as they left.

Vanutti and O'Brien faced each other across the table in the now silent room.

O'Brien wondered if he was supposed to start the conversation when Vanutti sighed.

"All right, tell me about this breakthrough."

"I think it is important," said O'Brien. "As I was saying, I really think I have found the location of the 'greatest treasure'."

Vanutti wasn't impressed. "Personally I doubt this treasure even exists. I have always supported your work but it is becoming increasingly difficult to assign any more funds to it."

Vanutti banged the table top with his fist.

"I need something substantial!" he continued, looking away in frustration. "Find me something like the Turin Shroud. Something tangible that people can see and believe in!"

O'Brien nodded calmly. "I will, your Grace, I promise. As you are aware the scroll describes this treasure as the Greatest Gift from God. Who knows what we will find? Perhaps even a new gospel."

Vanutti frowned. "Let's say we do. *If* we do. And I do admit that this lead you have, whatever it is, must be important, otherwise even you would not have presumed to interrupt my meeting. But I do warn you again; you must take the utmost precaution here. If a new scripture emerges, it is paramount that our people here interpret it first. You know what trouble the St. Thomas Gospel caused. We want no repeat of that."

"Of course, your Grace. I will report any findings to you directly."

O'Brien paused. "Does this mean that I have the go-ahead for more..."

Vanutti stood up. "I will give you three months to uncover this...treasure. Three months and not a day more. If nothing is found, I will have you cleaning books in the Vatican library."

Vanutti left the room, leaving O'Brien with a large smile on his face.

One month later

Ruins of Khirbet Qumran
July 1984

Ahmed and O'Brien stood facing the northwest end of the complex, as they had on so many mornings before this. It was two hours after dawn. The long shadows thrown by the uneven remains of walls and towers were disappearing as the sun rose higher and moved around to the south. The old priest was nodding quietly, smiling in expectation. He looked at the boy, who was also grinning and pointing to the remains of a low stone building to their right, giving the thumbs-up sign. That was where O'Brien had found that first incense jar, many years before.

The complex had once been a thriving community. In front of them they could just discern the remains of the northern gate, which two thousand years ago would have been buzzing with traders and flocks of animals.

Now, it consisted mostly of low, uneven ruins where there had once been walls, narrow alleyways and rectangular buildings. The desert and the wind had taken their toll, but most of the stone had been taken from here in the hundreds of years since it had been abandoned, to build Beth Shela and the neighbouring villages.

"OK, are you ready, my friend?" said O'Brien. He tried to project a calm impression to Ahmed, but struggled to conceal a huge grin. He felt a wave of excitement inside his chest, a feeling missing for many years.

Ahmed made a mock soldier's salute and grinned in return. He had his shovel on a rope slung around his shoulders and picked up his bag full of digging tools.

They followed a familiar route through the remains of the gate and began to pick their way through the complex towards the south end.

O'Brien felt a dull ache in his back each time he stepped over a chunk of masonry or turned an awkward corner. Last night he hadn't slept well, partly because of the excitement of today, but mostly because his bed, a rough mattress in a dusty hut outside the complex's compound, was so uncomfortable. It was ironic that, as they neared what might be the end of his quest, a hotel was just being built at that spot. Ahmed's father worked as the leader of the labourers at the site, apparently to be called the 'Elil Palace'. It was he that had told the priest of the boy's interest and asked that he let his son help out.

"Father! Come on!"

O'Brien shook the memories from his head, as he sped to catch Ahmed up.

"Jesus was not born here – but he stayed here – is that right?" the boy asked.

The priest smiled and nodded, again impressed by the boy's grasp.

"Yes, Ahmed. That is correct! He was born about sixty miles south of here. But he did come to live among the people here in the time before he became a famous teacher.

"Why here, Father? This is just a small place. Why didn't he live in Jerusalem?"

"Well, eventually he did go to Jerusalem, as you know," O'Brien replied. "But for many years he had to prepare himself for that."

"For what, Father?"

He thought for a moment, as they walked. "Well, like many people of that time, Jesus thought that the religious leaders then were corrupt and greedy." O'Brien sighed inwardly. How much had anyone really learned since that time?

"A lot of people who felt the same way decided to live separately, away from the large temples," he continued. "Those who came to live around here were called the '*Essenes*'. They were ascetics. That means they believed in living simple lives, with few luxuries. Jesus was welcomed here. Of course, as you know, one day he decided to preach against the temple elders and left to go to the great city."

Eventually, they reached the refectory chamber at the southern end of the ruins. Two of its walls still stood about four feet high, showing its shape and size. Just outside this area was the entrance to the tunnels that ran underneath.

"Do you have the torches?" O'Brien asked.

Ahmed had prepared thoroughly, as ever. "Yes Father. Two torches. New batteries. Large tape measure. Shovel, trowels. Notepad, pens. Camera. All set!"

"Very well. Good job," said O'Brien. "Ready? Let's go and see what we can find!"

They went down the steps and into the first tunnel, O'Brien leading the way. Their two torches played on the sidewalls, casting a shape like a huge distorted pair of binoculars. As he made his way, Ahmed brushed his hand against one of the stones in the wall, and felt a series of depressions in the hard surface.

"Father, there is something here. A sign."

They both shone light onto the stone.

"Yes, Ahmed, we know about these inscriptions," O'Brien said. "What do you see there?"

The young man tried to focus his eyes. They were not yet accustomed to the darkness in the tunnel, having just entered from the sunlight at the entrance.

"There is a circle, with a cross through it – I can just make it out."

The old priest smiled.

"You see better than I do, my boy. But we know these signs, they are the Templars' markings."

"What are the Templars?"

"They were religious men from the West. They conquered these lands and ruled here in the Middle Ages, about nine hundred years ago. Like us, they also searched for important relics. They lived here for a long time, in this area, and also held the area where Solomon's temple stood, in Jerusalem. So they were called the Knights Templar.

"Knights? Did they have swords and armour?" asked Ahmed excitedly.

O'Brien nodded. "Oh yes. Many of them were warriors who fought great battles with the Moslems. They were eventually driven out by the Ottomans – the Turkish Empire. They certainly found some things here, but I don't think they made any great discoveries."

Ahmed smiled, his eyes bright with enthusiasm. "But we will find great things, yes?"

"Yes. I hope we will, this time."

In a few minutes, they came to a large, rectangular chamber that opened off to the side of the tunnel. Ahmed and O'Brien knew it well. Either of them could probably have found their way around these passages without any light. This room was an ancient kitchen that had served the refectory chamber above. Another room led off beyond it and each had tunnels running from doors in the walls.

"What were these tunnels for?"

O'Brien smiled again. "That," he said, "we don't know. They are like corridors, but they don't lead anywhere. Perhaps they once did and were blocked up. Perhaps they were for storing things and keeping them cool. But now they have nothing in them. Just brick walls and floors."

Ahmed gave a cheeky grin. "But perhaps they do have something in them?"

O'Brien nodded and gave a cheerful shrug. Ahmed thought he could see a twinkle in the priest's eye.

"Yes, perhaps they do my boy! Perhaps they do! Come on, let's start."

Ahmed pushed past him enthusiastically to one of the openings. "This one, Father, yes?" he said excitedly, pointing his torch at the second doorway in the left wall of the chamber.

O'Brien was shaking his head. "No. We're going into the second one in the next room."

"But how can you be sure which is the right one? Did the man in Rome tell you?"

The priest smiled. "Not really, my boy. But he did tell me some very interesting things, and I have put together my own theory. It's a bit complicated for now. Do you mind if we just get started?"

Ahmed smiled in return, nodding excitedly. "Let's go!"

They stopped at the entrance to the second tunnel that led off from the antechamber to the kitchen. They unloaded their tools, maps, drinking water and other bits and pieces. The doorway was jagged and broken. Many of the bricks that had made its arch had fallen onto the floor beneath, half blocking the entrance. They climbed over and shone their torches inside. Walls of smooth stone blocks could just be seen, disappearing into the shadows.

"Now, let's stand at each side of the entrance arch. I want you to count as I do as we proceed into the passage. We must count along one hundred and forty stone blocks as we go."

They both walked slowly in, counting aloud. They reached one hundred and forty blocks and stopped. The tunnel here, like the rest of its length, was featureless and empty.

"There is nothing here Father."

"Well, my boy, what we seek must be hidden somewhere here. Let me look for a while."

O'Brien sat on the floor, patiently examining the walls on each side of the tunnel. Ahmed held the torch beam for him, having to be reminded every so often to keep it steady. At last, the priest shouted in surprise. "Ah ha!"

"What is it Father?" asked Ahmed excitedly.

O'Brien sat upright with a huge smile on his face. He pointed down towards two of the blocks.

"This is where we dig. Let's get out our tools."

They dug carefully for the next two days on both sides of the passage, digging pits in the earth floor and gradually exposing the stones in the foundations beneath.

Towards the end of the second day's painstaking work, Ahmed suddenly called out. "Father, there is something in the earth here."

O'Brien walked over to Ahmed's pit and aimed his torch at the small object Ahmed held.

"Well, my boy, that is interesting. It's metal, like a small hook."

"Is it valuable, Father?"

O'Brien laughed. "Perhaps worth nothing! Perhaps everything."

He turned it around in his hands.

"Do you see, it's the broken end of a tool, a crowbar."

"What is that?"

O'Brien stooped down into the pit and pretended to insert the fragment in between the blocks.

"This is what you would use to move these stones. And look at them."

He patted the two lowest blocks.

"Do you think they are straight? I'm not sure. They look a bit ragged don't they?"

Ahmed looked blank. O'Brien grinned.

"If I'm right, someone has pulled out these two stones and put them back again, only they haven't done a perfect job. We'll try to get them out. If I'm wrong, the tunnel will probably come crashing down on top of us."

Ahmed still looked nonplussed. The priest hit him playfully on the shoulder.

"Come on, I'm only joking! Let's get to it! This is where you can show me just how dedicated an archaeologist you are."

It was another two hours before the last block was heaved backwards and hauled, between them, up from the pit and onto the earth floor. Behind, as O'Brien shone his torch, there was blackness. Ahmed jumped up, ready to scramble inside.

"Now wait a minute!" O'Brien stopped him. "Let's have a better look before you go falling into a bottomless pit."

He lay down, his head almost disappearing into the hole, playing his torch down into the darkness. There was a rough floor, about six feet below.

"OK" he said, pulling himself upright again. "I'm going down into it. Take my hand. You stay up here."

Ahmed held the priest's hands as his legs disappeared into the hole. Then further, until he let go, and dropped in.

"Father, what can you see?"

O'Brien heard Ahmed's voice, muffled above, as he looked around the chamber. It was about eight feet in diameter with large rough hewn stone walls holding back the earth. He shone his torch around the inside for a few seconds.

"I'm going a little further in Ahmed. It's quite safe. It's a fairly small chamber. There's a great stone box here…"

Ahmed thumped down onto the floor behind him.

"I thought I told you to... Oh, never mind. Take a look at this."

They both played torches over the structure. A stone oblong, some four feet high, eight feet long, virtually filled the chamber.

"I am sorry Father. I was so excited! Is it in that block? The great treasure? Shall we open it?!"

"Shine your torch onto the side of it. There – look – some inscriptions. They…"

O'Brien stopped, silent.

"What is it Father?"

Ahmed could just see the outline of O'Brien's face. His eyebrows were furrowed. Gradually, his mouth opened wide. He whispered to himself.

"It can't be…"

Suddenly he stood up. Ahmed had never seen O'Brien like this. The priest shouted urgently. "Help me! We have to try to move the lid."

Together they pushed at the stone lid. It moved about half an inch.

"We must do this together Ahmed. It's very heavy. Come on. One, two, three…"

They both pushed as hard as they could and a corner of the old stone lid suddenly shifted, with a loud scraping, about a foot. They both recoiled, breathing hard.

O'Brien held both hands to his head for a few moments, reeling from the effort and trying to calm himself.

"OK. Let me have your torch please."

He took the light from Ahmed, who saw O'Brien look him in the face. He seemed terrified to look down into the opening. He had never seen the priest afraid in all the time they had worked together. With a shaking hand, O'Brien shone the beam into the box. He drew a sharp breath. "My God…."

ADVENT

ADVENT

DeLoitt Institute of Natural Sciences, Washington DC, USA. September 1984

Doctor James Van Doest finished his talk and waited for the somewhat muted applause to die down before he impatiently gathered his papers together at the large wooden lecturers' desk. It had not gone well. He had been expecting a rough ride, but he was disappointed that there seemed to be so little support, even open hostility from some of the audience. He looked up to see them filing out of the lecture theatre, some of them shaking their heads and laughing in his direction. He walked off the dais to his left where a sympathetic Professor Grant was waiting, ready to shake his hand.

"Well, thanks Jim. It was very…different!"

Van Doest scowled dismissively. "Bunch of idiots. Mediocre plodders. Just because something challenges their thinking, or because someone might just be able to do something revolutionary, they…."

He pursed his lips, perhaps out of respect for his host. Paul Grant shook his head, smiling. "Don't worry Jim. You ruffled a few feathers there! You sure made some challenging points – but science needs a bit of that! Seems sometimes that it's you against the whole of the academic community doesn't it?"

Van Doest just muttered and continued clearing his materials. The Professor put a hand on his arm.

"Look Jim, I really am grateful to you for coming – why don't you come for a drink when you've finished up here?"

Van Doest momentarily looked to the front of the stage. Two of the audience members had descended from the ranked seats and were waiting to speak to him. He looked back at the Professor.

"Perhaps I should get back to my smoking test tubes and bubbling flasks," he said sarcastically. "After all, these people think I am some kind of a monster."

Paul Grant smiled and turned to leave the room, shaking his head. "Come on Jim," he shouted back, "Lighten up a bit! I'll see you in a few minutes."

Van Doest climbed down from the podium and walked towards the men, half expecting more censure or criticism.

"How can I help you gentlemen?"

They looked decidedly odd for an Institute audience. They were dressed in almost identical long black coats, buttoned to the neck. Each held a wide-brimmed black hat. One looked like an old-fashioned Italian, the other, non descript, probably northern European. One of the men spoke, in carefully practised English.

"We were very interested in your lecture, Doctor Van Doest. We were wondering if we could perhaps have a private talk with you?"

Van Doest looked around the high, echoing lecture room. It was now completely deserted.

"Here's as private as anywhere. What do you want? Are you in the field?"

The other man shook his head. "Not exactly. But if you don't mind, we have a proposition for you." He looked at his colleague before continuing. "We may be able to offer you some…assistance?"

Van Doest shrugged. "Assistance in what? And who are you?"

The two men again exchanged glances before one of them continued.

"My name is Thommasen, and this is Frederico Grazzini. We are from the Vatican, in Rome."

"You are?" Van Doest replied, surprised and puzzled.

Grazzini continued. "Doctor Van Doest. Do you really think you can do what you proposed in your lecture?"

"Look, if you guys are trying to make some moral, religious point, I'm afraid you should have raised questions at the end of my lecture, now if you don't mind…"

"I'm sorry Doctor," the priest held up his hand. "Please, we are not interested in making any moral criticism. Just – how do you say it? – humour us, for a few moments. Can it be achieved, technically?"

Van Doest shrugged. "I wasn't lying back there. I think it can. But you may have noticed that most of my learned colleagues don't agree with me."

"Do you intend to continue? To prove them wrong?" asked Thommasen.

Van Doest shook his head slowly. "How? It would take considerable sponsorship. I'd have to get equipment, technical staff. And after today, I don't think I'll manage to get any funding from anywhere."

"Would you be interested in an opportunity to continue your work outside of this country?" said Grazzini.

Van Doest studied the men for a moment. He could not imagine why on earth these priests were interested in his work. But he smiled, if only faintly. "Everything has its price gentlemen. So do I. But mine would be quite high."

They looked at one another again, before Grazzini nodded to his colleague and spoke.

"We are prepared to fund your work, completely. Until you succeed, or if unfortunately you establish that it cannot be done. You would be able to acquire any resources you wish."

Van Doest opened his eyes wide. "*Any* resources? You…you're not serious?"

"We are entirely serious, Doctor Van Doest," Grazzini continued. "With certain conditions, of course... Are you interested in such a proposal?"

"Of course but," Van Doest still looked at them with suspicion, "what conditions? And why do you want to make this offer to me?"

"I'm afraid we cannot tell you about our particular interest at this time," Thommasen said, "but I assure you, it is a challenge that a man of your intellect receives perhaps only once in a lifetime. As for the conditions – firstly, we will require you to establish a laboratory within our premises, in Rome. I'm sure that will not be difficult for you?" Thommasen smiled. "But secondly, and this will be more…unnatural perhaps, you will need to work under conditions of utmost secrecy. Your work, for reasons that we will explain, may remain unpublished for some years, but you will be able to realise your scientific goal. And of course we will pay you extremely well for your services."

Van Doest's mind reeled with surprise. "I will have to give this some thought. If you're really serious I…"

Grazzini held out a business card. "We won't take up any more of your time now, Doctor Van Doest. Please call us when you have had time to think. If you are willing, we will pay for you to travel to Rome, where we can discuss this project in more detail."

Van Doest looked at the number on the card, then again at the two men, who were preparing to leave. He tried once again to elicit some information from them. "Can't you give me a clue? What have you got there that is so important?"

The men started up the steps that led to the high rear exit door from the lecture theatre.

"We will discuss all in good time, Doctor Van Doest. One more thing. We would appreciate it if you told nothing of this to Professor Grant or anybody else."

Van Doest nodded in agreement and the two men left, their steps echoing from the corridor that led away from the theatre doors.

Rome, October 1984

Father O'Brien sat in a backstreet bar finishing off his espresso coffee. He put down his cup with a noisy clunk and checked his watch. Almost 8 p.m. Time to go.

He looked around the room at the other customers, but they were all talking, smoking and laughing with each other. They were too busy to notice just another Vatican priest minding his own business.

Rain beat against the bar's windows. This was the first storm of the season and it was already dark. This made O'Brien feel more comfortable. He had to be so careful these days.

He stepped out of the brightly lit doorway and into the Roman night. The wind whipped the rain under his wide-brimmed hat and he had to hold on to it to stop it flying off onto the rooftops.

He set off down the street, hugging the sidewalls and walking under the shop awnings – not for shelter but to remain inconspicuous. He knew that Vatican security was looking for him, and he now had to turn to the only friend left that he trusted. Father Piali had agreed to meet him secretly and O'Brien looked forward at last to learning the truth.

Across the street he glanced at another man keeping pace with him. Was he a priest too? O'Brien peered into the blackness but he could make out only the man's black coat held tight against his neck.

Was he being paranoid? He stopped to look into the darkened window of a tobacconist's shop, long since closed. The footsteps across the street continued for a while and then stopped suddenly.

O'Brien glanced across in that direction but the street was deserted. A car rumbled past and sprayed water onto the pavement from a deep puddle in the road. O'Brien's feet were already soaked so he took no notice and started down the street again. Where was everybody? Just when he needed the public to be out and surrounding him, he found himself completely alone.

The gates to a small park appeared at last. With a last quick look around him, O'Brien disappeared into the darkness.

He approached a fountain in the centre of the park where four paths met. Huge, dark trees could just be seen against the dark sky, surging back and forth in the wind. He could just about make out a black figure standing waiting.

"Roberto?" whispered O'Brien, "Piali is that you?"

The man held out his hand. "Yes, Michael. Come quickly."

A rumble of thunder echoed overhead and the rain fell even harder.

O'Brien took the man's hand, which was trembling.

"Thank you for coming my friend," said O'Brien, speaking quickly and nervously. "Please tell me what is happening? Was it you who told me that I should stay away from the Vatican?"

Piali nodded, nervously looking from side to side.

"What is it?" said O'Brien. "This is crazy! What have I done? I cannot talk to anybody. Vanutti will not discuss anything with me. It was my discovery! Yet I've been virtually excluded. What is so secret?"

Piali pursed his lips, his eyes staring in fear. "They have…" he stopped, again looking to his right.

"I am sorry Michael. Please forgive me." Piali gripped O'Brien's other hand. In it he felt a small slip of paper.

"What is it?" the old priest asked.

Two black figures rose from the shrubs at the side of the fountain and approached them.

O'Brien was stunned. "Roberto! Surely you have not…you have betrayed me?" He slipped the paper into his trouser pocket as the two men quickly came towards them and took hold of each of O'Brien's arms.

"You are to come with us please, Father," one of them said. "The Cardinal wishes to talk to you about your absence."

They led O'Brien back towards the park entrance. He turned his head to his friend.

"Why? Tell me why!"

Piali raised his hands and shrugged. "Forgive me Michael. I had no choice. Please forgive me?"

O'Brien was disappearing into the shadows. He noticed rain running down Piali's face. Or was it tears?

12 months later

Basement Storerooms, The Vatican
October 1985

Cardinal Vanutti strode down the corridor, his shoes making loud squeaking noises on the polished floor. The storage areas below ground at the Vatican were plain, without any of the decoration above. Yet they were still massively built, with smooth stone walls, interrupted at regular intervals by huge wooden doors. A row of bare electric bulbs stretched into the distance. He stopped outside the one of the doors and gently tapped.

"Who is it?" a muffled voice answered, in a loud whisper.

"It's Vanutti. Open up."

A large metal bolt was unlocked and the door swung open. The quiet stillness of the corridor was washed with the hum of machinery and the smell of chemicals. Vanutti entered, blinking, suddenly having to cope with intense, blue brightness. The room resembled a science laboratory, with a central bench, surrounded by storage cupboards, with a sink, microscopes and a battery of electronic instruments.

Vanutti looked around. There were four men in the room, two wearing white lab coats, the others in simple workaday cleric's dress.

"His Holiness is not here yet?" asked Vanutti.

One of the priests frowned and shook his head. "From what I have heard, the Pope is – how to put it – somewhat reluctant to view this experiment."

Vanutti simply raised his eyebrows. His blank facial expression did not alter. He walked to the bench in the centre of the room and gazed down.

"We should not refer to it as an experiment anymore. This project has been a huge success!" Vanutti said. "I must say I never really believed it could be done." He shook his head, as if he still disbelieved it and whispered aloud. "Incredible. Absolutely incredible."

He looked up again and smiled at one of the men in white coats.

"Professor Van Doest. You are a brilliant man. And a very determined one."

Van Doest looked triumphant, but very tired. In the last weeks he had been working at least twenty hours a day. "Carlo, I can tell you now, a few months ago even I doubted whether I could really do it. But – well there it is!" He wiped his brow and took several deep breaths, staring down at the table. He mused to himself. "If only I could tell the world about this..."

"One day indeed, James," replied Vanutti. "But in the meantime, you are one million US dollars richer than you were two months ago. It has been worth every cent."

"That remains to be seen," said a voice from the doorway.

Vanutti turned. The Pope stood in the doorway. Unusually, he had come without any of his aides. Vanutti bowed. "Your Holiness," he said, reaching for the Pope's hand. "I am glad that you have at last come to see this marvellous achievement. Please come in!"

The Pope allowed the Cardinal to kiss the back of his hand. "So it is complete." The Pope's voice was slow, measured and flat. He showed no sign of being pleased. "But I am still very troubled by this whole project. As you know, my counsel was to tell the world about our discovery and accept the consequences."

If he was annoyed, Vanutti showed nothing but gentle dissent. "We have been over this many times your Holiness," he said. "Let us wait until the time is right and then the world can rejoice with us."

"And if this project does not work?" asked the Pope.

"Then who will know? It will be as if nothing had ever happened."

The Pope stood in thought for a few moments.

"Very well, but remember," he looked around at all present, slowly and carefully. "I know nothing of this at all. The Church cannot be charged with something as grave as this if it should go wrong. Do you understand?"

All in the room nodded in agreement. Vanutti smiled gently. "Of course, your Holiness. Only six people know of this. Oh and of course Father O'Brien, who made the discovery."

The Pope's face darkened. "I have been hearing things about this man. I gather he is not to be trusted with – important information? You have dealt with him I presume?"

"Yes indeed," nodded Vanutti. His silence is… guaranteed."

The Pope nodded gently and his frown softened slightly, to show agreement.

"Very well. I am sure you have. Thankfully I chose somebody for your position who is so…thorough."

Vanutti bowed his head by the smallest amount in acknowledgement and leaned towards the Pope to whisper into his ear. "I think if you remember, you had no choice Excellency? With respect."

The two men held each other's gaze a moment longer before the Pope relaxed.

"So, where is it? Can I see it now?"

"Certainly your Holiness."

Vanutti walked to the corner of the room and stood next to the table. On it stood a plastic box, covered by a blanket. He looked briefly at Van Doest to check if it was all right to pull it back. The professor nodded. The Pope moved closer and gazed down hesitantly.

His face changed to one of amazement as he broke into a huge smile.

7 years later

Catholic School – St. Assisi, Tuscany
June 1992

"Can I help you your Grace?" asked the young priest.

Vanutti had been lost in his thoughts, staring into the schoolyard.

"Oh! Yes, you must be Father Andolini, the teacher here?"

The young man nodded. "Yes, I am. But I am sorry – I do not know you? Please excuse me if I…"

Vanutti waved his hand to quell Andolini's concern.

"No problem Father. It is a credit to you that you protect the young children here. I am sorry to come unannounced up to the school like this. My name is Carlo Vanutti. From the Vatican."

"You are Cardinal Vanutti?" asked the priest with surprise. "I hope that you have not come all this way just for our little school?"

"No, not really Father. I have business with the Abbot at the monastery."

The schoolyard was a rough square of patchy grass in the centre of a group of low brick buildings. A leaning basketball post stood at one end and a small set of football goalposts at the other. There were about ten boys clustered around it, kicking an old ball. Under the shade of two large cedar trees that towered over the buildings, about eight girls were playing games of skipping and juggling.

Another young boy was playing on his own, kneeling in a corner of the quadrangle, pushing pebbles to and fro on the sandy floor with a stick. Vanutti was staring at him, nodding gently to himself.

"Do you know that boy, your Grace?" asked the priest.

Vanutti turned to face him and nodded more strongly. "Indeed I do, Father. I have a – concern for his progress. Do you know his mother?"

The priest looked down. "Of course. Signora Rossi. She has had a hard life here."

Vanutti put his hand on the priest's arm. "I know that Father. It was I who brought her to Assisi."

The priest looked up, open-mouthed. "You – oh, I am sorry, I did not know."

Vanutti smiled. "Perhaps I should have introduced myself before now. Yes, she came into my care by chance, as you know, pregnant, with the wretched father having deserted her. She was uneducated and poor. I managed to take a little time away from my work and arranged for her to be brought here and cared for by the monastery. The rest perhaps you know."

The priest smiled also. "That was a good thing to have done. Now they are members of this community and her past has been forgotten."

Vanutti looked down and nodded gravely. "That is good. And Father – I wish to keep it that way. But – well every so often when my schedule allows, I like to visit. Tell me, how is the boy doing?"

The priest smiled more widely. "He is a fine student! One of the best in the school. He...oh here he is."

They turned and looked down at the boy. He was standing straight and still, the stick still in his right hand. He had a quizzical, puzzled expression on his face. His large brown eyes looked directly at Vanutti.

"Who are you?" he asked quietly.

"My name is Carlo," said Vanutti, smiling down at him. "I am visiting the village. I heard this was a very good school and that you were one of the brightest pupils. I thought I would come and talk with your teacher."

"You are lying," said the boy. "I have seen you before. Why are you dressed like that?"

Vanutti raised his head to a haughtier angle, but still retained his smile. "I am a priest too, like Father Andolini. Only I am a different kind, a Cardinal. I come from the Vatican, in Rome. We are always interested in schools."

"Then why do you watch only me? I will tell my mother."

Vanutti laughed a little. "You can if you wish. I have heard about your mother. She is a fine woman. I hope you are a good boy for her."

The boy scoffed and puffed up his chest. "I am seven years old now. I am not a baby. I am a student. I am studying language. I am the best in the class! My mother is proud of me."

"And so she should be." Vanutti patted the boy on his head, then turned to the priest. "Well, I must go now. I am late for my appointment with Father Giovanni."

He looked again at the boy. "Goodbye, young man," he said smiling, and walked away towards the gravel path leading up to the monastery complex.

The boy spoke once more, this time more loudly. "You do not come from the Church," he said. "You are not a holy man."

Vanutti hesitated slightly, then continued walking away without looking back.

The Vatican, Antiquities and Theology Library
February 3rd 2003

Myron Wilson stood in the great library room. He could not help feeling in awe of its age, and its smells of polished wood and old paper. Along the walls were galleried shelves in three stories. In the middle of one long wall was a wooden spiral staircase that led to the upper balconies. Above these, giant sash windows rose up to the decorated ceiling. He slowly moved across the waxed parquet floor, taking care to keep the deathly quiet, which was being observed by all of the visitors and students here. He scanned the ranks of books in front of him. Each of the partitions between the shelves was finely carved wood. Beautifully bound books, some looking hundreds of years old, were tightly packed between each one. He browsed along row after row, pretending to be a casual tourist. He could feel the watchful gaze of the attendant on the back of his head and didn't want to raise any suspicions. What seemed to be a very old volume stood on a small table. He picked it up and opened the first page, smelling the musty odour that came from the decay of the old print.

"The literal interpretation of the Ten Commandments in Catholic Europe in the age of Enlightenment."

He sighed and replaced the book carefully.

There was a polite cough behind him and Wilson turned to see a small rather nervous man looking up at him. He was probably in his late twenties.

"Mister Wilson?" he asked, quietly.

Wilson nodded. "That's right, son. Where can we talk?"

The priest ushered him to a table in the corner of the room and they both sat down on the hard wooden chairs.

"I am Gianni Coppella. I understand you asked to see me?"

"I did." Wilson coughed and brushed his hand across his forehead, as if to clear his head. "Excuse me, my plane landed only a few hours ago. You see I am in quite a hurry."

The priest looked puzzled. "I really do not know how I can be of help to you. What is it you are seeking?"

Wilson leaned closer to Coppella and lowered his voice. "Let me come straight to the point. As I said my name is Myron Wilson. As well as running my oil corporation I am also the president of the Texas Culture and History Foundation. I am interested in acquiring some important religious artefacts, to establish the reputation of my museum in Dallas."

Coppella looked as if he was beginning to understand. "Ah, I see. Well, as you know, we have the greatest collection of such things in the world." He looked at Wilson quizzically. "It may be that you could arrange to borrow some things for a special exhibition? We frequently organise such things with museums around the world. Perhaps I could arrange a meeting for you with the Curator?"

Wilson was shaking his head slowly. "I'm afraid that's not quite what I'm looking for."

"Well Mister Wilson, I really do not understand. I'm sure that the Curator could help you more than myself. I am basically a librarian. I look after records, documents – that sort of thing."

Wilson smiled. To Coppella, it did not seem a nice smile. "Oh, Father, you are precisely the sort of man I am looking for. You see," Wilson leaned a little closer and lowered his voice to a near whisper. "I am indeed trying to find some documents. Things that may well be here, but – how to put it – the Vatican does not care to talk about."

Coppella's face changed suddenly. "What are you saying?"

"Well," Wilson's smile faded a little. "Let's start by discussing the scrolls, shall we?"

Coppella shook his head in annoyance.

"Huh," he said. "This is a waste of my time. I hope your journey was not made solely for the purpose of asking this? If so you have wasted your time also. Now I'm afraid that I have to go…"

Coppella made to stand up.

"Just a moment!" said Wilson a little too loudly, holding the younger man's elbow. All eyes in the library turned towards them. Wilson turned and nodded apologetically. People returned to their reading although he noticed that the head librarian behind the desk was dialling on his phone.

"Let me just ask you one more little thing."

Coppella looked disdainfully. "If you must. What?"

"I wonder," said Wilson, the sardonic smile returning to his face, "how is your son these days?"

Coppella stared at Wilson in silence for some moments, then tried to give a nonchalant smile. "How could I have a son? I am a Catholic priest. We are not allowed to marry."

Wilson was staring directly back. "Oh I know that Father. But I wonder," he made a gesture of looking around at the people in the library, "who else knows about your secret woman, and child?"

Coppella's forced smile disappeared. "How do you know this?" he whispered.

"Oh, I know a great deal about you Father. And do not take me for a madman or a fool. I suggest you sit down again."

The young man sat down. Wilson let go of his arm.

"My information tells me that your son is sick. That right?"

Coppella sat in silence for several seconds before responding.

"My son is suffering from a rare form of leukaemia. It is…terminal. He will probably die before the summer. What is this to you? How do you know these things?"

Again Wilson placed his hand on the priest's arm. "Like I said Gianni, I found out about a lot of things before I came here. Including the treatment. Very expensive, a lot more than you can afford."

Coppella was silent again a moment. It was true. The paltry salary of a Vatican librarian hardly paid the costs of living in Rome, never mind the escalating fees for his son's care.

"What about if I could help you?" Wilson continued. "I could fly your son to America for bone marrow treatment. I can have him cured and it would not cost you a cent."

The priest again stared at the Texan. How could he have discovered all these things – his secret 'wife', his financial problems, his son? Could he possibly be serious? His mind leaped at the possibility of Gino being cured. "What do you want in return for this?"

Wilson leaned back slightly in his chair and shrugged a little. "Information. The truth."

Coppella looked around warily at the various people in the library.

"We cannot talk here. Let us go outside."

Minutes later they stood in one of the cloister areas of a huge inner courtyard. A few tourists were walking around in small groups, far on the other side. Otherwise they were alone.

The young priest stood with his head down, facing the marble cloister floor for some while, the desperate thoughts racing through his mind. Finally he drew in a deep breath, looked up and faced the impassive expression of Myron Wilson.

"There is one sensitive area that I know about, relating to the scrolls."

Wilson leaned closer. "Go on."

"Do you know anything about them?"

"I know a little," said Wilson.

"Well, there are hundreds of fragments as you know. Ever since their discovery they have been pieced together, translated and documented. They are held in the Vatican but their contents have been widely published."

"Yes?" said Wilson.

"They have been studied for many years. We now understand a great deal about them, and…well, there is one scroll in particular that has fascinated academics and archaeologists the world over. Most agree that there are some important pieces of information missing, but they are presumed lost."

"And?" said Wilson.

"In public we agree with these conclusions. We share the view that this material does not exist – that it perished long ago. But," Coppella looked around nervously again and drew in another, shaking breath, "we have it. We always have had. It is kept here in the Antiquities department. Ever since it was discovered we kept it confidential, but about fifteen years ago it was placed under the tightest security. There is rumour that it tells of secret directions to a priceless treasure, yet to be found."

Wilson smiled and patted the priest on the back, to walk with him along the cloister.

"So. Tell me how can I get to see this document, Gianni?"

Coppella shook his head vigorously. "It is impossible for you to see it."

"Why impossible?"

"Only two men have access to it. Cardinal Vanutti and the current head of translation, Father Thommasen. You already know more than any man outside of the Vatican. Most of the internal staff do not even know about it."

Wilson pondered for a moment. "Are there any copies? Photographs or drawings?"

"No, no. Even I can get to see maybe one sentence in isolation. Privately I have put a few pieces together in my mind – but I have never seen the entire thing."

Wilson stopped and took a cell phone out of his jacket pocket. The priest watched as he dialled and pressed send. He held it in the air in front him, smiling. Moments later it began to ring softly.

"What?" Coppella asked. The Texan handed him the phone.

"I think you'll find that you are about to call your bank."

The young man moved the earpiece closer to his head. He heard a voice. "Hello? Hello? This is Lazio National Bank. Can I help you?"

Wilson was nodding towards him. "You need to ask how much you have in your account. Go on."

"Er…yes, this is Gianni Coppella," he said, by this time so numb with fear that he simply followed instructions. "Could I make an enquiry about my account balance please?"

He answered a few security questions to identify himself to the bank. There were a few moments delay. Then his eyes and mouth opened in shock. "Thank you. Goodbye," he stuttered, then leaned on a nearby pillar. Wilson smiled and took the phone back from him.

"I told you I was serious, didn't I? There wasn't very much in your account this morning. Now there's one hundred thousand dollars. By tonight it can be removed again. So listen. I want a copy of this information. When I get it, I will place another one hundred thousand dollars in your account, so that you can pay for your son's treatment. I will arrange transportation for you, your girlfriend and him to America in my private jet. I will have my people put you in touch with the best surgeon there is. Now, tell me, how can we go about this?"

The priest hung his head, breathing heavily. "What if I refuse to do this?"

Wilson's smile faded and he stared menacingly into Gianni's eyes.

"Then I'm afraid that your employers would have to know about your secret life. I should think you'd be disgraced and immediately dismissed. Your pathetic income would shrink to nothing."

Coppella sagged against the pillar, his face white.

"So it seems that you have little choice, my friend," Wilson continued. "Now, how do we do it?"

The priest looked up at the Texan for several moments in silence. Then forced himself to speak.

"I do not know. It is almost impossible to access the storage room. We are searched on entering and leaving. I would risk...perhaps my life. I would do that for my son, but even so – I do not know how to get what you ask for."

"What about computers," asked Wilson, "can you access it that way?"

Coppella thought frantically for a minute. He seemed to nod his head and shake it at the same time.

"Well, yes, in theory, I suppose. But it would all be password protected. I'm afraid that I am not an expert with computers," he was thinking hard, his hands pressed to his mouth. "Perhaps Alfredo..."

"Who is Alfredo?" asked Wilson.

Coppella pursed his lips and held his hand over his eyes for a moment, aware that he was about to drag someone else into possible danger.

"He is a young man. Well, almost a boy. He works with the computer systems in my department. He is very clever, impressionable. Very ambitious. Perhaps he could..."

"Can you persuade Alfredo to get a copy of this document?" said Wilson.

Gianni shook his head again. "I hope you appreciate the danger involved in this? We are not just talking about dismissal. Cardinal Vanutti is ruthless. We will be simply made to disappear. For me, perhaps it would be a necessary sacrifice, but to involve this young man…"

"I understand," said Wilson, and thought for a moment. "So I tell you what we'll do. Let's say that young Alfredo gets us what we need. If he wants, I'll take him to the US and get him employment in a computer firm that will value his talent. Silicon Valley, Hollywood, Wall Street – wherever. Plus I'll give him a starting bonus of fifty thousand dollars. Oh, and of course, you get to save the life of your little boy."

Both men stood, silent for a moment.

"Do we have a deal?" asked Wilson.

"Give me one week," replied Coppella.

Wilson grabbed the priest's hand tightly and squeezed. "Thank you Gianni. It will be a pleasure to do business with you."

He pulled a business card out of his pocket, showed it to the young man and pointed out one of the telephone numbers. "Call me there. It's a very secure connection. Use a public phone. Toll free."

Wilson strode away, out of the shade, into the sunlit area of the courtyard.

7 months later

State University, Columbus, Ohio
September 21st 2003

"Doctor Andrews?"

The professor looked up from his desk as his secretary called him.

"Mister Wilson has arrived. Shall I send him in?"

Andrews stood up and straightened his tie.

"Yes Jean, please."

With a resigned sigh he looked around at his office. At times like this, the professor always wished he had either a much larger room, or perhaps a more efficient regime of dealing with his filing. Piles of papers, drawings and site plans filled every corner. He took his jacket from its hanger, put it on, and vainly tried to smooth his white hair.

Myron Wilson strode in, a huge grin showing an impressive array of white teeth. He gripped Andrews' hand with both of his in a vigorous shake.

"Professor Andrews I presume! Good to meet you!" He spoke in a loud Texan voice.

"Well…yes, er, you're welcome Mister Wilson," Andrews replied hesitantly. "Please sit down. I apologise, I haven't had much time recently to…" his hand waved around to the piles of mess strewn around the office. He picked up a stack of folders from his visitors' chair, looked around the room for a suitable spot, then dumped them dustily on one of the smaller piles.

The Texan's smile grew even wider as he laughed and sat.

"No, no, Sir. No problem at all. One thing that never changes about archaeologists. They always get small offices, small budgets and they always have plenty of paper!"

Andrews navigated his way carefully past several pottery artefacts, resting on other stacks of files and sat back behind his desk.

"Yes, quite. But I'm afraid you have me at somewhat of a disadvantage Mister Wilson. I'm not sure why you asked to see me?"

Wilson's expression changed from the flashing grin to a more thoughtful look.

"Well, professor. Keith isn't it? Let me get to the point. You may not know me, but I am the owner of one of the largest oil corporations in Texas. I have been in business all of my life. I am sixty three years old and I am a very rich man."

Andrews didn't look impressed.

"Look, I'm not here to brag. I'm looking to invest some of my money in something more valuable than cars and swimming pools."

The professor now raised his eyebrows. Wilson leaned forward.

"To be frank with you...I don't have long to live. At least, that's what the doctors say. And believe me,

I have the services of some of the most expensive doctors around."

The professor looked puzzled and a little embarrassed. "I, er, don't think I..."

Wilson interrupted him, with almost a dismissive wave of his hand. "Just hear me out Keith. I've put money into genetics, cancer hospitals and heart clinics. I aim to live as long as possible, but I think I'll have to wait 20 years for genetics to advance enough and I don't think I've quite got that long."

Andrews was even more puzzled. "I'm sorry Mister Wilson but I still don't understand."

Wilson continued, leaning back again. "I figure that if the good Lord knows I've done something for Him, He'll do something for me. But you may ask what the heck that's got to do with you, yeah? Well I am interested in archaeology, Keith. Passionately interested. Your department here has a reputation, and your work coincides with the interest that I cherish the most."

"And what is that, Mister Wilson?"

Wilson's smile returned.

"Biblical artefacts, Keith. Important ones."

Andrews did not respond straight away. Uncertain, he toyed with a finger against his mouth as he regarded Wilson's rock steady gaze. Finally, he spoke.

"I cannot lie to you, if you are offering us funding, that is most attractive, but I'm not sure what you want or expect. We are a science institution, not a religious one. We don't do any – miracles – here, just painstaking investigation and academic study."

"You leave the religion to me, Keith," said Wilson. "Let's talk science for a minute."

Wilson reached into his jacket pocket and held up a CD in front of Andrews.

"This, Professor, is a miracle that will convince even you. Here on this disk is a piece of information I guarantee that you do not have and that you would never obtain if I walked out of here now."

Andrews looked dismissive.

"What is it?"

"You have presumably heard of the copper scroll?"

"Of course. Every archaeologist knows about it. It's in the public domain. Why should I be especially interested in another copy?"

"Well, you probably know that at least one important piece of it has always been missing?"

The professor rocked back in his chair and shook his head. "Come on, Mister Wilson. Don't play games with me. It's a very popular mystery on TV documentaries. Almost certainly that fragment was never found. Surely, you…"

There was something about Wilson that was, suddenly, deadly serious.

"You can't have found that particular missing piece?"

Wilson was nodding, gently.

"But, I mean, where on earth did you get it, if it exists at all?"

"Oh it exists, Professor. And I ain't about to tell you where I got it. Suffice to say that the owners have kept it secret since the day they found it, and I had to pay a whole heap of money to get a copy. The man who gave this to me had a son who was real sick, needed expensive medical treatment. If he got found out, he's now dead. Do you understand? And here it is. You want to find the Grail, or the Ark maybe, or the Spear, or the Crown of Thorns? I can help."

Andrews sat in thought for what seemed minutes.

"What do you want out of this? And why have you come to us?"

Wilson smiled again, even wider than before.

"I want to give this to someone I can trust to do a good job. And I reckon you're about the best in this field. Now I'll come straight to what I want in return. I will give you this information as soon as we agree. I want you to select a team of your very best people, and I will fund them for an expedition to find what they can. You get free rein to direct the work. You find anything important, you can announce it in the press when you're ready. I get first call on any artefact, to be housed in one of my museums, in the USA."

The professor sat back in his chair. After moments of silence, he raised his eyebrows, and with a small expression of resignation, nodded almost imperceptibly.

Wilson sensed his growing enthusiasm and held out his hand to shake. Andrews waited for a few moments longer and then placed his hand in the Texan's.

"Professor Andrews, this is a momentous day, which will be followed, I estimate, by many more. Now, do you have any half decent restaurants around here? I would like to buy you some lunch!"

One week later

State University, Columbus, Ohio
September 28th 2003

At the junction of another bewildering set of corridors, David found a wall-mounted map. When he'd arrived yesterday, he'd been shown to Professor Andrews' office, but he had no idea how to find his way back to it. He looked at his watch. Five minutes late. In the rooms he'd been taken to last evening, he'd been unable to sleep after the long flight. Consequently he'd overslept this morning. The cab had dropped him off at the sprawling campus and it had taken him ages, running in the hot autumn sun, to find the right building.

To the right of the map was a chart showing all of the staff in this department. Andrews' photo stood at the top of the tree. He looked for the person he'd said would be joining them this morning and found her on the next level down to the Professor. Dr Helen Ross, looking very attractive, and very stern.

"Are you lost?" said a voice close behind which made him jump.

David turned to see a wide-smiling female student with a mouth full of teeth braces looking up at him. "No. Well actually…yes!" said David, "room ninety seven?"

She couldn't decide if this man was a teacher or a mature student. His dark brown hair was tousled and unkempt, his jeans and jacket ill-fitting, yet she was attracted to his deep blue eyes.

David pointed to his left. "I have a feeling that it's this way…"

The student took hold of his finger and pointed it in the opposite direction.

"Oh, that way," said David. "Thank you."

"You're welcome," she said walking away and giggling.

David's anticipation and nervousness increased. He'd never been that good at meeting new people, especially women. But he mentally warned himself to speak directly and clearly, as he set off clutching to his chest a mass of papers inside a loose folder, somehow releasing one finger to push his spectacles properly into place. His feet echoed on the hard linoleum.

Yesterday, Professor Andrews had seemed very mysterious about the work he'd been hired to do.

David had been asked to meet with him and Dr Ross this morning and to bring along his recent work on the scrolls. That was all. Now, he reached the door, just one of many along the endless corridor. He had to put his folder down to knock, spilling his papers in the process. Jean opened the door to see him on his knees, scrabbling to gather them together again.

David stumbled through into Andrews's room, nearly tripping over a rug.

"David. Glad you could join us. Come in and have a seat."

Andrews showed him to a chair and the young Englishman sat down clumsily, nearly losing his sheaf of papers again.

As well as the Professor, there was a woman seated on the other chair, a tanned face, surrounded by curls of black hair. Late twenties, he thought.

"Hi," David said. She looked very surprised to see him, but seemed lost for words, as if she was carefully assessing how to respond. She looked away towards Andrews.

"Well, I guess you two haven't met," the professor continued, smiling from one to the other from behind his desk.

There was an awkward silence. Andrews spoke again.

"Yes, well, David, this is Helen Ross. She's our leading archaeology resident here. Helen, this is David Woodbridge, just arrived from England."

Helen managed a guarded smile. Her dark eyes looked at him briefly, then down at the floor, as she turned back to face the professor.

"David is Cambridge University's leading expert on ancient languages. Particularly from the Middle East. Or rather he was, until we poached him!"

Andrews laughed nervously at his own joke. David smiled weakly. Helen didn't.

"He should be the perfect man for our expedition."

David's eyebrows furrowed. He looked puzzled.

"Expedition? Do you want me to go on a field trip of some kind?"

Andrews nodded and pointed down to several maps placed on top of one another. They had obviously been spread on the desk after several piles of paper had been pushed dangerously close to the edge, to make room.

"Qumran! At least that's where we're going to start."

"Doctor Andrews!" Helen suddenly interrupted loudly. "I really can't understand what's happening here." She held a hand out dismissively to David.

"Look, no offence. I know about David's reputation. He's a scrolls boffin, right? But we have those all translated."

"Well Helen, if you'd let me..." Andrews didn't get to the end of his sentence.

"Sorry, Keith, but I thought you were consulting me about the personnel? There are some great archaeologists in the department that would add much more to the team. I don't think we should be discussing any details of the trip now."

The professor didn't react with the annoyance that she had tried to provoke. He sat with a silent smile and took a very deep breath.

"I'm afraid I haven't been quite honest with you. I did not call either of you here to discuss any details of the expedition."

"Sorry? What...?" said Helen. She and David looked at each other, then at the professor.

"David," he said, "Perhaps you can enlighten Helen for us. What can you tell us about the copper scroll? Fragment number six."

David thought for a minute, a little unsure of what was being asked.

"Er – right, what we call fragment number six is, or at least is suspected to be, a missing piece from the copper scroll, you know, the one that Michael O'Brien found in the 1940s."

Helen was nodding, not as if she was learning anything, but with an impatient expression. David stopped for a moment, looked to Andrews, who gave him no sign of help. He continued.

"As you probably know, the thing was rolled up, and it had sort of rusted into a solid mass. It had to be cut into fragments to unroll it."

Helen interrupted again.

"Look, I know this. We all know it don't we? We've all read the translations of the scroll, as much as any of it makes sense. What's the point of this?"

Andrews stayed completely calm.

"Just humour us for a moment Helen. David – why is the sixth fragment important?"

"Ah, well. Nobody knew anything about the copper scroll for years. The Catholic Church wouldn't talk about it. Then, about ten years ago, some people were allowed to have a look at the fragments. That's when they started translating it all. And the most mysterious puzzle is a phrase they found at the very beginning of one of the fragments. It says: '*you will find the greatest treasure of them all. God's gift to Man.*'"

"So?" Helen responded. "It's just a statement. There are lots of them. It's like a horoscope. They have those in the parchment scrolls, don't they? It doesn't mean anything."

David held up a finger, to disagree.

"Ah, well, if you look at the grammar, that phrase may actually be the end of a longer sentence. You know – 'go down to so-and-so village, go east for a thousand paces, dig here – and you will find the greatest treasure…' So you'd think we'd find that first bit on the end of the previous fragment. But we don't."

"And so?" Andrews gestured to David, encouraging him to reach his conclusion.

"It means that there's a missing fragment. In the running order, it would be fragment six. Everybody has asked the Vatican about it, but they maintain that no more fragments were ever found. It may be true, but that's unlikely, since the scroll was a continuous document when O'Brien found it. Since then they haven't let anybody look at them."

Andrews looked down at his desk. He reached beneath the overlaid maps, pulling something out from beneath. He took the CD in the fingertips of both hands and stood it on the desktop, facing them.

They both looked at it in silence for a few moments. David's mouth began to open. Helen's too. She pointed at the disk, which Andrews playfully used to reflect coloured sunlight from the high windows into her face, sporting a smug grin.

"Does this mean...?"

"Surely, you can't have…what is that…is it...?"

Andrews just nodded.

They sat for a few moments more in total silence, broken only by shouts from students out in the grounds, playing baseball on the lawns. They looked at each other, then to the disk. Helen spoke again.

"If that's what we think it is, where on earth did you get it?"

"From one of our benefactors, a very rich, and apparently very well connected one. He gave us this, and he's funding an expedition to find whatever it leads us to."

David was struggling for words and was able to close his mouth enough to form words.

"But...what's on it? Have you read it? Is it the missing fragment?"

Andrews shook his head.

"Of course I've tried. I understood some of it, but not much. But that..." he said, looking at Helen "...is why this young man is here."

Andrews and David both slowly looked around to the professor's desktop computer. As if in a panic, David grabbed the disk and the three of them scrambled around the screen as he put it into the drive.

Same day

State University, Columbus, Ohio
September 28th 2003

David sat alone, gazing at the screen. He nearly jumped out of his seat as Helen crashed in through Andrews' office door.

"How are you doing?" she said.

Andrews walked more soberly in after her, carrying a half empty cup of coffee, still trying to persuade her to wait.

"Helen, we've only given him an hour. I'm sure he'll get more done if he's left to get on with it. Come on, let's allow him to work in peace for a while."

But David wheeled his chair around to face them, nodding quickly.

"It's OK," he said. "I think I've made a breakthrough here."

"Excellent," said Helen, grabbing another chair to sit down beside him and ditching a small pile of the professor's papers onto the floor. Andrews closed his eyes and shook his head in mild exasperation. But he also carefully removed more paper from a small stool, and the three of them stared at the computer screen.

It showed a square-ish shape, obviously something that had been scanned. It was faded yellow in colour, green tinged at the edges, marked with lines like a sheet of crumpled paper. It was covered with symbols, in regular lines.

David hit a couple of keys on the keyboard and the picture zoomed in twice.

"Right," said David, "let me explain what I have so far. Can you read any of these symbols?"

Helen shook her head. "This? No way."

Andrews leaned towards the screen. "I know some of these words. That one there..." he pointed to the top section of the picture. "That's '*cross*' isn't it? And that's '*silver*'?"

David grinned. "Yeah. OK, so at least you'll know I'm not making it all up!"

He drew his finger gradually down the screen. "Look here at this section. I think I can isolate three separate clues on the page. But let me check them with you as I go, all right?" They both nodded expectantly, encouraging him to continue.

"So. If we look at this top section, I'll read off some of the words that I can translate. First, as you said, '*cross*'. Then a word, perhaps a place name – '*Patro*' or something like that."

"*Petra*!" Helen interrupted.

"Oh. Yes of course," David said. "Sorry, I'm afraid I'm a bit rusty on the geography. OK then there's '*Babylon*' and something about the '*Empire*' – Rome I suppose. And a '*stop*', or '*command post*'. Then there's something about the '*east wall*', then '*silver*'. And '*magic bird*'. Perhaps '*phoenix*'."

Andrews thought for a minute. "Right – let's see if we can piece it together. '*At the cross – crossing – of the roads to Petra and to Babylon….*'"

"*…a Roman way station* – yes!" Helen interrupted. "There's something like that about twenty kilometres from Qumran! It's a Wadi…Bebn al Nizir, or B'Elan! That's it. I was there in '98. The roads would cross about there."

"*…and somewhere around the east wall, there's a… silver phoenix*!" continued Andrews.

Helen reached for a piece of paper from Andrews' desk. "Let's get it down!"

David looked at them both, unsure for a few moments that he'd quite understood. Then Helen finished writing and showed him.

"Right, OK. Well, there's more." He turned back to the screen. "Look at the middle section of the fragment." They stared for a short while.

"Is that '*rock*'?" said Andrews.

"Yep," David nodded. "Actually it's '*great rock*,' followed by '*under*'. Then it says, '*east, two thousand cubits, Mithras temple*'. Hmm. There were a lot of Mithras temples in the Roman Empire weren't there?"

"Does it say where?" Helen asked.

"Well, there's a word here," David continued. "Something like '*Berinium*'...perhaps a Roman town name?"

They all sat in silence for a minute.

"*Ber sheba*?" Andrews asked. "Could it be? Wasn't that Berinium in the Roman period?"

Helen was nodding enthusiastically. "Must be!" She scribbled it down, she and Andrews trying to puzzle the jumble of words.

"What about this?" she announced. "*Under the great rock, which is two thousand cubits east of the temple of Mithras at Ber Sheba*...you will find something. What?"

"I have it..*a centurion's gold amulet!*" said David proudly, having just read this while Helen and Andrews had been working.

They sat back for a few moments to breathe. David was not looking so confident now. "The last bit is harder. I had more trouble reading this section. Do you want me to work on it a bit more by myself?"

Both Helen and Andrews were shaking their heads firmly, smiling, yet disagreeing.

David smiled too. "OK, you asked for it. Here goes."

He pointed at the lower section of the picture. "There's all sorts of words here. *'Home'*, then something strange – *'people with nothing'*."

The other two looked at him blankly.

"There's lots more. *'Holy place'*. Then the word *'blessed'*, or *'anointed'* perhaps."

Once again they stared blankly, trying to link the words. Helen had written them all in a circular pattern, and was drawing lines between them with her pencil.

"Oh hang on, I remember," David said. "It could be *'friends'* instead of *'blessed'*. Yes. *'Friends...people with nothing...Holy place'*. Yeah. That's the order of it."

There was silence for a few minutes, before Helen suddenly shouted to herself.

"Ha! It could be!"

"What? What do you think?" said Andrews.

Helen looked up at them and smiled. "*'Friends'* could mean disciples! And *'holy place'* – that would be a temple of course."

Andrews still looked puzzled. "But that could be anywhere?"

Helen shook her head. *"'Home'* what if it means *'our* home' – see? The *'people with nothing'*."

Andrews' mouth opened in recognition. "Of course! I see. You could be right!"

David looked from one to the other in total ignorance.

"I'm sorry David!" said Andrews. "We mean that it could be Qumran itself. The people there didn't approve of worldly goods or riches – so they were *'people with nothing'*. They're trying to tell us that the place they refer to is their own home – where some of the disciples – *'friends'* – once stayed. We know that's true!"

But Helen was starting to doubt her prior confidence. "It could be Qumran, but there are a few more places around that area that could fit that description."

David once again turned to the screen.

"Well that was the easy part I'm afraid," he sighed. "There's some other stuff here that's really complicated."

"Tell us David. Perhaps we can help."

"OK. Well look here," he pointed to a set of symbols about an inch from the bottom of the fragment. "There are some measurements. *'Ten cubits'*. *'Left wall'*. Then there's another distance measurement. Or perhaps an instruction? *'Go one hundred and forty cubits'*. Then it says *'doors'*. Oh, the last one. *'Passages'*. Does any of that make any sense?"

Helen looked up suddenly from her paper. "Passages? What about passages? Is there any more?" She sounded suddenly excited.

Andrews also was starting to realise something. "Yes David. Is there any more about that?"

David furrowed his brows and stared for a few moments, concentrating. He moved a little closer to the screen. "There's a little fold – look, just there," he pointed with his pen. "Where the scroll sheet hasn't quite been straightened. It could be... Well perhaps the word '*under*' again. Then...'*kitchen*'?"

"Yes!" both Andrews and Helen reacted almost simultaneously. David turned around. "What?" he said. "What is it?"

Helen's smile was now beaming at him. "The Kitchen! We know that!" She sounded triumphant. It's Khirbet Qumran itself, I'm almost one hundred per cent sure about it. And we know exactly where! There's a communal dining room there, with tunnels underneath it, and a known kitchen area. And it has passages leading off of it! Perhaps it means that there's something in one of them – a hundred and forty cubits in! But what?"

David grinned at them. "Well, that's the end of the fragment, isn't it?"

Helen sat back in her seat. "Oh," she said, disappointed. David and Andrews were smiling at each other.

"What?" she said.

David left her in suspense for a moment. "Remember, where we came in? This is the end of the fragment, where it's cut, and at the start of the next one..."

She broke into a laugh and jumped forward. "Of course! What an idiot!" she shouted, then her voice calmed, almost to a whisper. *"The greatest treasure of them all…"*

"God's gift to man," Andrews concluded.

"Look, I need some time to make sure of all this," David said. "There's a few things on here I can't work out yet. But I think I could get much more detail if I worked at it a bit."

"How quickly can you do it?" asked Andrews.

David was taken aback. "Er…well I suppose it won't take me too long."

Andrews looked from one of them to the other.

"The reason I'm asking is that unless you find anything contrary to what we've seen so far, you two have got two days to get yourselves ready. Then, go and find the Holy Grail!"

A few moments later, David and Helen stood in the corridor. She held out her hand and David took it.

"Well, David, I'm sorry if I was a bit short earlier. Perhaps I should start again. It's good to meet you."

He smiled and lunged to hold all of his papers in the other arm, almost dropping the precious disk.

"Whoops! Yes, you too! Don't, er...well, no need to apologise. I'm sure it wasn't personal."

He looked into the strong, dark eyes. It was almost impossible to predict whether she was going to be annoyed or amused.

"Of course it wasn't," she replied, with a benign smile.

He was a little surprised by the strength of her grip. She looked down at his hand, then back up.

"You can let go now, David. We're going to be partners, but only working partners."

He looked up at her face, now smiling a little, and jerked his hand away.

"Oh, sorry! Yes, of course."

"Well, I have plans to make. Do you think you'll have discovered anything more on that disk by tomorrow?"

"Well…I should think so."

At last her mouth widened into a grin. She had very white teeth.

"Come and see me tomorrow afternoon. My office is on the ground floor."

She shouted the last part as she turned down the corridor. David's eyes followed her slim body, her black wavy hair falling gently over her shoulders as she walked away.

She stopped and turned around to face him again.

"One more piece of advice David?"

"Yes, what's that?"

She tapped the skin of her arm, just above the wrist, with three fingers.

"Get some sunscreen before we go. You know, mad dogs and Englishmen?"

Four weeks later

Elil Palace Hotel, Dead Sea, Palestine
October 30th 2003

David cupped his coffee in both hands. It was just getting dark. The last of the sun's rays illuminated the tops of the hills across the valley. He looked at his watch. Five o'clock. The distant sounds of chanting began from the mosque in the town, some hundred yards behind the hotel. It pierced the still air, which otherwise was virtually silent.

When he'd first sat down there earlier that afternoon, there had been a cacophony of noise from the plot of land next to the hotel where another house was being built. But the labourers were finishing up now and the cement mixers and pumps were quiet.

About half an hour ago, a shepherd boy had passed by on the road, leading about a hundred goats. Now they'd gone far into the valley and he could just hear gentle, dull chimes from the bells some of them wore.

Only a few hardy tourists ever came to this spot. This was one of only two hotels, both two-star and very much the worse for wear. However, the Elil Palace did have this terrace, covered above with a ramshackle pergola, with grape vines twining around the frame and overhead, making a natural roof of cooling green leaves.

This was his favourite place and he loved this time of day. There were five tables on the terrace and he was pleased to be the only customer out here. There were very few guests at this time of year. Helen would be back soon and he didn't mind admitting to himself that he'd started to miss her when she was away on her daily digs.

In the last week, it had occurred to him every day that, when they talked or dined in the evening, he should take a chance – perhaps compliment her in some way. Even tell her how attracted to her he was. Of course he hadn't done anything of the sort. What about tonight? He looked at his watch again and as ever, his earlier confidence was evaporating as the time of her likely return approached. How could she ever want a clumsy Englishman like him? Best to wait for her to make the first move if she really was interested. He sighed and wished, not for the first time, that he could be more confident with women. And he didn't want to lose this opportunity with Helen now.

Idly he flicked through the notes he'd been working on earlier that day. He strained to read in the failing light, holding the papers to catch the glow from the dining room, through the glass doors at the back of the terrace. In the end he gave up and picked at the bread and olives the waiter had brought him with his coffee.

He pondered on their time here, which up to now had been a total disappointment. They had eagerly

143

probed the tunnels in the Qumran complex, the key clue from the disk, and found nothing. Helen seemed to take these failures very personally, whereas he kept working, looking at things from different angles and suggesting new ideas for her to try out the next day.

His eyes fixed on the workmen finishing off for the day. They were laying a large concrete block, having winched it into place with a wood-and-rope hoist. Building methods had hardly changed here for hundreds of years. Indeed, these labourers might very well be the descendants of the Qumranis who had built the old town.

David rose from his seat and ambled over to the workmen, nodding a greeting. They replied briefly but did not stop to chat. They were brushing the dust from their clothes and downing tools for the night.

Something had occurred to him early that day when he was poring over transcripts of some old documents. He crouched down to study the blocks nestling in fresh wet cement. He'd heard that in some parts of the Middle East, local factories still produced 'cubit' sized blocks. Was this a notional measure, or a real one? He placed an arm against the new wall. These blocks did look smaller.

"Hmm," he mused. "I wonder."

He went back to his seat. Idly, he scribbled a few calculations while he waited for Helen.

In the dusk, he saw her approaching along the road from the direction of the complex. She did not look pleased. She walked up the steps to the terrace and dumped her rucksack angrily on the floor beside his table.

He spoke without much enthusiasm.

"Hi…er...how've you got on today?"

She looked at him for a brief moment, frowning, then shook her head.

"Rethinking my life, mostly."

David looked at her in awkward silence, as she sat down opposite him, folded her arms and looked down at her old sneakers, thick with dust. She took a deep breath and looked at him with a small, resigned smile.

"Sorry, I'm just tired of trailing around after that damned priest."

"You're not insulting the reputation of the great Father O'Brien?"

"Yes, the great finder of treasure and the keeper of secrets. Why couldn't he stick to hearing confessions in Dublin instead of hoarding his discoveries without publishing anything?"

David smiled. "Well he did work for the Church. The Vatican aren't very open about these things."

The old waiter came out to the terrace and approached their table. He said a polite good evening to Helen.

"Mohammed. Hi, how're you doing? Can you get me a coffee and some hummus with bread please?"

The waiter bowed slightly and walked back into the hotel building.

Helen sat up, pulled off a piece of David's bread, and chewed it idly.

"Look, how long have we been here? A month?"

"Just over," David replied.

"What have we found? Empty tombs, robbed-out pits. Our wonderful new information puts the great treasure, whatever it is, in the corridor over there in the complex and it's as bare as a subway tunnel. We spent two weeks at Ber-Sheba, finally found the gate to the temple, dug it out and found nothing but an empty chamber. We've just trekked for two days to find the right spot in the Wadi Belan, lifted a ton of rocks and found a perfectly carved square hole – with nothing in it. I half expect to find a calling card next time with '*Father O'Brien was here*' written on it."

David swallowed his mouthful of coffee.

"Well, perhaps we're in the wrong place," he said. "There's a hundred thousand archaeology sites around here, remember."

She shook her head.

"No way. I'm sure we were right. You're doing your job. You've read those clues perfectly. That jar should have been there. It was there. Until Mister O'Brien collected it and so conveniently forgot to tell anybody."

"Father O'Brien, you mean?" David said, grinning.

"Pah!" Helen threw her bread at him, as he ducked. They both sat up, giggling, caught like naughty schoolchildren, as Mohammed arrived with Helen's tray.

"So where have you been this afternoon, sulking?" asked David.

She flashed a pretend angry glance at him.

"David, I do not sulk!" then she shrugged a little guiltily.

"Well, it was hot when we returned today, so I went for a shower, then I watched TV for a while."

He nodded: "The Arabian soaps, eh?"

"Actually I watched MTV. Sorry, I needed a break. After that I just went to the diggings to think for a while, about an hour ago. Perhaps for inspiration. I don't know."

She took a sip of her coffee and flicked her fork around in the plate of hummus and salad.

"So, my calm and collected partner, what have you been doing today?"

"Oh, sorting through bits and pieces, looking over the stuff from the disk, trying to make sense of it." David was vague, as usual. He shuffled with his papers. "I've had a few little insights."

"Such as what?" She spoke through a mouthful of hummus.

"Oh, nothing very sensational. I think there are a few mistakes in translation of some of the Qumran words."

Helen raised her head just a little, gave him a small smile, with suspicious eyes.

"Tell me. Where it says 'treasure', that actually means 'pile of dust and stones'?"

He ignored her sarcasm.

"Well, no...but take 'treasure' for example. When you're looking at a historical document you have to consider the meanings of words as they get translated. Also, what's in the mind of the original writer? What's his intention? When he says 'treasure' he may not really mean that."

"So we've spent all this time searching for treasures, and in fact the Qumranis are writing about cakes, or something?"

"No, of course not. I didn't mean..."

David struggled to find the right words for a moment.

"...yes, they did mean treasures. As you say, O'Brien seems to have found some of them. Perhaps that was a bad example. I meant more ordinary words. Nothing really exciting."

"Well, I'm up for anything right now."

David pointed down at his papers.

"Well, for instance there's a word here '*shaba*' that was thought to mean 'wedding dowry', when I think it just means 'present'."

Helen smiled. "I'm going to be sorry I asked, aren't I? Are there any others, preferably not related to getting married?"

"Well, there are some things that are more complex. You know the building works over there?"

She looked to her left then back towards him, with a quizzical smile. "The ones that have woken me up every damn morning since we've been here? Yes. What on earth are you talking about?"

He went on, somewhat embarrassed. "Sorry. It's just that they triggered some thoughts. Like '*qaba'*, which is their word for the length measure, the 'cubit'. It's not so much the word, rather the way they use it. It seems to be used as 'cubit' some of the time, and 'stone block' at others."

Helen leaned forward in her chair, looking more interested.

"Go on," she said.

He gestured to the building site next door, now almost invisible in the dark. "Well they still use cubits around here, and their standard building blocks seem to be quite a bit shorter than that. The ancient builders probably charged their Roman employers by the cubit, but built by the block."

David continued to explain. "Builders haven't changed much over the centuries you see! Or it's become some sort of notional reference. So...just a minute..."

Their eyes met. David's mouth fell open as the implications of what he had just said struck both of them. She stood up and gripped his hands.

"Do you know what this means?" she shouted at him, laughing.

"Oh, good heavens! That's the answer! Good heavens!"

Helen pulled his head towards her and kissed his cheek.

"Eureka might be a better word!"

She reached excitedly into her bag and pulled out a sketchbook and pencil. She started drawing hurriedly.

"OK, this is the kitchen area. What did the disk say? *'Go ten cubits along the wall of the kitchen and you will find an entrance...'* She looked up. That would still mean the second door, whether it was one measure or another."

"'Then one hundred and forty cubits along this passage you will find the greatest treasure of them all. God's gift to man'."

"Wow!" said Helen. "If that was in blocks instead? We'd be in a completely different part of the tunnel!"

She pulled away. David stared at her, smiling.

"Well, what now?"

Helen held her chest as she took another deep breath.

"Let's try to keep calm. What I mean is, *I* will try and keep calm! We could check it out with torches but...no, we can't. It's pitch black. It'll wait. Let's try and get some sleep shall we? Start at first light?"

David hesitated for a few moments, as he always did when preparing to say anything that contradicted Helen's suggestions.

"Perhaps...a small drink? You know, just to make you drowsy?"

Helen took his arm.

"Lead on, Archimedes."

They went together into the hotel. David secretly enjoying the feeling of her fingers on the crook of his elbow.

Ten minutes later they were in the bar of the Hotel.

"Hiya Rami! We're celebrating!" said Helen, approaching the barman.

The man looked puzzled and looked from one of them to another.

David immediately fumbled in his pocket, eager to pay for the drinks. "Drinks, Rami. I'll have some red wine, I think. Do you have a Beaujolais?"

"Pardon sir?" The barman looked puzzled again.

"Just...red wine for me then. Helen, will you have some as well…?"

"Jack Daniels on the rocks," interrupted Helen as she walked towards a free table.

David raised his eyebrows and looked back to Rami.

"OK! One red wine and a Jack Daniels. On the rocks."

"Sorry, what sir?"

David looked around the ramshackle bar. He realised that he needed to make some allowances. He spoke again, pointing at the relevant bottles.

"Whisky, on its own. With some ice." He lowered his voice. "A large one."

He carried the drinks to the table and sat right next to Helen. He was pleased to see that she made no objection to this. She sipped her drink, before looking through the side of the glass at the size of the measure. Rami was very generous with his drinks.

"Are you trying to get me drunk David?" she said with a smile.

"No, no honestly," he said, not seeing the mischief in her eyes.

"Well, here's to us! To our great find."

They chinked glasses together.

Helen sighed. "Do you realize that this may be the first time we have out-thought Father O'Brien? You don't think he would have worked this out?"

"I hope not. But you never know. He was a clever man."

Helen looked cheekily at David. "Not as clever as you though."

She sank the whisky in one go. "My round I think?"

"Umm I've only had one sip." But Helen was already advancing on the barman.

An hour later, they stood outside Helen's room.

David felt somewhat awkward. "Thanks for a lovely night."

"Thanks for making my decade!" said Helen throwing her arms around David and hugging him.

She opened her door and stepped inside, turning to face David.

"Well goodnight."

"Yes goodnight," said David and made to kiss Helen on the cheek. She grabbed his neck and pulled him to her, planting an almost-jokey kiss quickly on his lips.

"Six o'clock sharp!" she laughed and closed the door in his face.

David stood there awhile, not quite knowing if he was thrilled or disappointed.

The same day

Vatican City, Rome
October 30th 2003

Six men, all priests or bishops, filed into the office of Cardinal Vanutti. He sat at the head of his deeply polished, antique meeting table, frowning and silent. Several of them wished him good morning. He did not acknowledge them with more than a brusque nod. They all sat down and within a few moments he closed a folder of papers and placed his gold pen neatly by the side of it.

"Gentlemen, as you know, we as members of this committee have the privilege of supervising the most important project that the Catholic Church has ever been engaged in."

This put the others off guard. Several leaned forward, not knowing why Vanutti had begun with such an obvious statement.

"Recently," he continued, "I have been undertaking a review of security, which as you know is of paramount importance."

"Has there been a problem, your Grace?" One of the priests looked puzzled.

"Should there be, Monsignor Garcia?" Vanutti was accusing in his reply.

There was no answer from anyone. Vanutti continued.

"Let me remind all of you that the truth of this project is supposedly known exclusively to those in this room, His Holiness, and a few staff who are under the closest supervision. There has never been any hint of a leak in the Vatican at large..."

The group waited, in silent expectation.

"Until now."

There were astonished looks around the table. A babble of discussion arose. Vanutti finally stilled it by raising his hand. His eyebrows seemed to darken and lower even more and he spoke with a menacing tone.

"At present I am acting on the merest hints and suspicions. I have no concrete evidence. But let me re-emphasise to you all. This information has been given to you under a sacred trust. Do I have to spell out the consequences should I discover that any one of you has broken it? I promise you, I will personally silence anyone who has betrayed us. Do I make myself clear?"

There were looks of surprise and fear, plus general mutterings of understanding.

"Thank you gentlemen. That is all. Please keep me informed of the slightest news."

One day later

Ruins of Khirbet Qumran Temple, Palestine
October 31st 2003

The first rays of the soon-to-be fierce sunlight played through a hole in the drapes, onto Helen's face. The room was small, basic and scruffy.

For a while she dozed, half awake, and stared at imagined patterns in the plaster ceiling. She let a beam of sunlight play over her eyes, moving her head backwards and forwards and feeling the warmth there. The first call from the local mosque echoed in the distance and suddenly she awoke fully. She sat up in bed and reached for the ancient telephone on the battered cabinet beside her. She dialled David's room number.

The phone rang seven times before a bleary sound could be heard at the other end.

"Hey!" she shouted. "Are you awake?"

There was a pause as she waited for David to get his brain working.

"What do you mean it's early? Yes, now! Come on, I'll see you down there."

She put down the phone and sat for a moment hugging her knees and smiling to herself, as well as trying to smooth the curls of dark hair out of her eyes. Then she threw back the bedcovers and dressed as quickly as she had ever done.

Thirty minutes later they stood amid the ruins of the old town. The low, wind-smoothed remains of the walls cast long shadows across the scrub floor of the valley, with the sun still low in the east. A light breeze whipped a little sand into the air. In front of them were some worn steps, leading beneath the refectory area into the dark entrance to the kitchens tunnel.

David yawned wearily. Helen was jumpy and alert, like an excited schoolgirl.

"Have you got the flashlight? Are you sure the batteries are OK?"

"What?" David replied, briefly puzzled. "Oh, the torch, yes. I changed them two days ago." He fumbled in his kit bag, brought out the torch and she grabbed it from him. She playfully shone it into his eyes. He winced and made a pretend lunge to admonish her, but she giggled and jumped away towards the steps.

Some eight feet down, the tunnel stretched away into the distance, only the first twenty yards or so illuminated by the torch. It felt cool and damp and was completely silent. Helen went first, preceded by the wash of torchlight; David followed touching the sidewall. He had to concentrate on peering over her shoulders to see anything ahead, and not on the dimly lit outline of her behind, very roundly pressed into her tight-fitting jeans.

They passed several openings to the right and left.

"Is that where we were before?" he whispered, tapping her arm.

"Nope. It's a bit further on," she replied, not stopping. "And there's no need to speak quietly. We're not in a church!"

As they went on, he began to recall the layout of this maze of tunnels from when they'd first explored it a month ago. Helen seemed to have a map imprinted in her head.

"Here!" she said, and they stopped as she shone the torch to the right, into the opening space of the kitchen chamber.

The kitchen was roughly square, about thirty feet on each side. There were still benches around the walls, built from stacked mud bricks and stone tiles. In the right hand corner nearest them was a deep hole in the ground, the remains of an old well. In the center of the room was an oblong raised platform, the base for the cooking fire. It was covered with a small mound of earth and stones. Looking up, they could see the old chimney hole from where this fall had descended, now blocked. Directly opposite them was a dark doorway, and in the wall to their left, a further two. They picked their way across the floor, shining the torch down to avoid the tumbled mess of rocks and broken tiles, and stood on the hearth platform.

David pointed at the doorway facing them. "Was it that one?"

In the dim light, he could just see Helen shaking her head. She could barely conceal a nervous smile and was breathing heavily with apprehension. "No. That's the dining area, remember? This is the one. Come on." She flashed the torch at one of the doorways to their left and went in.

David stood still for a moment, lost in thought. "Eating area. Hmm. I wonder..." he muttered to himself. The light vanished.

"David! Come on!" Helen shouted back to him.

As carefully as they could, checking on both sides of the wall, they counted one hundred and forty blocks along the tunnel. They stopped and Helen played the light around the walls on both sides.

"Where were we before?" David asked.

Helen ignored him for a few moments, crouching down to examine the stones. "Further up there. Forty feet or so," she pointed into the darkness of the tunnel without looking, still focused on her task.

"Trowel," she said, and David rummaged in his kitbag for the tool. He sat silently for several minutes while Helen poked at the stones on both sides. Finally, she slammed the torch down onto the floor and sat down, back against the wall.

"Damn it! Nothing! Absolutely nothing."

David was puzzled and tried to offer some words of encouragement.

"Er...look I'm no expert, but what if something is behind the stones? Here or at that spot along the tunnel where we were before? Shouldn't we dig a bit, or something?"

Helen sighed as if trying to be patient with a naughty child.

"David, all these stones are undisturbed. Completely. They are virtually the oldest bits of this structure. They were built six hundred years before the scroll artefacts were concealed."

"Oh," David replied.

She hit out at the wall in anger. "There's nothing here! Look, if we don't find anything today I swear I am packing up and going home. I've had enough."

David thought for a moment. "What about that room that leads off the kitchen? Couldn't we check in there?"

"Of course," Helen replied, sarcastically. "We could check everywhere. Every brick and stone in the place. *If* we had the rest of our lives to spare."

"What is that room, did you say?"

Helen forced herself to be patient. "It's an annexe of some kind. A storeroom. Or perhaps an eating area, where the cooks would eat. Staff dining room. That's what people think, anyway."

"Aren't there tunnels leading off that room as well as from the kitchen?"

"Yes. Well, long store cupboards probably, but now they look like tunnels, just like this," she replied impatiently. "But what's the point? We don't know it's a dining area because any wooden table they might have had would have rotted away. But we know the clue says 'kitchen', and that the room behind us *is* the kitchen. Everybody who's studied this place agrees." Then her voice changed, as she saw David furrowing his brows in thought. "What are you thinking of?"

He thought for a moment longer. "It's just something that occurred to me yesterday, while you were away. You know, as well as the cubits thing."

She sat up, now more animated. "What?"

"Well," he went on, trying to choose his words carefully. "I've been thinking about the wording in the scroll. 'Kitchen; eating area' – they could easily be confused in the dialect that we're translating from."

She pressed two fingers to her mouth and touched his lips with them. "My hero to the rescue again! I should really learn to trust you shouldn't I?"

She smiled again and stood up. "Follow me," she said, walking back down the tunnel to the kitchen area.

"Wait for me!" shouted David. Then a little quieter he added "You know I hate the dark."

They entered the second room, which was almost featureless, apart from a litter of broken tiles and earth on the floor. To their left were two openings in the wall, smaller than those that led from the kitchen. The furthest entrance was not an evenly cut doorway, but ragged in shape, with fallen masonry across the threshold. Helen entered, ducking under a giant cobweb straddling the top of the hole. David followed, breaking it and flapping his hands in case there was a spider still there.

Helen laughed. "Onward brave explorer!"

A rustling noise from the floor made them jump. A small dark-ringed snake started crawling away from the torchlight. David guided it towards a hole in the wall with his foot. "C'mon little fellow, time for bed."

The snake disappeared from view.

Helen stood with her hands on her hips and a slight smile on her face. "Do you know what that was?" asked Helen.

"A snake?"

"It was an Asp. Little one. Still deadly."

David laughed a little too loud. "Oops," he muttered.

They carefully worked their way along the tunnel, once again counting blocks from the entrance.

"One hundred thirty-eight, thirty-nine, one hundred and forty. It should be here."

David looked from one side to the other as Helen played the torch around. "It looks just the same as all the others."

Helen held out her hand. He could just see the almost-resigned expression on her face as once again he pulled her trowel from his kitbag.

He sat again as she poked around where the wall met the floor on both sides.

"I guess my theory was wrong then," said David apologetically. "There's nothing here either."

Helen didn't reply. There was complete silence, apart from her careful stone-scraping down near the floor.

He pressed one of the large blocks in front of him and whispered "Open Sesame!"

The noise stopped. "David, I don't mind the jokes, but could you just hold the flashlight steady please?"

"Oh, sorry. Yes." He felt stupid as she continued for several minutes. Then she stopped again. She was staring hard at something.

"Yes!" she cried out suddenly, making him jump.

"What?"

He leaned over and put his head next to hers, staring where she was pointing the light.

"Look at this! Mortar!"

"What, like cement? What does that mean?" he replied, puzzled.

She was becoming more excited by the second.

"David – these two stones have been set with mortar. The original people here built this structure without any! Look at the other stones around them. See? Normally they just lie on top of one another. This is incredible!"

She leaned over and hugged him, then let go and continued talking excitedly.

"The Romans invented cement. This means that these stones have been disturbed and reset at least…well, hundreds of years after this place was built! There's an artefact here!"

"Possibly here," David said.

"Oh come on, don't be so pessimistic! Let's get some help." Helen pushed the trowel back into his bag and guided him back along the tunnel.

"Let's go and get the digging team, my genius-like partner!" She took his arm in hers and clamped them together, side by side, as they picked their way across the debris of the tunnels.

David smiled to himself as they walked out. He wasn't really pessimistic. And he did very much like the way that Helen had hugged him.

They were back in three hours. Five men from the local village, Beth Shela, had arrived with stone-cutting tools, shovels, buckets and rope for ferrying loose earth. They walked slowly up to the outer walls of the complex, smoking and talking in rapid Arabic. Their leader came up to them, smiling, and bowing a little. Helen was almost jumping up and down. He was a little surprised as she briskly stepped towards him and grabbed his hand to shake it.

"Youssef – great you could get here!"

"Hello, madam, hello sir. Well, here is my team as you requested. We have done the digging work for many scholars. We will help you find what you seek. Which is the place for digging?"

Helen was unstoppable. She shook the hands of all the men and led them like a US cavalry captain over the rocks towards the entrance to the complex.

In the tunnel, Youssef surveyed the area around the mortared blocks. He nodded reassuringly to David and Helen and was about to speak to them, when an argument suddenly ensued amongst his men. He turned to them and they all debated fiercely in Arabic for several minutes. Helen looked at David, smiling and raising her eyebrows despairingly.

After Youssef had raised his voice finally, one of his team stamped out of the tunnel, shouting back to the rest of them. Youssef turned to David, who hadn't understood a word.

"I am sorry sir. He wished to make trouble. He has gone now. We are ready."

With hammers and chisels, they hacked out the mortar that had sealed the stones. Two of the men jammed crowbars into the cracks on either side of one stone and heaved. The stone came out of the wall by about half an inch. Youssef shouted to the others to come and assist. They laboured for over an hour, gradually hauling the two stones further out into the corridor.

A cloud of dust filled the air. Finally, four of the men drew back, sweating and coughing, speaking excitedly. As the dust settled, they could see the large, earth hole laying behind the stones.

"OK!" Helen asked Youssef and the others to move back. She shone her flashlight into the hole. It was very dark. She could just make out an earth floor about six feet below.

"Let's see what's in here!"

She climbed into the hole, feet first, holding her hands out for Youssef and David to help lower her in. She gradually wriggled downwards until only her head and arms protruded above floor level.

"Right guys, you're gonna have to drop me!"

They expressed some concern about this. She nodded vigorously.

"It's OK, I've seen the floor down here. It's only about another two feet down."

They let go, and she whooshed out of sight.

"It's a small chamber." They could hear her muted voice coming from below. "It's real dark down here. I'm trying to see the size of it with my flashlight."

David lowered his head, to try and see down inside the hole.

"Helen, what's down there?

Helen sounded sombre. "There's a great stone box here. It fills up most of the chamber. I can just see some inscriptions on the side of it. There are some broken pots lying about, and some old tools. OK come down, I'm out of the way."

David wriggled down into the hole, with Youssef holding onto his hands.

"OK your feet are nearly there." He felt Helen grabbing his ankles. Youssef let go and he jumped down.

The chamber was just big enough for both of them to stand together. He patted the earth and dust from himself. There was the dimmest light from above as the scant illumination in the tunnel above filtered down through the hole. They played torches onto the stone box.

"Is this it?" asked David.

Helen lowered her voice, whispering. "It's like a sarcophagus. Look at this lid, it's two inches thick. Do you think we can open it?"

David had an experimental push at it.

"Perhaps. I don't know. If we push together. Maybe we can move it enough to peek inside."

"Look, it's covered in funerary inscriptions isn't it?" Helen said, excitedly. "What do they say?"

"Well, there are some familiar characters. I don't know. I'll need to think."

"Come on then. Hey – will any of these tools help?" Helen stooped down into the dark. David heard clanks as she picked up various metal objects. She stood up, with one in each hand.

"Here we are. A chisel, and some sort of digging tool."

David played his torch over the objects. Helen was already trying to prise one of them under the huge stone lid.

"Wait a minute. Don't they look in rather good condition?" he said.

She stopped, and held the digger up into the beam. It looked like a trowel, with a fine coating of dust. The edges were straight, the wooden handle rotten. She closed her eyes and blew the dust away. There was writing on the metal. They both peered closely at it. A few letters were obscured, but it was clear. '*Sheffield steel. England. 1946*'.

Even in the dim light, David could see the enthusiasm draining from Helen's face.

"O'Brien!" they both said together.

She shouted in anger as she put her hands against the sarcophagus lid. "Open, damn you!"

David pushed as hard as he could to help. There was a shriek of stone against stone as the lid shifted four inches open at one corner. Helen shone her torch into the blackness and nervously peered into the interior.

The box was completely empty.

"He's beaten us to it again!" Helen threw her torch into the sidewall of the chamber and pushed past him, shouting for Youssef to help her out.

"Helen, hang on, be careful," he called after her. "Look, at least we can check out these inscriptions! Don't be so..."

She was gone. David sighed and turned his torch on the shapes carved into the stonework.

The side of the tomb was covered in very old symbols in the Qumrani dialect.

He muttered to himself as he ran his fingers along each symbol, like someone reading Braille.

"A King? This must be the tomb of a King. Israel. Jews. But what is this first part…?"

Helen sat on the floor of the tunnel lifting pinches of earth and throwing them back down in frustration.

Youssef was talking to his men, further down the tunnel. He approached her and crouched down. Helen looked up, with a wry smile.

"Sorry Youssef, you'll still get paid, I promise."

Youssef shook his head.

"You are kind, miss, and we are grateful. But there is something else. A thing that may be of use to you."

Helen looked faintly surprised, but not terribly excited.

"Yes? What?"

"The man who left the tunnel earlier," Youssef continued, "he would not dig here. He says it is cursed. But he knows a man, Ahmed Mossadah, in the village near here, who he says was digging here in the past. Perhaps you would like to meet him? I can arrange it."

Helen sat up.

"David, what do you think? This could give us a clue. David?"

She noticed for the first time that he was still down inside the tomb.

"Helen! Helen come here quickly!"

David sounded scared.

She lowered herself into the darkness again and stood next to him. "What is it? Another snake?"

David gripped her arm too tightly.

"Ouch! David what is it?"

"The tomb. Look on the side of the tomb!"

"What David? Calm down!"

"I know what we have found." He held the torch as steadily as he could, and tracked along the carved symbols with a shaking finger.

"Look here. '*He was the Messiah*'. And here – '*Killed by the Romans, betrayed by the Elders of his own people*'. And here, '*the true Son of God*'."

He looked up at Helen with fear in his eyes.

"And the last line…" he gulped. "It says, '*Jesus. King of the Jews*'."

One day later

Beth Shela Village, near Jerusalem
November 1st 2003

It was just after dusk. The amplified chants from the village's two mosques broke the silence, thin and crackly over the megaphone speakers that were tied to the minarets. They were grim concrete buildings with makeshift towers. This village had none of the grace and attraction of towns on the middle-eastern tourist trail. Youssef led David and Helen down a side road. The road beneath them was uneven and made of packed earth, with discarded household refuse littering the dark alleyways between the houses. Harsh brightness of bare electric bulbs came from glassless windows. They reached the last house. Youssef knocked on an ill-fitting, ramshackle door. A young man answered, welcoming, obviously expecting them. Youssef said something in Arabic to him, and he ushered them inside. He disappeared through a further door. David went to follow, but Youssef shook his head and motioned for them to sit. There was an old wooden dining table in the middle of the room, surrounded by a small, torn sofa and various rickety chairs. Around the walls were photos, Islamic art prints, faded and obviously damp.

Youssef whispered: "This is the house of Ahmed. He is here, but he will not see you without his son bringing some tea. Wait a few moments, have respect for his home."

David gently touched Helen's shoulder.

"What?" she said and looked in his direction as he motioned her towards one of the photos framed on the wall. They could just make out two men posing for the camera, a young Arab resting his feet on a shovel, next to an older man, dressed in western clothes, with a clergyman's dog collar.

"Ahmed and a priest," said Helen.

"O'Brien, I presume," David whispered.

They were interrupted by sounds from the back rooms, of cups and scraping of plates. Then someone moving, and a steady click of wood on the stone floor. The young man reappeared with a tray, followed by another, older man. He had a stick with which he felt his way into the room.

"Greetings, my friends." He hobbled into the light. He looked about forty years old. His son, about seventeen, held the older man's arm and guided him to a seat. In the harsh wash of light from the bulb above, they could see his eyes, glazed and opaque with blindness. He reached out, searching with his hands. Helen and David shook hands in turn, introduced themselves and sat around the table.

"You will have some tea? Hecham, pour some tea for our guests."

172

The boy poured thick, sweet tea into small, cracked glasses. There was an awkward silence as they took a first sip. Youssef sat in one corner of the room smoking a cigarette and saying nothing. Then Ahmed broke the silence.

"Youssef tells me that you are archaeologists, working at the temple?"

"Yes, er, that's right," David replied, "We've been...er..."

"Mister Mossadah," Helen interrupted, "We believe you were digging at the same place as us about nineteen years ago. With Father O'Brien?"

Ahmed was silent for some moments. He lowered his head, took a deep breath.

"So. It is a secret no more. You have found the chamber."

David looked at Helen, then back at Ahmed.

"Well, we've found something. Something incredible. But it was empty. Can you tell us what happened? What did you find?"

"If you have found the chamber, then you saw the sarcophagus. Father O'Brien and I were the first to find it. As soon as we had lifted the lid, he said that we had to leave. He said that it could not be disturbed without more scientists being told."

"So what happened next?" Helen asked.

Ahmed frowned and shook his head. The fingers of his right hand made a fist, which he pressed onto the wooden tabletop.

"We had worked for years up until that moment. We were friends. So I waited for a few days. I honoured his request. Then, many men came to investigate the diggings. Father O'Brien's masters, from the Vatican. He came to see me here and told me that we could not work together any more, that it was finished. He said that I should never tell anybody of what we had done. I should never dig there. So I watched from a distance. They had guards with guns outside of the entrance. They brought transport vans and helicopters. Then, after two weeks, they were gone. I crept into the tunnel and it was just as if we had never been there."

Helen and David looked at each other again, uncertain of what to say next. Finally, David spoke softly.

"When you first opened the tomb, you must have seen what was in there?"

Ahmed put his head into his hands.

"I have been wishing for twenty years that I had not. Can't you see I'm blind? I used to be healthy and strong. I was a clever young man, perhaps like you. I wanted to be a scholar. An archaeologist. I believed in science. But because...of what we found, I was cursed." He raised his head. "I see nothing but phantoms. I have not been able to look into the eyes of my wife or my son for ten years. Now, I wish to let the past lie. Perhaps God will forgive me."

David made to speak, but Helen stopped him with her hand against his arm.

"Mister Mossadah. What if I was to say that your blindness was not caused by any curse?"

Ahmed looked sneeringly at them.

"I would say that it is not you who are blind. Why should I care to argue?"

"I was born in a very poor district, in Detroit, in America. My father was a doctor who would treat many local people who could not afford health insurance. I have seen eyes like yours before. I think you have cataracts, and they can be cured."

Youssef looked up suddenly. Hecham saw the surprise in Ahmed's face and asked his father in rapid Arabic what had been said. Helen continued.

"You need an operation, in hospital. Not a major one. They can remove the cataracts and you will see again."

Ahmed looked at once excited and puzzled.

"But are you sure in what you say? I am a poor man. I do not know if I can get treatment at a hospital. There are long queues for anything."

Helen spoke again.

"You have something that we need. We have access to whatever resources we need from America. Please tell us everything you know. I promise that you will get the hospital treatment."

Ahmed nodded slowly.

"Very well." His voice was shaky. "I saw into the sarcophagus for only a moment. But it was enough."

"What did you see?" David leaned forward.

"It was a body. Very old. I have seen lots of bodies, with Father O'Brien, but this one, he was certain. He was frightened... he knew what it was."

Helen was almost afraid to confirm it. "It was...?"

"Yes," Ahmed nodded once more. "We found the body of Jesus Christ. They took it away. To the Vatican. I never heard anything about it again."

EPIPHANY

EPIPHANY

3 days later

Columbus University, Ohio
November 4th 2003

Keith Andrews looked across his table at David and Helen.

He detected subtle changes in the two of them already. David seemed much more self-confident than before. He didn't appear to stumble over his words as much as he had before. Helen on the other hand was more quiet and introverted somehow. He put the folder down onto his desk, giving a low whistle as he closed it.

"Well, that is some report!" he said, then tilted his head a little as they heard a booming voice from the outer office. The door opened and Jean popped her head in.

"Professor?" she said, looking somewhat flustered. "Mister Wilson is here. He…"

The door opened fully and the Texan strode in past her, radiating an air of excitement.

"Thank you my dear!" He beamed at Jean as she left.

"Helen! David!" It's great to meet you at last!" He tried to shake hands with both of them at the same time.

"I've read the report. This is fantastic news. Let me tell you – you two have done an amazing job!"

David nodded. "Well we still don't actually have it. We haven't seen it yet."

"No but just knowing it exists, it makes me buzz with electricity! I feel alive again."

"Sorry?" said David, somewhat puzzled.

"What? Oh – just my turn of phrase, son! What I mean is, I've been real impatient for news. This is beyond all my expectations!"

Andrews raised his hands as if to calm the Texan a little. "Well, I apologise for sounding a little sceptical Mister Wilson, but we don't know what happened to the body yet. It may not even exist anymore."

"You kidding?" Wilson waved Andrews' objections away with a flourish of his arm. "Why would they get rid of it? It's the body of Jesus, for Christ sakes! Come on folks, why are y'all being so damned miserable?!"

"But why would the Vatican keep this a secret?" Andrews continued. "Why not announce this to the world? It's such a fabulous find to share."

"It was also nearly twenty years ago," said David. "Why would they have just hidden it away for so long?"

The Texan smiled broadly. "Now that, I intend to find out!"

"Well, perhaps now you need to go and talk to a private investigator?" said Andrews. "I think our department has helped you all that we can now."

Wilson shook his head emphatically. "I think not! These guys have done a better job than any private eye that I've met." He looked down at Helen and David. "I want you two to continue with this work. What d'you say?"

David looked alarmed. "Er...No, I don't think so Mister Wilson. I don't think I'd be any good at...detective stuff."

"Nonsense!" Wilson boomed. "You two are the perfect choice for this job. You have all the background information. You know O'Brien and his work. Hell, he may even be alive still!"

They sat in silence for a moment.

"I want to go."

All three men turned to look at Helen.

"I want to go and find out what happened," she spoke quietly and defiantly. "I think we should go to the Vatican and find the body if we can."

Wilson beamed at her.

"That's my girl!"

"David?" said Helen. His face still showed alarm and confusion. She was smiling with a hint of coyness. "You won't let me go on my own, will you?" she said, but somehow that was for the benefit of the other two men. To him, her eyes were appealing and demanding, holding him in their gaze. She spoke softly to him. "You know we've got to do this. If I have to I'll go by myself, but you're part of the team."

David exhaled and hung his head as he reluctantly agreed.

Wilson was triumphant. "That's what I needed to hear! Now, when can we start?"

The two of them looked up at Wilson, then at each other, shrugging their shoulders.

"Tell you what," the Texan continued. "I'll call Dallas immediately. They can fuel up my private jet and have it ready in a couple of hours. You can be gone in a day. What d'ya say?"

They nodded in surprised agreement.

"Well, this is a great day," Wilson boomed. "I wish you Godspeed over the Atlantic! And Keith?" Andrews looked up. "Let me tell you, I don't forget my friends. You and your college here are gonna benefit big time from this!" He put his arm around Helen's shoulders and the two of them walked towards the door, Wilson talking excitedly into her ear. "Now, you go and make your preparations. You bring me some news as soon as you can. And whatever you need – you just call me, anytime. Deal?"

"It's a deal!" said Helen.

David looked sheepishly at Andrews, and with a nervous smile, followed them out.

2 days later

Approaching the Pallacio Hotel, Rome
November 6th 2003

The cab wound its way through the back streets near the Vatican. The driver seemed to speak little English beyond understanding their hotel destination and he was in any case preoccupied with muttering and sounding his horn at the crazy Roman drivers that seemed to lurch out of every side street.

"So what do you think they did?" Helen said. "I mean how did the body get to the temple?"

David was shielding his eyes from the sun slanting in the rear side window.

"Well, Jesus had a lot of followers, didn't he? Don't forget the story of his tomb being empty after his death. We're pretty sure it was buried outside the walls of Jerusalem. When the flak died down they could well have taken away his body and concealed it. They must have decided that they needed a hiding place and put it in the Qumran complex. Who knows? It could have been in a dozen places before that."

"But how did it get into the scrolls?" Helen took a turn to shield her eyes and the cab turned a corner.

"The Essenes – you know, the people who moved away from Jerusalem to Qumran – they were the real zealots, the people who wanted the Jewish Temple

Elders out as well as the Romans. They would have had a lot in common with the crowd that followed Jesus just before he was arrested. After he died, some of those may well have gone to live at Qumran, and told their hosts the full story. They wrote it down and locked it away. Somehow it got lost."

Helen touched David's arm as they struggled to carry their luggage up the small cul-de-sac, from where the cab had dropped them.

"There – that old fashioned looking place up at the end – that's the Pallacio."

She pointed to the end of the street, to a thin, tall building. Its yellow paint was faded, typical Roman, and at each of the upstairs windows, tiny, rickety balconies teetered over the street. There were flowers on the mesh of leaves, climbing around all of the window frames."

He turned to smile at her. "It's lovely."

The sun was almost setting, illuminating the tiled roofs.

"'See Rome and die happy', they say, don't they?" Helen said, as they approached the hotel entrance.

"Actually they say that about Naples," David replied. "I can't think why though!"

They clattered into the lobby. Marble floor. Plants in huge, old pots. There were large, old mirrors on the sidewalls, and at the end of the corridor, a tiny desk. Helen went forward and hit the bell. A dour, very Italian man shuffled out of a side office.

"Si?" He looked as though they had just interrupted his dinner.

"Ross. Helen Ross and David Woodbridge. We made a telephone reservation?"

The man looked through the scruffy papers on his desk.

"Ah, yes. I have a note of your call. What...er...you want? One room?

David nodded enthusiastically, if not very seriously.

"Yes. One room. Mr and Mrs Smith."

The receptionist did not see the joke.

Helen pushed David out of the way.

"Don't listen to him! We want two separate rooms please."

"With adjoining door?" David chipped in.

"Preferably on different floors." said Helen.

The man was looking from one to another, completely mystified.

"I'm sorry!" Helen was apologetic and began to speak more slowly. "We want two rooms. Anywhere is OK. Thanks."

The man gave her a key. She turned to David, pointed at him and pretended to be angry.

"Now you. Behave yourself! I'm going for a bath. I'll see you for dinner. Eight thirty down here. Don't be late!"

She walked off, up and around the small staircase. David took his room key and whispered to the man, with a knowing glance. "That may be best. She snores loudly anyway."

He grabbed his bags and set off up the stairs. The receptionist shrugged his shoulders, shook his head and went back to his dinner.

They sat in a small bistro, a few streets away from the hotel. There were a few other customers. It was cramped, dim and last decorated about thirty years ago. A perfect Roman restaurant.

"So, what are we going to do tomorrow?" Helen asked, sipping her glass of wine.

David picked at his bread. "I suppose we'll just have to go to the Vatican main entrance and then ask for O'Brien. Any other approach you can think of?"

"No, I don't think so." She put both elbows on the table and rested her chin on her hands, smiling slightly. "Anything else on your mind?"

He hesitated, nervously smoothing the tablecloth.

"Well, my father always says 'this is my body' when he breaks bread in church."

"He's a pastor?" Helen asked, her eyes widening a little.

David spilled breadcrumbs all over the table. "Ooops. Yes. In England we'd say 'Vicar'."

She laughed. "Well well. It's creepy isn't it? Anything else?"

"Er...no. My mind is blank. Well...blank-ish. I'm still wondering whether or not to have pudding…"

He looked up at her, his words trailing off. She sat looking at him with a smile and eyes that he thought twinkled a little in the candlelight.

"Well," he said, "I suppose there are always things on one's mind. Aren't there?"

She continued to look at him, her smile growing.

"What?" he asked.

She laughed gently. "You're not going to be the first to say anything are you?!"

She sat back slightly with her palms on the table. He looked down at the table and saw that her left hand was snaking slowly towards his.

"Erm…well, there was actually something I was thinking about," he said.

Her fingers brushed the side of his hand.

"I know what you're thinking David. I'm thinking the same. There's something special between us, isn't there?"

Her hand moved to cover his, steadying it on the table.

He shrugged, then nodded, smiling.

"I just wanted to say something before we get back to the hotel," she said.

"You're really a man in disguise?" David joked, laughing nervously. She smiled and shook her head.

"I like you, even if you are a stupid English geek! Look, I am a loud, modern American girl but I had a pretty moral upbringing. My parents weren't religious but they were a great example. So I don't do casual stuff. I just need a little time. How's about

I don't let you in my room just yet, but you keep on doing what you're doing?"

He took her hand and kissed the back of it. "It's a deal, partner."

She laughed out loud. Several of the other customers looked round and she covered her mouth in mock guilt.

"Remind me to tell you about my parents some time." David said, suddenly.

Helen looked up at him, expectantly. "Great. Tell me. What are they like?"

He pursed his lips. "It's a bit complicated. Like I said, let's leave it for another time."

She pointed at him with a piece of bread. "What is it about you English guys? Why do we bother?!" she said cheekily.

He shuffled uncomfortably in his seat. Then she touched his hand again, playfully pulling hers away before he could close his fingers around it. Her white teeth beamed at him.

"OK, you keep your secrets! Now come on, what are you going to have to eat?"

One day later

Vatican City, Rome
November 7th 2003

David stood in the visitors' entrance hall, hands on hips, looking gradually around, trying to think of the best place to start. Groups of tourists thronged on all sides, with guides shouting to make themselves heard

Helen walked up to him.

"At least they have modern bathrooms here! I was thinking they'd be holes in the ground. So – you found out anything?" She finished tucking a tissue back into her purse and clipped it shut. They both looked around the hall.

David pointed to a far wall. "What about over there? It's an enquiry desk of some kind."

They walked across the stone floored space to a long row of desks, waited in line for a few minutes, before they faced a young woman behind a desk, piled with guidebooks.

"I wonder if you can help – we are looking for someone who perhaps is based here, a priest." David said.

She turned to her computer screen and clicked the mouse. "I have a directory of all the staff who work in the Vatican. Do you have his name please?"

"O'Brien. Father Michael O'Brien." David spoke slowly and carefully.

The woman studied her screen for a few moments. She tapped at the keyboard, obviously trying different spellings, then turned back to David and shook her head.

"I am sorry. There is no one here of that name."

"Perhaps he is retired? Left?" Helen said. "Can we find out where he is?"

"Well, I will try the administration office for you."

She picked up the telephone, and gabbled in Italian for a moment. They couldn't discern any words apart from an 'O'Brien' somewhere in the middle. She was holding on, waiting, for about a minute. Then she seemed surprised.

"Somebody is coming down to help you. Will you wait over by the magazine kiosk please?"

They had been waiting about ten minutes, leafing through books of paintings, guides and tourist maps, when a man approached them. He was around sixty, with dark hair, streaked with grey. He had very dark eyebrows. He wore a black suit and underneath it a purple tunic, with dog collar.

"Greetings, my friends. Welcome to the Vatican. I am Cardinal Carlo Vanutti. I understand that you were asking for a priest named O'Brien?"

David answered, with some surprise at the rank of the man who had been paged. "Oh, yes…sorry, David Woodbridge, and this is Helen Ross. We're from Ohio University in America. Is Father O'Brien still at the Vatican?"

Vanutti sighed and shook his head.

"No, I'm afraid no more. Father O'Brien worked in my department for many years. But he passed away several months ago. He was an old man, you see. But what was your interest in him?"

Helen interrupted, as David was about to speak. "We're students from the archaeology department at Ohio. We've heard about Father O'Brien's work – we were just interested to meet him."

The Cardinal smiled. "Yes, he was an interesting man. A great loss to us. I'm sorry that your journey has been wasted. But perhaps, if you wish, you could visit our museum? Some of the work that Michael O'Brien did is on display there."

David nodded. Helen was tugging at his arm, out of sight of Vanutti.

"Perhaps, yes." she said. "It was nice of you to come personally, thank you."

"You are most welcome. I will leave you now. Goodbye, and enjoy your visit here."

He strode off, crossed the hall and disappeared through a door on the far side.

"Do you really think O'Brien's dead?" Helen asked.

David pondered for a moment. "I don't know. What did you think of the Cardinal? Did you believe that story?"

"Of course not!" Helen snorted. "There's something a bit spooky about him. He wasn't telling us everything."

"So what are we going to do now?"

"Let's explore a bit. You never know what we'll find."

She sped off to the ticket office. David struggled to catch up.

They walked through room after room of the Vatican's lavish galleries, alongside the tourists following directions to the Sistine chapel. Eventually they came to a junction of corridors. The tourist route led in two directions. Through the vast doorways they could glimpse more paintings and sculptures, in ornate glass cases. The third direction, off to the right, was a bare passage, in the middle of which was a sign saying 'Staff Only'. They looked at each other and then around at the people passing. No one was taking any notice. Helen nodded. Quickly, they walked past the sign and into the staff area.

They walked around a maze of corridors, looking at one office door after another. Several people passed them by, busy with their own conversations and seemingly unconcerned about David and Helen's presence.

David was shaking his head as they rounded another corner.

"Is this getting us anywhere? We don't even know what we're looking for."

Helen had stopped.

"What?" David asked her. She pointed to one of the doors. Like the others it was large and heavy with a huge brass knob. It was ajar. David looked at the gold-lettered sign on the door – '*Cardinal C. Vanutti*'. They peered gingerly into the opening. David jumped as Helen pushed the door, which creaked open further. They tiptoed in.

They were in a large room, obviously converted from a minor palace chamber into an office for the Cardinal. There were gold-leaf plaster mouldings on the ceiling, in octagonal patterns. Large religious paintings, with carved gold frames, hung on every wall. High windows were surrounded with thick drapes of red velvet. An antique desk dominated the far end of the room. They walked across the thick carpet and Helen stared out of the windows, down to one of the Vatican courtyards. Tourists milled around the statues and fountains. David ran his hands softly over the green leather surface of the desk. There was an immaculate gold pen set and a neat in-tray, with a small pile of official-looking papers. A computer sat at the other end of the desk, with a swirl-patterned screensaver playing on the monitor.

"I wonder…" David said and pushed the spacebar on the keyboard. The screen jumped into life.

"I don't believe it," he said with some surprise. "It's unlocked."

Helen turned to look.

"Should we?" She came alongside the desk chair. David sat down hurriedly and she knelt down beside

him. They looked at each other, then at the door.
There was no sound, no one near.

"Up to now we're almost tourists who've got lost,"
David replied. "Now we're…"

He held his hands, in suspense, above the keys.

"Do it." Helen said.

His hands jumped onto the keys and the mouse.

"OK. What have we got? An email screen here.
Let's have a look at his correspondence."

He scrolled up and down. There were hundreds of
messages.

"Wait!" She put her hands on his. "Look at that
one. It's got a similar title to a few of the others."

The title line read '*St Assisi Project: Update
20/02/01*'. Another read '*St Assisi Project: Progress
query, Dec 00*'.

"Open that one!" Helen said, pointing at the
screen. David double-clicked it. A warning box
appeared: '*This has been sent from a member of a
secure discussion group. It must not be forwarded to
unauthorised persons, copied or printed. Any
violation will be reported immediately to the list
owner. Do you wish to continue?*'

They both opened their eyes wide, turned and
smiled at each other.

"Wow. Important stuff. Let's see it." Helen
encouraged him to go on.

The note opened.

'In answer to your query, I made careful observations during my last visit to St. Assisi. I do not think the item is showing any signs yet. Perhaps it is a little early. It may be some years, in my view.

On another matter, Fr Roberti is asking some awkward questions. Suggest we discuss asap.'

They both looked at the message. It meant very little.

"So, what else can we do?" asked Helen.

David looked around the screen. "Look! This icon – *Library Information System*."

He clicked the link and a search window appeared.

"What shall we search for?"

"What about 'St. Assisi'?" Helen replied.

David typed it in and clicked the mouse. The system responded. '*28 documents found*'. Many had titles that meant little. But number seven on the list said '*Project summary as at June 1999.*' David clicked it. Slowly, the program opened.

"Come on, come on." Helen kept looking to the office door as the document loaded.

They scanned the text on the first page. It was a menu of contents:

Section 1: Laboratory work
Section 2: Selection of keeper and carrier
Section 3: Security implementation
Section 4: Environmental monitoring

"Perhaps it's the body! They're storing it in secret!" Helen said. "Let's see more!"

David stopped before turning the page.

"Look, how long do you think we've got before someone comes? Let's see if we can...."

He clicked a few more options.

"Yes! We can send this document! I'll mail it to my email address at Columbus!"

Another warning appeared on the screen, asking if he was sure he wanted to send a secure document. He clicked 'yes' and it disappeared.

"Done it! Now, let's see if there are some more we can get."

They sent another five documents in the next few minutes.

The telephone on the desk suddenly rang, bursting the silence and making them both jump.

"Shall we answer it?" David said in a loud whisper. "Somebody may come."

"Of course we won't answer it, you idiot. Let's carry on. See what you can find out about Father O'Brien."

The telephone stopped ringing.

Fredo, an analyst on one of the support desks, put down the telephone. No answer. Very strange, he thought. Perhaps Vanutti didn't want to be interrupted – no surprise in that – but there were some very strange messages on the screen in front of him. The Cardinal seemed to be sending files from the most secure of his databases out over the Internet. Surely he shouldn't be doing this? It was Vanutti himself who had instigated the last security review. He hesitated in thought for a moment. Then he called the Antiquities Admin office.

"Hello? Fredo here, from the support desk. Is Cardinal Vanutti with you? Yes? Can I speak to him?"

There was a pause.

"Yes – it is most urgent, I want to speak to him now if possible."

There was another pause. More odd messages popped onto his screen.

"Cardinal? I have been trying to call your office. Have you left your desk without logging off your computer?"

Fredo pulled the telephone a little way from his ear as the Cardinal's voice barked from the receiver.

"I am sorry – but there is something unusual happening. Do you have an assistant who is working there? There are files being sent outside of the network."

The receiver went silent.

"Cardinal? Hello?"

Then Vanutti's voice shouted out of the receiver.

"Meet me at my office. Now!"

The phone was put down abruptly. Fredo left in a hurry.

There was a sound in the corridor outside. They froze, holding their breath. Footsteps approached the doorway. Slowly, they walked past and faded.

David hung his head, and breathed out.

"That was close. Look at this stuff on O'Brien. Tons. Reports, discussion papers." David's head scanned from side to side as he read the entries. Suddenly his eyes opened wide. '*Report on Michael O'Brien's work in support of the St Thomas Gospel*'.

"Helen – look at this! Do you realise how secret this stuff is? The Catholic Church denies the existence of this thing!"

She had her hand at her mouth.

"David…sorry, I know how much it must mean. But I've just realised – could we search for O'Brien's location on this machine?"

David nodded and furiously began tapping keys.

"Yep. Back to the email program. Search for him in the address book. There!"

The entry showed '*O'Brien, M. Tel: ---. Location: Wing 4; Museum Archive Rm 3.*'

"Got him! Okay David, go back to your St Thomas stuff…"

The screen suddenly changed. '*Forced logoff by system at 14:35*'.

David stood up quickly. "That's it! They've spotted us! Come on, let's go!"

The two of them ran across the carpet to the door and out into the corridor. They half walked, half ran along to the main hall they'd left and finally back into the bustle of tourists.

They both stopped and smiled at each other, breathing heavily.

"Now, let's look for a plan of this place." Helen said.

The archive room filled most of the first floor of a whole palace wing. High windows illuminated hundreds of objects: sculptures shrouded in dustsheets, paintings leaning against one another along the walls. Huge tables were piled with archaeological junk. David and Helen picked their way along an aisle, towards the far side. There were small rooms leading off the large one, some open, filled with more bits and pieces, some locked.

Helen suddenly stopped. "This is it, room three."

The door had a grille and a bolt on the outside.

"It can't be. It looks like a prison door." David said.

"It's creepy," said Helen. "Something is wrong here. What's inside?"

David put his nose up to the grille and peered inside. A silver haired old man was hunched over a small table, studying a book. There was a bed in one corner. Bookcase shelves, stacked with old volumes, took up another entire wall.

Helen knocked gently.

The old man looked up puzzled, not used to anybody knocking. David pulled back the bolt and opened the door. They both stepped inside and walked towards the old man. He looked up at them, obviously very puzzled.

"Father O'Brien?"

"Yes, that is my name," he said getting up slowly. "I am not used to visitors."

Helen helped him to his feet. "I am sorry Father, but we don't have much time. We are being looked for as we speak."

David held out his hand. "This is a great honour Father, we have followed in your footsteps for a long time now."

"You have?" said O'Brien, confused and slow, as if he was coming out of a dream. "Who are you?"

"Forgive us, I am Helen Ross and this is David Woodbridge, archaeologists. We really don't have much time Father. We have found the secret tomb, the one that you found years ago. We know that you took the body of Christ. We talked to Ahmed."

O'Brien's face changed. "Ahmed? He is still alive? I thought they had…Oh…"

O'Brien was lost for words for a moment. He sat down again, looking down at the table, his mouth working soundlessly.

"This is…this is wonderful news. At last…"

"At last what Father?" said David.

He looked up at them again, with pleading in his eyes.

"I have waited years to tell the truth to somebody."

"We only have a minute or two," said Helen, glancing at the door. "What happened to the body?"

"The body was brought here of course. To the Vatican." O'Brien pointed towards a bookcase full of old leather bound books. "See the red book on the top shelf? Look behind it. A small diary."

David reached to where the priest was pointing and pulled out a small, dusty green book.

"I knew that one day somebody would come, but in case I....well, I wrote everything down. Take it. It explains everything."

Suddenly they heard running feet and shouting at the far end of the large room outside.

"We have to get out!" shouted Helen. "Father, come with us!"

"No!" O'Brien was suddenly animated. He held both hands up in front of them.

"I won't be able to go fast enough. You must barricade the door."

"We'll be trapped!" David said.

O'Brien hobbled over to the back wall and pulled back a curtain. There was a small service hatch built into the wall. "This was installed last year. They send my food up here every day. It leads straight to the kitchens."

"We can all escape this way!" Helen said.

"No, no, no! I can hardly walk let alone squeeze into that tiny box. You go and I will try to hold them for a while."

David pushed the diary into Helen's hand and grabbed the priest's old chair, wedging it under the door handle.

"It won't hold them for long! We have to go now!"

Helen pushed David forward. "Get in!"

He hesitated.

"Just go," she insisted, "I'll come after you. I have to ask Father O'Brien something."

"Well hurry. I'll send the lift back up."

David squeezed into the wooden box elevator, creaking and straining on its pulleys. Helen helped O'Brien pull on the rope. The elevator descended – too fast for David's liking. It jarred to a halt in a noisy, steamy kitchen.

He got out and brushed himself down, pulling on the rope to send it back up. Four Italian cooks stood and looked at him with their mouths open.

"Health Inspector," said David looking around and dusting off his clothes. He touched several of the tables, with mock disgust. "This is filthy!"

Helen turned to O'Brien as they heard beating on the cell door. "Are you a prisoner here?"

"Yes unfortunately I am. I have been for a long time."

"But why?"

"Partly to keep all this a secret." He paused. "And partly because of what I did."

There were shouts now outside the door and loud knocks. The handle rattled.

"What did you do Father?"

O'Brien shook his head.

"Something unforgiveable."

"What, Father please tell me!"

"The body...I..."

The elevator clattered back into place in its hatch. The door to the cell was being forced.

"You must go!" said O'Brien.

"What about the body? What did you do?" Helen held both of O'Brien's elbows. He was pressing his lips tightly together, fighting with himself to speak, shaking his head.

"I destroyed it! I destroyed the body of Christ," he blurted out.

Helen stared incredulously at him. She looked to the door. Men were hammering at it, the wood splintering. Then, in a daze, she backed away from O'Brien's desperate eyes towards the elevator. She climbed in, oblivious to the lurching of the box.

O'Brien grabbed the rope.

"Do something for me. For everyone," he said as he began to lower her.

He turned his head as the door flew open. Two men crashed into the room.

"Tell the people. Tell the whole world. Jesus Christ is alive...and walking the Earth..."

O'Brien disappeared from view as the elevator dropped.

David pulled Helen out. He was talking what sounded like nonsense to Helen.

"No that's OK. Just a little grease here and there. But otherwise – fine job chaps!"

The chefs stood around the kitchen, in complete puzzlement, as an extremely unlikely looking English food inspector had clambered out of the service lift. Then a very attractive woman in a state of some dishevelment also climbed out. They looked at each other with open mouths, shrugging their shoulders.

David led Helen briskly through an open door out of the kitchens into a busy courtyard at the back of the Vatican.

"Walk slowly," said David. "Let's make sure we look like tourists again."

She pulled his arm to hold her around the waist as they walked and pushed her head against his shoulder.

"David, I can't think. Father O'Brien's trapped there…I..."

She stooped, looking back into the building.

"We have to keep moving." David grabbed her arm and pulled her forwards again. "We can't do anything else here. We're not safe yet. We've got to go."

He shook her shoulders. "Look, are you going to be all right?"

She looked up at him. There were tears in her eyes.

"Yes, I'll be OK," she said. Then shook her head and looked down. "No. I'm scared. What will they do to him?"

David looked up at the first floor windows, with a grim frown on his face.

"I don't know. I'm scared too. But there's nothing we can do. And I think that somehow he was waiting." He looked down at the diary. "He knew what would happen."

He put his arms around her. Briefly she gripped him hard. Then he took her hand and they walked away to the exit.

Cardinal Vanutti stood head to head with Father Michael O'Brien.

"Where are they?"

O'Brien shrugged, "Who?"

Vanutti looked at his security team.

"All clear sir. Nobody here. They must have gone down the hatch."

"Then go after them!"

Vanutti stepped forward until his nose was almost touching O'Brien's.

An outline of a smile crossed O'Brien's face. "It's too late. They know everything. The story will soon be out and you will have to answer for it."

Anger flashed across Vanutti's face. "Fool!" His fist clenched and there was a flash of steel as his arm struck out at O'Brien. The old priest gasped.

"You have freed me at last."

"I should have killed you years ago old man. You have troubled us too long."

O'Brien sank slowly to his knees, clutching his chest. Blood poured out onto his hands and dripped down onto the threadbare carpet.

"Lord forgive me my sins and accept me into your…"

Vanutti pushed the body away with his foot, a look of disgust on his face. With a sweep of his black robes, he strode purposefully out of the room.

They sat inside a café sipping a hot cappuccino, not speaking.

There was no sign outside of anything out of the ordinary. In the streets around the Vatican, bustling life continued as though nothing had happened.

"What did he say?" he asked her.

Helen looked down at the table, shaking her head slightly from side to side.

"Something strange. That he had destroyed Christ's body, but then I think he said 'Jesus is alive'."

She looked up at him, puzzled. David furrowed his brows, considering for a while before he spoke.

"Odd. I know he was a priest, but…well I always thought he was a bit more of a scientist than a preacher."

Helen held the diary in her hand. "Perhaps there are some clues in here."

"Yes I suppose," said David. "Shall I?"

"Yes. Please. I'm still shaking."

David took the book and began to thumb through the pages.

"Looks like he's kept this for the best part of twenty years. It starts in the mid-eighties."

He looked around the café. There was a group of tourists a few tables away. They moved their heads close together, David speaking in a whisper.

"Look at this…"

11ᵗʰ November 1984

I am becoming very concerned. The senior members of the Research Council have decided to keep the body a secret. This is against my wishes. This is the greatest archaeological find there has ever been. It should be published. Let them take the credit if they like, but the world has a right to know.

"There's some stuff about how he misses his travel, ….*I miss the sands of Israel and Jordan, the dry heat and the warmth….* Nothing very significant…."

David continued thumbing through the pages.

"Here – listen to this…"

18ᵗʰ November 1984

I talked to the scientists performing the carbon dating tests on the body. They told me they are being moved off the project. Some new people are being brought in. It is getting harder somehow for me to get answers. I repeatedly ask Vanutti what is to be done with the body and he evades these questions.

24th November 1984

I am trying to discover what is happening with the experiments on the body. They have flown in an expert on genetics from America. Dr Van Doest. I know nothing of this science. What are they doing? I accept that Christ's body should merit the world's best scientists, but I have forebodings about…

David looked up from the book.

"You don't think…"

"What?" Helen leaned forward towards David, as he sat, temporarily motionless. He looked down at the book, almost frightened to turn the page.

"Here's the next entry, the next day…"

25th November 1984

I cannot believe this news. I have just heard from Monsignor Piali, my one friend on the Council. They intend to…

David stopped reading, his mouth opening in utter astonishment.

"My God."

"What ?" Helen asked.

"No…I mean…I don't believe it." David continued, rapidly shaking his head as he was clearing his ears.

She shook his arm.

"Tell me David. What does it say? What?!"

"They've made a clone," he whispered.

Her eyes gaped wide.

"They've made a..." her voice descended to a whisper also, "clone...of Jesus?"

David read more.

...he has told me that they are having great problems with the process, but that the American scientist has almost solved them. Have they any idea what they are doing? What could this 'thing' turn out to be but an abomination?

22ⁿᵈ December 1984

Piali has told me that they have found a virgin host willing to be impregnated and that the genetic code of Jesus has been successfully cloned. I have been sworn to secrecy. Piali says that Vanutti has threatened all the Council members, and that my life would be in danger if I took any action. God help us all.

15ᵗʰ August 1985

They seem to have finished with the body now. Day after day I go into the cold storeroom and stare at it. I don't know if I still have faith or not. I fear that I am losing my faith in science as well as God. Yet there seems to be an odd feeling growing in my soul. It frightens me. Although I am growing old, there may still be work to do, for which I will need all my strength.

The clone will soon be born. What could it turn out to be? Piali tells me it will be exactly like Jesus physically, but how can it be Jesus a second time? He says that the Council is divided over this. They have started this enterprise simply because they can, not because they know what they are doing. So they keep the project secret. If the clone shows powers, they will announce it to the world, and the Catholic Church will stand glorious above all other religions in the world. However, if the clone is just flesh and blood they will kill him.

23rd April 1986

I have found out where he is! The clone has been born and taken to a monastery in Tuscany – St. Assisi. He is to begin his learning there, until he is old enough to be tested. His mother has gone with him. Even the monks will not know his true identity. How many years have I spent without a single prayer? Yet I pray for all of them daily. And, even though I am terrified to even write it down, I know now what my final act must be...God knows if I can do it.

"What does he do? Does he say?" Helen craned over to see the pages that David was flicking through.

"He keeps on and on about his fear of this great act..." David replied, intently scanning pages. "May, July, *I cannot... I must...* he keeps repeating it. Wait, this is it. Listen..."

15th October 1987
It is only now that I can write about what I have done. It was in January. Vanutti at first said he would kill me, but he did not. He locked me into this room, and now I am kept a prisoner. I have lived for months with the horror and guilt of what I have done. Yet I could not stay my hand. I had to put an end to any more research. There will be no more cloning. I broke into the storeroom and took Christ's body. I destroyed it. May God forgive me.

David and Helen looked at each other, silent for what seemed ages. Neither could fully absorb what they'd read.

"What are we going to do?" said David at last.

She sat back in her chair, for a moment, staring into space. Then she looked him in the eyes.

"We've got to go and find him. What else can we do? We must talk to him."

David stared at her, seemingly in horrified surprise, for several moments. His voice was shaking. "I...er...I guess..."

"David." She put her hand on his and lifted his chin, smiling at him. "Come on, we're scientists. Researchers. How can we not follow this up?"

211

His face relaxed, a little, with a wan smile. "I suppose so," he nodded.

"Come on. What is it?" she asked. "It's some religious stuff, yeah?"

He hung his head slightly, fiddling idly with his coffee spoon. "Not really. Well perhaps. I know you'll probably think I'm stupid, but I was a pretty convinced Christian when I was younger."

She raised her eyebrows, saying nothing.

"Not anymore," he continued hurriedly. "I mean, well that all faded away at college really. It's just, the idea of meeting…" he hung his head.

She smiled gently. "Is this a parents thing too? You were going to tell me, remember?"

He thought for a few moments. Then nodded slowly. "Yes. As I told you, my father's the village Vicar. You can imagine, that atmosphere. My mother too. It's not that they were – you know, strict, or crazy, with me but…" he looked up, with a nervous laugh.

"David. Look at me." Her big, brown eyes were fierce, but she still smiled at him.

"You grew out of it didn't you? Of course you did," she spoke quietly but in a deadly serious tone. "What do you think all this Vatican stuff is? And all the Catholic or Protestant or Buddhist teaching? With all their chants, robes and cathedrals? It's a way of keeping the poor, peasant masses happy and ignorant while they rob them blind. It always was." She spoke slowly and deliberately. "Jesus Christ was a historical figure. A famous preacher who died two thousand years ago. If there's a clone of his body, we need to find him, and speak to him."

David took in a deep breath. He looked away for a few seconds, then returned Helen's gaze.

"Then we need a map. We need to find this village," he said.

Helen smiled and relaxed. "Yes. Good. Look, I'm sorry for the lecture. These things just get me…well, I guess I'm pretty outspoken sometimes! But don't be fooled about one thing…"

"What's that?" David asked.

"I'm still scared. Perhaps I don't show it. But I couldn't do this without you."

He gripped her hand with both of his. "That's wonderful. Same for me. But we'll set off as soon as we can. There's just one minor problem."

"What?" she asked.

"Those guys from the Vatican will also be heading straight for St Assisi. We have to set off right now."

Same day

Vatican City, Rome
November 7th 2003

There was a hushed atmosphere in the darkened room. All the Council members had their eyes fixed on the defiant face of the Cardinal.

"You have gone too far this time Vanutti!" One of the elder priests was pointing at him, hand shaking.

Vanutti stood up. "I have called this emergency session not to be reprimanded but to resolve the crisis!"

The council members looked nervously at one another.

"As for you, Cragnotti, let him without sin cast the first stone." Vanutti continued. "Or do you forget how I protected you from all the accusations about the boys youth camp?"

Cragnotti looked down at his feet and said nothing further. Vanutti paused for a few moments to gather his thoughts and drew a deep breath.

"Now as you all know by now, we have a delicate situation at hand. Father O'Brien is no longer with us." He looked around to see if there were any faces still showing animosity.

"But two people are now aware of our most important secret. I have decided that the best course of action is for me to terminate the project as soon as possible."

There were gasps of astonishment from the gathering.

Another priest spoke up. "Is that wise your Grace? I mean we have not had time to test…."

"What do you think will happen if the world's press gets to know about this?" Vanutti interrupted. "We will be ridiculed for not 'sharing' this discovery with the rest of the world.

Worse still, if they test the clone and he shows no sign of miracles or powers, they will say that the original Christ was the same. Just a man. So what are we worshipping him for? That would be a disaster for the Catholic Church. I cannot allow this to happen. I will travel to St. Assisi and kill him myself."

Vanutti sat down, his face red. The other priest spoke up again. "Forgive me Cardinal. I still think that we should give the clone a chance to prove himself. We have been nearly twenty years preparing for this. I accept that the knowledge of the existence of this boy could be a problem, but he is still only young. We may yet be able to contain the news until he has had time to develop. Can we at least test him?"

"Very well," said Vanutti reluctantly, looking around at the assembled members. "Any other opinions? Or should we go with Father Thommasen's suggestion?"

An air of resignation and fear hung over the meeting. Most of the members nodded, some in reluctant acceptance, others in relief that another killing may be stayed, at least for a while.

"I see," said Vanutti. "I will leave at once, in that case. But I warn you I may have to act quickly, to protect all of us. Personally, I do not now hold out much hope for this ... clone."

Vanutti gathered up his notes. "Good day gentlemen."

Two days later

The road to St Assisi
November 9th 2003

The ramshackle bus drove along the stony road, its engine coughing periodically. For almost two hours they had rumbled through farmland and vine orchards, as they rose into the mountains. The passengers talked incessantly, carrying faded bags overfull with provisions. There were at least two chickens clucking at the rear.

"I still can't quite get used to this," David said, raising his voice above the noise of the motor. "How can we meet this boy? It's unreal."

Helen laughed gently at him. "What is he going to do? Strike you dead with a bolt of lightning? He's just a boy. Good pedigree, but he won't be much different from you or me."

"Yes, but…" David struggled for words, looking down at the litter-strewn floor of the bus.

"But what?"

He looked up at her.

"You didn't grow up like I did. My father's a vicar. Yours is a doctor – a scientist. You don't know what this would mean in the circles my family inhabit. They wouldn't know what to think. They couldn't reconcile it. To them it would be something that just shouldn't have happened."

She took his hand and smiled at him.

"But we can, David. We can reconcile it. Together we're a strong team. Can't you feel that?"

He gripped her hand, closed his eyes and breathed in hard, nodding.

"Yes we are. Thank you. Look, I'll try to keep myself under control. I might just have to rely on you to do the talking a bit, you know?"

She smiled again.

"That's what a good team does, yeah? No problem."

Suddenly she looked beyond his shoulder, stooping to see out of the bus's window.

"Hey, look!"

They saw hills above them, and the white dots of the monastery of St Assisi, nestling against the slopes above.

They stepped out of the bus, which had at last come to a halt in the central courtyard of the monastery buildings. David lifted out their bags and dumped them on the dusty ground, then sat down on a stone seat of a small, ancient fountain. The bus engine revved, and it slowly turned around the courtyard, taking the rest of the passengers back down the hill track to the tiny village, about a quarter of a mile below. He took off his glasses and shook the dizziness out of his head. Helen stood next to him, her eyes closed, breathing deeply. Sunlight played on the small trickles of water, dappled from the lime trees that nestled against the buildings.

"If they want to keep people away from here, they ought to advertise this bus trip. I thought it would never end!" David said. He stood up to straighten his crumpled trousers. "How are you doing?"

Helen stayed quiet for a few more moments. She gradually opened her eyes and smiled.

"Fine. I...I don't know, I should be feeling much worse after that trip, but I feel great! Listen – what can you hear?"

David tilted his head. "Nothing. No, wait a minute..." he screwed up his eyes, "in the distance – some bells, perhaps like they use on goats, or something?"

"Yes, isn't it wonderful? So peaceful! No car horns. Just birds singing, sunshine. Cool mountain air! Can't you feel it?"

David looked around, then up, past the tops of the high trees, into the sky.

"Well, it's a nice place," he agreed, but not really sharing the same delight in their surroundings as was Helen. A rusty pick-up drove past them, groaning with it's load of watermelons. The driver looked at them for a moment, unconcerned, then the vehicle disappeared down one of the tracks that exited from the courtyard. They both looked around. All of the buildings were white and plain, in need of repainting. One had an ornate pair of wooden doors and was topped with a small bell tower.

They walked over to the entrance.

"Well this is it," said Helen as she stroked her hands over the deep carvings in the surface of the door. David half-smiled at her, then noticed her flushed red cheeks. She looked very nervous.

"Are you OK?" he asked.

"I don't know," she replied. "I feel strange. It's difficult to explain. It's…like when you wake up on the day something really big is happening."

She placed her hand on her chest and took long breaths. David's eyes flicked down to her loose white shirt, with her tanned skin rising and falling beneath it, then back to her face, smiling, yet vulnerable, just as she'd been in the Vatican courtyard.

"I thought I was the nervous one!" he said.

She shivered a little and shook her hair around her face, gradually calming herself.

"Sorry, I don't know what's got into me!"

Her arm moved to the rusty iron bell pull hoop that hung down on a rope by the side of the massive doorframe. "Look at this," she said, holding her hand out to him. It was shaking slightly.

"What if *he*…opens the door?" David said, once again trying to smile.

She bit her lip a little as she looked at him. "Well, we'll just have to see what happens, yeah?"

David drew in a breath. "OK. But…well, just one thing before we pull the bell…"

"What's that?"

"Well, I wanted to say that I…" What he wanted to say was ringing clear in his mind. The thing he'd never said to anybody in his life. *I love you.*

"Yes?" She was smiling.

"I…I'm glad you are with me."

She smiled, puzzled but happy and accepting.

"Come on. We've got to do it," said Helen. She took his hand and both of them pulled on the bell. Somewhere far away inside, they heard it ring.

She gripped his hand, harder and harder, as they heard footsteps slowly approach from within.

The door groaned on its hinges and opened outwards. Both of them breathed out in sudden relief, as an old man peered out into the sunlight. He had white hair and a dark, heavily lined face. He wore a shin-length brown monk's habit, and rough sandals on his bare feet.

"Buon giorno?"

Helen stepped forward. "Hello Father. I wonder if you can help us. We are looking for somebody here."

"Please come inside," said the monk and invited them to enter the dark interior. They were in a bare entrance hall, with a long, empty table against one of the walls. Their feet echoed slightly on the stone floor. The old monk turned to them.

"Who is it you seek?"

"A young man. Perhaps about nineteen or twenty years old?" David replied.

The old monk thought for a minute and then shook his head slowly.

"No, none of the monks here are young men."

Helen glanced sideways at David.

"Do you mind if we look around anyway, Father?"

The monk bowed slightly. "You are welcome, but please respect the sanctity of our monastery. All the brothers are in the chapel for Matins. If you wish you can come and see?"

They nodded and the monk strode away further inside the building, his leather sandals flapping on the stone floor. They heard music growing louder and emerged at the back of a tall chapel.

Beautiful chanting filled the room. Light flooded in from high windows. They were mostly simple, without much decoration, save a few panes of stained glass that threw coloured beams onto the black and white tiled floor. The assembled monks stood with their eyes closed, around the carved stalls flanking each side of the altar. Helen lifted her eyes to the ceiling, which was covered in faded paintings, her face smiling as the monks sang and harmonised.

David studied the faces of all present. Most of the monks were middle aged or old. One or two looked to be in their thirties, but none at all matched the description of the man they were looking for. He turned to their guide. "Is there nobody here under the age of twenty five?"

The monk shook his head. "All are present in this chapel... but perhaps you search for somebody who is not a monk? There are a number of young men in the village here. Most of them are farm workers. The will be out in the fields at this time of day."

David turned to Helen. She didn't seem to be paying attention to what the old monk was saying. She staggered slightly, steadying herself on one of the nearby wooden pews, before sitting down. He went over and crouched down in front of her.

"Helen? Are you all right?"

She sat with her eyes closed, half smiling.

"Are you OK?" David asked again.

Slowly she opened her eyes, but they weren't focused at first. Then gradually, she returned from her reverie, looked at him, and nodded. A tear ran down her cheek.

A few minutes later they were back in the strong sunshine outside the chapel.

Despite the harsh light, her eyes were wide. A look of rapture was on her face.

"What happened in there?" he asked.

"I don't know," she looked puzzled, and elated. "But it was wonderful. It was the music. It hit me as soon as we walked in. A sort of…I don't know how to describe it. Like a rush of electricity went through me! Didn't you feel it?"

He shook his head. "No, not really. But I've been around church music all my life. I've got a bit bored with it."

She didn't look as if she was really listening. Instead, she stared up at the sky. Through the canopy of one of the lime trees, spots of sunshine waved over her face.

"Wow. It's crazy," she said. "We could be in the middle of the biggest religious event since the crucifixion."

"I thought you weren't religious?"

She looked down at him, staring for a while before responding, realising what she'd just said. "I'm not. Well, I never have been before. Nothing like this has ever happened to me. Is this what being religious feels like? Aargh!" She shivered again as if trying to shake something off, not being able to tell if it was good or bad. "I just don't know!"

She lowered her head. David tried to lift her chin, but she resisted him, hiding her eyes.

"Look, I...are you crying? I thought I was the one that was uncertain about all this?" David said.

She raised her head again, wiping tears from her eyes.

"Well now I'm uncertain too. All my life I've not believed in anything spiritual because there's no scientific evidence, no proof. Now I'm like doubting Thomas. I feel guilty that I needed to be shown something physical first, and...."

"What?" David asked.

"Nothing. Perhaps I'm not as tough as I thought," she replied. "I don't know, it's just since we got here. I was really terrified in the Vatican, but now...perhaps it's this place...it's so peaceful somehow. I should be as nervous as hell. But I feel really happy inside. I can't work it out."

David couldn't help laughing as a flashing smile broke through her tearful face.

"Come here!" he said, holding his arms out to embrace her. She hugged him, but, just at this minute, there was something not quite…right about it. It was almost imperceptible, but she was not hugging him as hard as he'd thought she would. He dismissed it from his mind. Over her shoulder, he noticed something.

"Ah ha," he whispered.

"What?" she pulled away from him and looked behind her.

"I think there are some people over there we could talk to."

They looked past the monastery buildings, down a roughly gravelled road, where a few people were working in distant fields. She gazed at them, shielding her eyes from the sunlight.

"David, he's down there."

"What? How do you know?"

She smiled. "I just know," she said, and set off walking.

After ten minutes of stumbling and avoiding knots of vegetables, they reached a small group of people. Two men and two women, middle aged, chatted to themselves in between scratching at the dry earth with hoes. The men wore ill-fitting trousers held roughly with their belts, crumpled shirts and wide cloth caps. The women wore old black dresses, covered with rough aprons. They seemed little interested in the two strangers. Further on behind them, a young man was tilling the earth, his back to them.

Helen walked straight on towards him.

When they were ten yards away, the man spoke without turning around.

"Welcome my friends."

They stopped in their tracks as the man turned to face them. His hair was black and short. He was young, perhaps nineteen or twenty. He wore rough black trousers, like the other men, and a white T-shirt.

He looked at them both with clear blue eyes. He seemed to gaze without glancing away, yet without malice. His face showed both an eagerness to be hospitable, and patience, waiting for one of them to speak.

David spoke first. "Er...Hi. Are you, er...part of the monastery here?"

He waited until David had fully finished bumbling through his words.

"Yes. And no. We are farmers. We provide food for the monks, in return for accommodation and teaching."

David was about to ask more when Helen held him back.

"What…is your name?" she said, stammering.

"Julius," the man said and smiled. "Can I help you at all?"

"How did you know we were English?" said David.

"You look like travellers to me. And English is a universal language. I learned it when I was at school."

Helen was looking agitated. "Excuse us. We have not introduced ourselves. We are researchers, we have come straight from the Vatican to see you."

"To see me?" said Julius, "But why?"

"We have information for you. Your life may be in danger."

Julius looked down at the ground and carried on pulling out stones with his hoe.

"I am afraid that you have the wrong man. My life involves no complications and little argument. I have no enemies."

In the distance, a sorrowful bell started tolling.

Julius laid his hoe on the ground and faced them.

"You must excuse me. There are some things I must take up to the chapel. Perhaps I will see you both later."

He started walking towards the monastery. David called out. "Who is your father?"

Julius hesitated and turned around.

"Why do you wish to know about my father? He died when I was a child. I do not remember him."

Helen ran to catch him up. "We know all about you and your parents. Everything. You must let us talk to you. We are running out of time."

Julius stood still for some while, looking a little frightened and suspicious, but he spoke calmly.

"I promised to take some fruits up to the monks' kitchens. But go to my mother's house." He pointed along the track that ran alongside the field. "She lives in rooms above the bakery. I will not be long. Wait for me there."

He walked away towards the monastery buildings and out of sight.

Helen sighed. "What do you think?"

David shrugged his shoulders. "I don't know. He's just a man. You were right."

Helen looked puzzled. "But couldn't you *feel* anything?"

"Feel what? He seemed a nice chap. A bit serious. Old for his age," said David, a little surprised at Helen's question. "What did you feel?"

She looked aside, as if she was irritated with him.

"Never mind. Come on, let's go," she said brusquely, turning away. She quickly stepped through the vegetation, towards the track. David followed, wondering whether to say anything. She'd never been like this with him before. He felt suddenly jealous, then annoyed with himself for being so selfish, as he struggled to catch her up.

Twenty minutes later

Via Pedruza, St Assisi

They walked down the gravel track that led slightly downhill and away from the monastery. Overhead, darkening clouds had obscured the sun. David looked to the horizon where a flash of lightning had caught his eye.

"There's a storm coming," he said.

Helen looked in that direction. The strengthening wind caught her long hair and whipped it around her face. She smiled at David.

"A very big storm," she said.

Twenty minutes later they arrived at a tiny village of around ten stone buildings. The walls had once been brightly painted, but most were peeling and in need of repair. They passed a workshop, full of old hand tools, oilcans and motor parts, where a dilapidated truck was in the midst or repair. Along the middle of the road, an old man led a donkey, pulling a rickety wooden cart piled with carrots and potatoes. They crossed to the other side, to a building with double doors, partly open, the smell of freshly baked bread filling the air. An iron staircase led up the sidewall. They climbed it to a small dull red painted door. There was no lock.

"Let me deal with this David. It needs a gentle touch."

"Oh, meaning that I have no tact?"

"Sorry, look, I just think I can find out what we need – a gentle touch…"

The door to the small apartment opened before they had knocked and a grey-haired woman dressed all in black looked them up and down.

"Si?" she enquired.

Helen offered her hand and the woman took it. "We'd like to talk with you about your son Julius."

The woman's face softened at his name, though she still looked uncertain.

Helen smiled at her.

"Well…all right, Please come in Miss…?"

"Ross. Helen. And David Woodbridge."

"I am Maria Rossi." They followed her into her sitting room, dark and simple, adorned with religious pictures, rosaries, beads and books.

"How can I help you?"

"Julius asked us to come here and wait for him. We need to talk urgently."

She looked puzzled.

"Why? What do you wish to talk about?"

"We have come from the Vatican. We have some…news for him."

The woman smiled. "Ah! I was sure there would be something! He is such a good boy. Do you know that five years ago the Pope himself came to St Assisi and spoke at length to my son! Imagine that. The Papa talking to my son!" She clutched at the wooden cross around her neck with her hand, crossing her arms as if hugging a baby, closing her eyes and smiling.

"We wanted to ask you about his father." Helen said quietly.

The woman's eyebrows lowered. Her smile disappeared. "What about his father?"

"Well who was he and what happened to him?"

"Why do you want to know this? It brings back painful memories to us both. I do not want to talk about this. You must leave now." She stood up and walked towards the door. "I am sorry."

David and Helen got to their feet as a man stepped into the doorway.

"Mamma," said Julius, "it's OK."

"Son?"

"Let them talk to us. If they have news about my father, it is time we heard it."

Helen glanced at David and he cleared his throat.

"Maria, do you know a man called Cardinal Vanutti?"

Once again, her face fell. She nodded. "Yes, I know him. He visits me maybe twice a year, although I do not...look forward to his coming. I think he is a very important man in the Vatican. I...cannot say anything more."

David continued. "I'm afraid we have discovered that Vanutti has manipulated your life and especially your son's life. That's why we need to know more about your husband."

She was silent for some moments. She looked across at Julius. He nodded to her almost imperceptibly.

"I was never married," said Maria bitterly. "There, does that satisfy you?"

"Then what about the father of your son. Who was he?"

Maria stood up. "I will not talk about it. I am sworn to secrecy!"

"To whom?" asked Helen.

"To the Catholic Church. To his Holiness."

"Maria, these are the very people who threaten your son's life," said David. "We know the truth, Maria. It's time you told your son."

She looked from David's face to that of her son and thought for a few moments before putting a hand on the young man's shoulder.

"Stop, Julius. I will tell you what you should have been told years ago."

Julius gazed up at his mother.

"I do not know who your father was. I was never told. I was an apprentice nun when Vanutti sought my help in a project that he said would help the Church. I could not refuse. I have been faithful to the Church all of my life, and he said that this project was more important than me taking holy orders."

Julius looked around at David and Helen.

"Then do *you* know who my father is?" he asked.

Helen looked puzzled. "Maria, is that the truth? Is that all you know?"

"Yes, of course. Vanutti said that I needed a medical examination at the Vatican hospital. Then I was brought here to live. All I know is that a month later I found out that I was pregnant. Yet...."

Her voice broke a little as she began to cry. "...how can you believe me? I had never been with a man. I swear it."

Helen reached out and held her hand. "Maria. We have to tell you our news. I'm sorry for this, the news may upset you. But I'm afraid we do not have much time. You are both in danger."

Julius got up to sit next to his mother, as Helen looked at David. She motioned him to speak.

"Maria, we do believe you. We found an old priest in the Vatican who told us there was a medical experiment. Julius was implanted into your womb."

"Then he has a father and a...another mother somewhere?" Maria said, with fear in her voice. "He was a...how do you say it...a test-tube baby?"

David held a hand to his brow and shook his head slightly.

"No, I'm afraid not. You see...your son does not really have a father, and technically, he does not really have a mother either. He was conceived as a...clone."

Julius lowered his head. Maria looked at them with wide eyes, still not understanding.

David continued. "He does not really have a ...biological mother. He was conceived by...an

233

experiment that sort of…makes a copy of a single person. They used a… dead man's body."

They all sat silently for what seemed an eternity. Maria had both hands fixed over her mouth. Her eyes showed fear and incomprehension.

"There is one person who I trust in this matter," said Julius. "The Abbot knows of my early life. I must go to see him straight away."

He stood up and hesitated. "There is more isn't there?" he said, his calm eyes searching into Helen's.

After several moments, Helen cleared her throat. "Yes, there is. We know the identity of the man's body who you were cloned from."

"Please tell us."

Helen hesitated. She reached into her bag and showed them O'Brien's diary. "The proof is in here, and confirmed in documents we saw at the Vatican. We're one hundred per cent certain."

Julius's clear gaze did not change. "I do not need to look into that book. I can tell that you are convinced. Now please tell us the name of the man that I came from."

"Your DNA was taken from the bone marrow of a man who died two thousand years ago."

Helen looked once at David, then back to Julius.

"It was Jesus Christ."

The same day

The road to St Assisi

Father Cuccini looked across at Cardinal Vanutti in the back of the car as it sped up the foothills above Florence. Since they started out, the sun had disappeared and now rain beat against the windows, only serving to darken Vanutti's mood.

"Your Grace, perhaps you should brief me a little more on your intentions when we reach the monastery?"

Vanutti's dark eyes wearily scanned the cleric. "Very well. But do not play political games with me, Father. You are one of the Holy Father's secretaries and our liaison for this matter. I'm sure his Holiness has asked you for a full account of the happenings at St. Assisi. I also need to have a witness present. But I am in charge here, and I will take whatever action is necessary. Unless you have no stomach for whatever may have to be done. Shall I stop the car?"

"Oh no your Grace, I will abide by your wishes."

"Good. Now let us try to be honest with each other. Tell me truthfully, Father, what are his Holiness' most current views on this project?"

Cuccini looked uncomfortable for a moment, then decided to reveal his thoughts.

"He is greatly troubled. He cannot decide, do we announce this boy to the world and risk the anger of world governments, keep it forever a secret, or destroy it? I should tell you, your Grace, that I do not think he will take kindly to you…how can I put it…taking urgent action without consulting him."

Vanutti raised his eyebrows. Cuccini had clearly been informed of the Council meeting proceedings.

"Do not be too hasty to pander to his Holiness, Father," Vanutti replied. "If we had always waited for permission from Popes we would not have achieved anything. Remember that the Holy Father is old. His health is bad. He will be replaced before long."

Cuccini nodded. He thought for a minute, before speaking again.

"Cardinal, may I ask you a question?"

Vanutti impatiently tapped on the glass behind the driver. "Can you go any faster?"

The driver shrugged. The rain had begun to fall much heavier and he was already taking the sharp corners as fast as he dared.

"Yes?" growled Vanutti.

"Do you think that this boy really is Jesus Christ?"

"He has the same body. The same brain. He is an exact copy. This is the same man that lived two thousand years ago."

"Yet I have to say that I have my doubts, your Grace. What if you had made a clone from Mozart's body? Would he now be composing works of genius? Or if Michelangelo had been unearthed from his grave. Would he now be painting great frescoes in the Sistine chapel? Somehow I cannot believe that it would happen. We live in different times."

"Perhaps you will change your views when you meet this boy. But I doubt it," Vanutti replied.

"What do you mean your Grace?"

"I am saying that this so-called Christ has so far turned out to be nothing out of the ordinary. Probably like the first one."

"What are you saying?" Cuccini said, startled. "Do you not believe in the very thing that our Church stands for?"

Vanutti was growing irritated. "You play the innocent priest very well Father, but I suspect that your true beliefs are little different to mine. What I stand for is the power of the Catholic Church. For the faith of the masses who embrace His Holiness as their spiritual leader."

"So if this clone turns out to be just an ordinary man…."

"I will do whatever is necessary to make sure that peoples' belief in Christ continues. Can you imagine that news leaking into the press? I curse the day we started this experiment. I will terminate him unless he can convince me by tonight that he has -" Vanutti's tone became mocking "- miraculous powers."

He turned away and looked back out of the rain soaked window.

Via Pedruza, St Assisi

Maria was sitting almost catatonic with fear in her armchair. Julius sat motionless, with his eyes staring blankly and unfocused. Eventually he took in a deep breath and looked at Helen and David.

"I must go and talk to the Abbot about this."

"No," Helen disagreed firmly. "We must all leave this house now. Vanutti will be coming here as we speak."

Julius held up his palm in a blocking gesture. "Father Giovanni has known me all of my life. He is knowledgeable and wise. However much you impress on me the urgency of leaving, I must talk to him first."

Julius got up and knelt facing his terrified mother. "Mamma, whatever they say, I am your son, and I always will be. I will be with you again very soon, but I must go to see the Abbot. These are good people, you must trust them." He got up and hurried to the door. "If there is danger, will you make sure she is safe?"

"We will. But please hurry," implored Helen.

Fifteen minutes later

The road to St Assisi monastery

The Cardinal poured himself a whisky from the drinks cabinet as the driver pointed to the Abbey just appearing in the distance. As they rounded a corner, the driver swerved to avoid a young man running at the side of the road. Vanutti cursed as his drink was spilled, turned around to look at the man and cursed. "Peasant!"

Julius kept running, his hair drenched with the rain, as the big black Mercedes sped past him, spraying him with water.

Ten minutes later, the Abbot faced an angry looking Vanutti in his vestry.

"Your Grace!" exclaimed the Abbot, "Nobody informed me of your visit?"

"This is a most urgent situation," said Vanutti, "and one of the utmost secrecy."

The Abbot shrugged, a little puzzled, then looked startled as a knock sounded on the door.

Vanutti placed a finger on his lips and shrunk back into the darkness of a corner.

Out of breath from running up the hill, and soaking wet, Julius had walked quickly to Father Giovanni's door. It was open slightly, but he'd still knocked and waited, out of respect for the Abbot.

"Please come."

The kindly face of the old man was smiling as he beckoned Julius to take a seat. His office was a stone chamber, containing a rickety wooden desk, with a heavy Bible and a few other books. A bare bulb hanging from the rafters dimly illuminated the room.

"What is it my son?"

"Forgive me for asking Father, but I need your advice."

"You know that you can always come to me for help, Julius. What is troubling you?"

"I have learned something today. About my father. He did not die when I was small, did he?"

The Abbot sat down.

"The two Americans that came here earlier today," he sighed. "I knew it would cause trouble."

Julius hung his head.

"I know you well my boy," the Abbot continued. "You would not come to me with this question if it was an idle one, would you?"

Julius looked into the Abbot's weary eyes.

"No Father. I think you have been hiding the truth from me. Perhaps it was necessary until now, but I am an adult and I think the time is now right for me to know."

Father Giovanni nodded slowly "Nearly twenty years ago I received a message from the Vatican; that a novice nun had been…led astray and was with child. This was somewhere she could be taken in, away from gossip and scandal. She could earn God's forgiveness and her child could have a fair chance.

We value charity above all else. We were pleased to take you in and teach you as part of our community."

"So you do not know any more than that? Not who my father was?" Julius said, his eyes narrowing.

The Abbot smiled and gently shook his head.

"I am sorry my son. But if your father is still alive, he is probably a weak and wasteful man. Your mother was best encouraged to forget him. But with the gifts you have developed...well, as far as such a thing is possible I cherish you as my own son."

"My gifts?" said Julius surprised.

"You have a great appetite for learning. You seem to have insights that most do not possess. You have a remarkable aptitude for languages. You have strong views, yet are gracious to everyone. All the Brothers delight in your company. These are gifts that cannot be disputed."

Julius looked down at his feet, his rough shoes dripping a small pool of water onto the stone floor, and then he looked up, into the Abbot's eyes again, and spoke calmly.

"What if I said to you that I were...Jesus Christ?"

The Abbot moved back in his chair. For a moment, anger flashed across his face. His mouth opened wide, then closed. He took a moment, staring at Julius, to grasp what he'd said.

"I...Julius, if anyone else had said that to me I would have thought him insane. But you...what are you saying?" Giovanni said, still trying to compose his words. "Are you playing games with me? What on earth do you mean?"

He looked at Julius hard. This was no theological riddle. The boy looked deadly serious.

"Because I was told today that I have no mother or father," Julius replied, "that I was cloned from another human body. From the body of Jesus Christ. I have the evidence here." He held up O'Brien's diary, the pages damp and swollen.

The Abbot looked horrified.

"That is preposterous! How on earth..."

Cardinal Vanutti stepped forward from the shadows. "I believe that is Vatican property." He snatched the book from Julius' hand and stepped into the middle of the small room. He looked at Julius and the Abbot in turn, who were both equally frightened by Vanutti's presence. They could see another, equally sinister looking priest step into the doorway on guard.

"What you have heard is true," said the Cardinal. "You are an exact copy of he who was born two thousand years ago."

The three stood in silence for several moments.

"My mother was right never to have trusted you." Julius stared fiercely at Vanutti. "Why was I not told of this?"

The Abbot sat to one side, unable to comprehend what was happening.

"You are a part of our project," Vanutti said. "We decided that you should be unaware, just as we think that the first Jesus did not know who he was until he was your age. You have learned of your origins much earlier than we planned, but no matter now. I am here to test what powers you have."

Vanutti turned to face the Abbot.

"What do you think, Father? You have lived with him all of his life. Do you think that he is anything more than a man?"

The Abbot spoke with panic in his voice. "I do not know. But the more I think about it, the more I realise that I have known it since he was a child. There is something about him. He can resolve an argument between two people with scarcely a word. He is always calm. There is an attraction to him. Perhaps if I were younger, I would be tempted to…follow him."

Vanutti raised his eyes to the ceiling in irritation, and then looked back down at Julius.

"What is so unusual about these things?" Julius said angrily. "Of course I am an ordinary man! No greater, no less. I cannot work miracles. I am here to serve God and my fellow men. To show the right path."

Vanutti smiled, with the menace of a cat stalking its prey. "Very eloquent, Julius. But you know that you are not ordinary. We made you. We will decide what happens to you."

Julius shook his head. "Then do you expect me to turn that glass of water into wine? To raise the dead?"

The Cardinal laughed, almost sneering. "Of course not. You are not stupid, my boy, and neither am I. But nevertheless you may have some powers that may yet be useful to our Church. I intend to test you before a decision can be made about your future."

"And what if I refuse?" Julius asked.

"Then I will make sure that your existence is hidden from public knowledge forever. You will be a prisoner. How would you like to spend your life in a small, secure room deep in a cellar of the Vatican? With perhaps your mother for company?"

"Bastard!" Julius spat his words at Vanutti.

Vanutti's mobile phone suddenly rang. "What is it?" he barked into the mouthpiece. He listened for a few moments and then rang off.

"I have to speak to His Holiness at once. You will wait here." He waved O'Brien's diary in the air. "I will return in a few moments and you will begin by telling me where the stupid Americans are who brought this to you."

Vanutti marched towards the door.

"See that he does not leave this room!" he said to Cuccini, slamming the door shut.

The Abbot looked around at Julius, who sat, calm once again, considering his thoughts.

"My son…" he said, struggling for words, and shaking his head. "Jul…I…"

Julius reached out and put a comforting hand on the old man's arm.

"Father. Somehow, though I do not know how, I can sense what is in your heart. You are a good man. I know that you did not have a conscious part in this."

The Abbot dropped his gaze to the floor, shaking his head.

"I remember you as a boy. When you settled the argument between old Petrocelli and the Baker. All of the questions you would ask me about the Bible. How you led the other boys when you stopped that runaway bull! Now, if we only had time to talk. But you must go. You and your mother must leave at once."

"They were right. Now they are in as much danger as I," Julius sighed to himself.

"Who, the two that came here earlier?" Giovanni asked.

"Helen and David." Julius looked up at the Abbot. "They told me not to come here. Now we are trapped."

"They were right, my son," the Abbot said, then continued, whispering. "But trapped? Perhaps not."

Julius looked around the room, and then spoke quietly. "The door is guarded. The window is small. We cannot get out."

The Abbot moved his chair as silently as he could, then pulled away the square of rush matting that lay on the floor. Underneath was a trap door.

Julius' eyes gaped wide in surprise. "Monasteries have always needed escape routes," whispered the

Abbot. "Help me! The hatch is heavy and we must try to lift it quietly!"

Together they slowly lifted the large, rusting iron ring from its recess in the wooden hatch. They pulled hard, and with just one loud creak it opened. They stood, silent for a few moments, waiting for any reaction from outside, but there was none.

"The steps lead to the crypt under the chapel," the Abbot said, searching his bookshelves. He found a key. "This will open the door that leads on to the old grain store. There is a hatch that comes up in…"

Julius stopped him, nodding and quietly mouthing the words "I know where."

Julius hugged the old man. "You have been like a father to me. I don't know if I will ever see you again, but I will always try to follow what you have taught me."

"God be with you my son," the Abbot replied. He had tears in his eyes. "Now I know that it is I who should be following you. But not at this moment. I am old and frail. I will delay Vanutti as long as I can. Go quickly, Julius."

Julius climbed down the steps, and looked up, also with a tear running down his cheek, as the Abbot lowered the trapdoor.

By now, it was dark. It was easy for Julius to escape from the monastery grounds and run down the road to the village. He jumped up the steps and into his mother's house, nearly bumping into David, who was speaking on his mobile telephone. His face shone with relief as Julius entered. Maria was rushing around the tiny apartment, collecting her religious mementoes into carrier bags. She dropped them onto the floor and hugged Julius.

"Yes, fine. OK we will. Thank you. Goodbye." David said.

Helen politely pulled Maria back. "Hurry, we don't have much time. Get your things." Maria nodded and quickly carried on collecting her things.

"What is happening?" said Julius watching his mother pushing shut a battered suitcase.

Helen handed him a bag. "We are getting out. Now."

Julius looked slightly overawed.

"Come on!" David said, taking Julius by the arm. "If you have anything you want to take, find it quickly."

"Where are we going?" said Julius.

"We are taking you and your mother to America. Our Texan friend has diverted his private jet from Rome to Florence airport, the military section."

Julius looked puzzled. "What friend?"

Helen stopped for a moment at looked directly at Julius. "Look, we probably don't have very much time. I don't know what the Abbot said to you, but you must trust us."

Julius shivered. "Vanutti has probably discovered my escape already."

"He is here? Now?" said Helen. She looked in panic at David, and back to Julius. "If he finds us he will kill us all!" she said.

Julius nodded emphatically. "I know. Let us go. Mother?"

"Yes I am coming son. I am already packed." Her eyes shone with pride as she looked at her son.

"But what about passports or visas? We do not have them."

Helen smiled. "It's OK. Our friend has 'bought' your passage out. Some hands have been greased! There will be no problem."

Julius was looking out of one of the high windows at the back of the room.

"I can see the lights of a car coming down the track," he said.

"Pick up your bags!" David shouted and turned off the lights. "Quiet everyone!" He peered out through the curtains, and breathed a sigh relief as the car pulled up outside. "It's OK, it's our taxi, let's go."

They scrambled out of the door, feeling their way down the staircase. Bundling in to the battered old cab, they sped off down the stony road.

"Five kilometres to go." The taxi driver pointed to the lights twinkling ahead. They were nearly down into the valley and the hypnotic swish of the windscreen wipers clearing the rain kept everybody silent.

David sat pressed against the window, next to Helen. His hand found hers and he wrapped his fingers around her palm. She looked at him, uncomfortable. Her face seemed to say 'not just at the moment' and she withdrew it.

Helen, sitting in the middle of the back seat, turned to Julius.

"Are you OK? Your mind must be spinning," she said.

Julius remained silent, but brought both his hands up to press the sides of his head, closing his eyes. Then he looked up at Helen, with a forced smile, and returned to his thoughts.

Suddenly there was a flash of bright lights and a loud bang from behind them. A large black car was ramming them.

"It's Vanutti!" shouted David. The taxi took a sharp bend and the car fell behind, racing to catch up again.

"What is happening?" yelled the driver.

David thought quickly. "It's the father-in-law. He is trying to stop us. But they are in love!" said David pointing to Julius and Helen in the back.

The car rammed them again, nearly forcing the taxi off the road.

"He is wrecking my car!" the driver complained.

David dug into his pocket, bringing out a handful of dollars.

"There's over three hundred dollars there," he shouted and stuffed the notes into the driver's hand. "Take it."

"Mamma Mia! For that I will drive you to America!"

The driver floored the throttle as the black Mercedes pulled level. The car swerved right and knocked the taxi off the road and onto a grass slope. The driver cursed and used the slope to speed past the Mercedes. They had reached the outskirts of the city.

David looked behind. "Hold on everybody, he is gaining on us."

The taxi driver jumped a red light and the black car swerved to avoid an oncoming truck.

There were signs appearing already for the airport.

"Can we make it?" asked Helen. David looked worried. "If we can get to the gates first, they won't let him through."

The cars were racing side by side down the main road. The black Mercedes swerved again as the taxi driver turned sharp right. "Short cut!" he said smiling.

They turned the wrong way up a one-way street and screeched onto the main airport approach road. The black car roared straight up behind them.

"There!" said David pointing. "The military entrance."

The taxi squealed to a halt in front of a barrier. A young soldier jumped out of a hut, rifle raised. "Hey! What are you doing?"

A senior officer appeared and pushed the young soldier away. He shone his torch at all five faces in the car.

"Andiamo!" he shouted at the hut and the barrier was raised.

The taxi screeched through as the barrier fell behind them.

The black window of the car glided down and Vanutti leaned out into the rain.

"Open it now!" he barked.

"Just one moment," said the officer, "this is a military installation."

"Vanutti's face was twisted in anger. "Open it now! I am Cardinal Vanutti of the Vatican! Those people must be stopped!"

"I will need to make an enquiry first…"

But Vanutti was out of the car, ducking under the barrier and running towards the runway.

"Over there!" said David, pointing to a small jet on the runway, its lights flashing. The taxi drew right up to the plane's stairs and they hurriedly scrambled out into the pouring rain. A steward appeared in the doorway of the jet. "This way quickly!" he shouted.

They boarded the plane and the door was closed. "Seat belts please," said the steward as the jet began slowly moving forward.

Vanutti carried on running towards the plane, even as he saw it taxi towards take-off. As the jet's engines reached full thrust, he stopped, holding his chest. He watched the jet lift off and soar into the sky. He stood alone, panting, hair soaked by the rain. "May God help us," he whispered.

REVELATION

REVELATION

Myron Wilson's Private Jet, flying to the US November 9th 2003

Red light filled the plane's cabin, as it flew west, cheating the sunset for an hour or two. Julius had awoken, his bleary eyes searching for any detail on the clouds below, as they slipped into darkness. Helen had been sitting next to him since they'd taken off, watching his face as he slept. David and Maria sat close on other seats. Maria did not stray from the small table in front of her and gripped it hard whenever the plane moved.

"How are you?" said Helen to Julius. He nodded slowly.

"Rested a little," he said. "How long have we been travelling?"

"Seven hours. One to go," she said.

He looked surprised. "I thought it would be much quicker, in a jet plane?"

She laughed and then stopped, embarrassed. "I'm sorry. You've never been in a plane or anything, have you?"

There was a moment of awkwardness, before the matter was dropped. Julius gazed out of the window once more. The moon was visible now, as the sky deepened to darkest blue.

"I was wondering. Do you mind me asking…" she began.

He turned and smiled at her. "I don't mind. What were you wondering?"

"Right." She spoke deliberately, but got stuck repeatedly. "How do you…I mean, are you…look, with what we told you…" until he raised his hand gently.

"Are you asking me whether we are really closer to God, now that we are far up in the sky?" he said with amusement. She lowered her eyes, embarrassed at her sudden failure to speak her mind. He reached out and put his hand on her arm.

"I am sorry," he said. "Forgive me for being sarcastic. I know what you were really asking me. I suspect that a lot of people will want to ask me the same question. Is there a God? Do I have a direct line to Him? Yes?"

She nodded, nervously.

He raised his hands as if in blessing. She shifted backwards as his face assumed a look of holy reverance. Then it deflated and he smiled softly again.

"No," he said. "That is, I don't think that I have any special connection. Tell me, what does God mean to you?" he said, looking into her eyes steadily and calmly.

She thought for a minute and then replied. "I always found it hard to accept the vision of God in the sky looking down on all of us."

He continued looking at her, with a small laugh, then his face became serious again.

"Tell me what you do believe, rather than what you do not."

Helen squirmed imperceptibly in her seat, as Julius asked her to reveal her most private thoughts, yet she was drawn, as she had never been before. Once again she stuttered a reply.

"I...I'm not sure. I don't think I believe anything that strongly."

As he smiled at her, she felt her body involuntarily relax into the seat, but her heartbeat quickened.

He said nothing for a few moments, shaking his dark curls very slightly. "Yes you do," he said gently. "You have...strong feelings. They surge within you, fighting to be expressed. You're scared, aren't you?"

Helen stared down at her clasped hands for what seemed ages. Julius waited in silence. She slowly looked up at him, with a tear in one eye.

"How did you know that?" she asked. "Damn."

She raised a hand to her mouth, breathed in hard, stopping herself from breaking into more tears. "I didn't really know that myself. But it's true. It's absolutely right. Can you read my mind?"

"I don't think so," he said, "but somehow I can feel your emotions. I can feel the turmoil of conflict, between your rational mind and the spiritual experiences that you have had."

She spoke, more insistently. "So which one is right? Which path should I follow?"

He simply shrugged. "The one you feel is right. All you can do is try to understand yourself and what will bring you happiness. If you are a Muslim, Hindu, Jew, or if you believe in…." he held up his palms ironically, "Christ. Or even if you have no religion. There are many paths, but all lead to same door. To God's house, if you like."

"I don't understand," she said.

He smiled gently again. "Well, you were asking about God, weren't you? I'm afraid I'm not a qualified expert on God. But I've lived all my life in a place where lots of people think and talk about God. I had a great deal of time to study, and think." He paused for a moment, unsure, then continued.

"Can I share something with you? Something important?"

She nodded. He took her hand in his.

"Close your eyes," he said. "Try to imagine. You can see inside your own head. Imagine it like a room, with a domed roof. Can you?"

She nodded again, eyes closed. "Yes, I can."

He spoke, softly and slowly. "Go to the back of the room. There's a spiral staircase there, going down. Deep into your mind."

She drew a sudden breath.

"If you never go down, you can't see what's there. But there's a whole world down there, the last great unexplored territory. A psychologist would call it your subconscious. A priest would say it's your soul."

"And what would you say?" She opened her eyes.

"That they're both right. But there's something else. That's the important part."

"What is it?" She was intensely focused on him.

"Well, when you look into your subconscious, you're not alone. It's a space you share with everyone else."

He let go of her hand and she sighed, her body tingling. He angled his head to lean against the dark window behind him.

"I'm sorry if I am not making much sense. It is hard to explain. But I don't think God is out there in the sky," he said, making a fist and placing against his chest. "He's in here. A little bit of me, of you, and of everybody else…that's what God is. The connections between all of us. In the Bible it says 'God's mansion is infinite' – that is because everybody has one of His rooms inside them. You don't need to have expensive churches, priests and bishops. People need to look inside themselves. I…"

He lowered his head. She looked at him, still spellbound by what he was saying.

"Tell me, Julius."

"I'm rambling now, I apologise". He stared into her eyes once again. "Do you realize how you have helped me?"

She was surprised. "Me? Help you? I think I'm the one who needs help."

He took her hand again. "We all do, Helen. But in talking to you, I have just started to realize why I'm here. My purpose in life," he said. "The things I've just said. What I've learned about myself. I have to teach. To help people to find God for themselves."

Helen jumped as the door at the front of the cabin opened. The co-pilot leaned out of the cockpit and shouted to them.

"Folks, we're landing in twenty minutes."

The plane rolled slowly to a halt. The engines cut and whined down to silence. Julius sat expressionless. Maria craned her head to see out of her window, dazzled by what appeared to be arc lights mounted outside. Helen tapped David on the arm as he rummaged in his bags. He turned, surprised and uncertain, having watched her and Julius locked in animated conversation.

"Hi," he said. "OK?"

"Yes," she nodded. "Do you think that Wilson will be waiting for us?"

David nodded his head. "I think that he will be here to claim his prize."

He stood, waiting expectantly for the conversation to continue, but Helen turned again to whisper to Julius.

"David, are we going to get out now?" Maria asked from behind him, holding several plastic bags in each hand.

"Oh, yes! Sorry!" David replied, suddenly realising he was blocking her path in the small aisle of the aircraft.

The side door of the plane opened with a rush of humid air. The four looked to each other, then went towards the exit, feeling the hot atmosphere of Texas seep into the air-conditioned interior.

David hung back until last, just behind Helen.

He touched her elbow.

"What is it?" she replied

"I…well, I wondered, can we get a chance to talk?"

The look on her face was as if he'd reminded her of some unpleasant duty; it was as if she was acknowledging the special trust they'd shared, yet not wanting it now. She looked at him for a few moments, then spoke quietly.

"Perhaps later, OK? Let's see how it goes."

David nodded reluctantly as she turned back.

They walked out onto the exit ladder. Bright lights illuminated the plane and its immediate surroundings. Beyond that was darkness, punctuated by distant lights of airliners and airport buildings in the distance. Next to the plane was a gas tanker and two long, black limousines. Three men in black suits stood by the cars. Another, older man, with immaculately styled white hair, dressed in a white suit and wearing a huge Stetson hat, approached them.

"Welcome my friends. I am Myron Wilson!"

His face showed the largest smile imaginable, his perfect teeth flashing. He held his arms wide and his eyes settled on Julius.

"I don't believe it! I just don't believe it! It is an honour and a privilege to meet you, my boy!" Wilson stood for a moment, shaking his head, his smile still visible through pursed lips. "Well, what do I call you?"

Julius managed a half smile. "'Julius' will be fine, thank you."

"OK," said Wilson, "you can ride in that limousine over there. I'd like to speak with you on the way to the hotel." He pointed to one of the cars and the suited men jumped to open the doors.

Wilson turned to Maria, crouching a little to see her face.

"Ma'am, you're the boy's mother?"

Maria nodded, looking around in vain for some guidance on what to say.

He clasped her hands "You are my honoured guest, Maria. You have a fine son!"

He turned to David and Helen, putting his arms around both their shoulders.

"What can I say to you two? You've done the damned finest job I could imagine. When we get some time, you let me know how I can reward you. You think of anything, you hear?"

Wilson virtually pulled all of them to the cars.

"Anyways, let's get going! I have y'all in the finest hotel in this city. Course I own it, but it's still the best!" Wilson laughed out loud.

"Aren't there any customs, passport control or anything?" asked David.

Wilson laughed again. "I have a lot of influence around these parts, my boy. No need for any of those. Now you three get in, and me and Julius will see you there."

The same day

The House of Vincente Tardelli, New York City
November 9th 2003

In the garden, the last few leaves on the trees and shrubs were falling to the ground with the freshening breeze. The sun was about twenty degrees above the high walls and illuminated the apple trees.

Vincente Tardelli watched the young boy playing for a moment. He was running around the pond, weaving in and out of the stone statues with his arms outstretched, pretending he was an aeroplane. Memories returned of his own children at that age playing in the same place. He finished his cigar, extinguished it in the ashtray on the pine table and hugged himself a little against the chill. He stepped back into the conservatory and saw the woman approaching. She was dark and pretty, about twenty eight. He smiled broadly.

"Claudia, nice to see you again," he said, kissing both of her cheeks. "You have come to collect your little terror?"

Claudia looked out through the high windows of the conservatory, to where her son was now fishing in the pond water with his hands. "The terrible two's have turned into the terrible three's!" she said. "He is as stubborn as his father."

"If Roberto turns out to be half as good as his father, I will be proud of him. Paulo is the most faithful of my employees. I treat him as my own son."

She smiled at him. "Thank you Don Tardelli. You are very kind."

The Don nodded. "I keep telling you, call me Vincente! Now what can I do for you?"

Claudia looked slightly nervous. "It's about Irena's baptism next week."

Tardelli's face fell. "Do not say that you cannot come? You are organising the whole thing."

Claudia urgently held up her hands to reassure him.

"Oh no! Of course I will be there! It is my greatest pleasure to plan your granddaughter's service. But…well I wanted to ask you about…well a request to mark the day?"

The Don relaxed and smiled.

"Of course. You can ask me anything you wish. You know it's a tradition and I honour all our family traditions."

"Thank you," Claudia replied, but once again looked a little nervous. "But can I say that my husband does not know about this. He would not have allowed me to ask you."

"Just ask my dear! It is my pleasure and your entitlement."

Claudia took a deep breath, calmed herself and spoke.

"Well as you know we live in a two bedroom apartment that you provided for us. We are very grateful. But we would like to stand on our own two feet. It would be perfect for us to own our own house, maybe three bedrooms, but modest…"

The Don was nodding slowly. "It is good to think of your future, and that of your children who will benefit in the end. But it is expensive to buy houses, especially in a neighbourhood like this one. Claudia, you are not happy there? It is a very large apartment."

Claudia smiled gratefully. "It is a beautiful home, but…we will need another bedroom."

"You will?" The Dons eyes twinkled. "Are you hoping to expand your family then?" he asked smiling.

"Well, not hoping. I *am* expanding it."

There was a pause as the Don pondered this.

Then he gripped her shoulders and laughed. "You mean you are pregnant? Maria Madonna! Let me hug you!"

Claudia laughed. "Not too tight!" she said.

"Does Paulo know yet?" asked the Don.

"No, I will tell him at the baptism. He longs for a little girl. I will keep my fingers crossed."

"I hope my christening favour is not to make the baby a girl?" said the Don chuckling. "Even that may be beyond Vincente Tardelli!"

They both laughed.

"No, but if I could be so bold as to ask…well, could you perhaps lend us the money for a deposit, to get a mortgage?"

"Ah I see," said the Don. He stood in silence for a minute.

"I am afraid I cannot lend you any money," he said at last.

Claudia's eyes dropped to the floor.

The Don held up a hand. "It is not good to be in debt to anyone."

"You are right Vincente, forgive me for even asking."

The Don smiled widely at her. "Instead, I will give you your house. I own a four-bedroom villa not too far away. It is yours."

Claudia took a few moments for this to sink in and then looked up with tears in her eyes.

"Oh Vincente that is fantastic!" she said and hugged him.

"Not too tight!" he said, laughing.

"How can we ever repay your generosity?" she said.

"To be truthful, I will feel more comfortable if you are both living closer to me. There, it is done. Let me have my driver take you home. You need to rest in your condition, no?"

"We can walk," she said. "It is not necessary to drive us."

"No, Luigi will take you in my own car. Franco?" he called.

A man of about thirty, expensively dressed in suit trousers and a cashmere sweater, appeared from the hall. "You called father?" he said, then recognising Claudia, greeted her with a hug.

"Franco, be careful, your friend's wife is pregnant."

Franco smiled from ear to ear and was about to speak, but Claudia quickly put a finger onto his mouth.

"Ssh!" she said. "It's a surprise for Paulo – he does not know yet."

The little boy came running in from the garden. "Mama!" he shouted. "I saw a fish!"

They all smiled. Claudia made signs at Franco to the effect that "he doesn't know either!"

"Is Luigi here?" said the Don.

"Yes, he has just finished cleaning the limousine," replied Franco.

"Excellent!" said the Don. "Please take these two out and make sure she accepts a lift home!" Then he turned to Claudia: "You should take things easy from now on."

"Thank you so much," replied Claudia, kissing the Don's cheek. "You are as a father to us all."

"That is the way I like it," said Vincente, with a smile and satisfied nod.

"Now off with you. Tell Luigi to drive carefully!"

Claudia, Roberto and Franco left, she talking excitedly about the forthcoming baptism of Franco's daughter. Vincente sighed happily, went to a bureau and selected another large cigar. Outside, the last rays of sunlight played on the garden. He opened the conservatory door. Blackbirds sang in the apple trees.

In a split second, the Don saw a bright flash of light, just before a loud explosion blew him off his feet as the blast rocketed in from the hall, where the front door had been torn off its hinges. Glass from the conservatory windows smashed in all around him.

Alarms were ringing all through the house and there was the sound of running feet.

The Don crawled to his knees and hauled himself to the hall door. He looked at a scene of carnage where the massive front door had blown in and smashed one wall of the entrance hall. Beyond the hole where it had been, he could see his car, a tangled mess of twisted metal, lying on its side, burning.

"No, no," he whimpered and headed towards the door.

Franco rushed towards him, frantically looking in all directions. He held a handkerchief to his head, which ran with blood.

"Papa! Papa! Are you hurt?" he asked.

"I don't think so. Let me get up," said Vicente. He staggered as he tried to get to his feet, and made to lurch towards the front of the house. Franco held him back.

"Let me get out there," said the Don trying to push past.

"No Papa, it is not safe," said Franco. "Our men are searching the grounds."

The Don looked questioningly up at Franco, then at the burning wreck.

"What was it, a bomb?" said the Don, incredulous.

"Yes, we think so. And meant for you no doubt. Thank the Lord that you…."

"Do not thank the Lord for this. Were they in the car?"

"Yes Papa, I saw them," Franco shook his head. "They had no chance. They were killed. They are all dead. I am sorry."

The Don closed his eyes in anguish. After a few moments he turned and walked quietly to the phone, took a deep breath and dialled.

"Hello? Paulo?"

Later that day

Downtown Dallas, Texas
November 9th 2003

The interior of the limousine was dark, spacious and cool. Julius watched endless blocks pass as they sped along the outskirts of the city.

"My boy…Julius, I…"

Julius turned away from the window as Wilson leaned towards him and spoke hesitantly in a low voice.

"Between you and me, I am not a well man."

Julius looked him up and down. "You look very healthy to me, Signor."

"Well, that may be so," Wilson continued, adjusting his sitting position as if to ease some discomfort. "I guess I put on a show. But I have cancer. My doctors tell me I could die by the end of the year."

"I am sorry to hear that Signor," Julius said, not volunteering any other comment. Wilson was lost for words for a few moments.

"I…well I wondered, if you could perhaps help me?"

Julius stared at him in silence. Then spoke softly.

"Do you think I can perform a miracle?" He held out both his hands, palms upward. "Perhaps I can help. Take my hands."

A little of the colour drained from Wilson's face. He offered both his hands excitedly, which Julius gripped, sitting in silence with his eyes closed, before opening them again and speaking steadily.

"You are afraid, Mister Wilson. You are in fear of many things."

"Go on," Wilson said, his voice shaking.

"You worry that your rivals will take over your position. You are frightened to lose even a tiny part of your money and your power. You think that when you die, nobody will remember you. Your desire is to control everything, to protect yourself. Perhaps you should let go of some of these things, to make peace with yourself."

Wilson backed away, pulling his hand from Julius' grip. He stopped himself shaking, composed himself, and then wiped his brow with a handkerchief.

"I was right about one thing," he said, forcing a half smile for a moment.

"What is that?" asked Julius.

Wilson pointed at him. "You are going to create quite a sensation!"

He rapped on the drivers' window behind his head. "Lewinski!"

"Yessir, Mister Wilson?" the driver shouted from the front.

"How long to the hotel?"

"About ten minutes, sir."

Wilson nodded and watched Julius quizzically, as the young man gazed out again at the city traffic.

One day later

Presidential suite, Wilson Dallas Plaza Hotel
November 10th 2003

David stared out of the penthouse windows, across the skyline of Dallas. The sun cast a red glow all over the mass of buildings and roads he could see, spread out below. He had slept only a few hours, before rising and wandering around the corridors and empty rooms. Wilson had reserved the entire top floor of the hotel for the four of them. Last night, Julius and his mother had been billeted in adjoining bedrooms. Once they were installed, Helen had quickly found another room, very obviously shutting herself off. David was left to find another bed, which he did, falling asleep through exhaustion rather than any sense of comfort or contentment.

He walked across the thick carpet, back to the central lounge area. It had a massive four-piece suite of furniture, which faced a large TV system. Paintings of past US presidents hung around the walls. Just by the double doors to the corridor, there was a breakfast trolley, which a porter had delivered a few minutes ago. He turned his head, hearing a noise from somewhere, and his heart thumped as Helen walked into the lounge, yawning.

"Hi!" he said.

"Hello." She rubbed her eyes and ruffled her hair with her hands. "Are Julius or Maria awake yet?"

David shook his head. "I don't think so."

"Oh. OK." She turned to back out.

"Helen…I…well, can we talk for a minute?" David said. She turned back, with a look as if he was a naughty child, irritating her by doing something he'd just been told not to.

"It's…I told you last night, it's not the time now," she said.

"What about later then, tonight perhaps? Can't we go out to a bar or something? Just for an hour?"

"Look David, I…" she was trying to find words. "I'm really confused at the moment. I don't think I can talk about this right now. Something's happened to me and…well I just can't focus on us right now. I need to be with him, can't you see that? He needs me right now. I'm sorry."

David shook his head angrily.

"OK. That's it then. I'm going." He walked away, out into the corridor towards the lifts. "I'll see you later. If you have any time, that is!" he called back.

Helen stood for a moment, with a hand over her eyes.

"Damn!" she said, softly but harshly.

"You have a lot of affection for David, don't you?" Helen jumped as Julius spoke to her. He stood in the entrance to the lounge, smiling sympathetically.

274

Helen's face instantly brightened. She smoothed her hair.

"Oh, hi!" she said. "I thought you were asleep."

"I awoke about half an hour ago," said Julius. "I was watching television."

Helen gestured to the trolley. "Do you want some breakfast? This was just delivered, I think."

"Thank you." Julius took a plate, picked some pieces from the trolley and sat down on one of the plush settees.

"I was asking you about David. He seemed upset?" Julius asked again.

Helen shrugged, then shook her head. "It was nothing. David's a little immature sometimes."

Julius looked at Helen in silence, waiting for her to say more. She didn't, looking obviously like she wished to change the subject. She sat down opposite him, taking a fruit juice. Julius sensed her mood and changed the subject.

"On some of the TV channels I saw Christian preachers, in business suits. They seemed like politicians."

Helen laughed. "Were they asking for money?"

Julius' eyes opened wider. "Ah, was that it? They showed telephone numbers on the screen. You would call them and use your...credit card?"

Helen smiled and nodded. "Yep. You're getting it. That's the American Church!"

Julius considered a blueberry muffin for a few moments before pulling off a piece and popping it in his mouth.

"I'm afraid that the Americans do not have a…how would you say…a monopoly on that," he said. "All Churches collect money. The Catholic Church takes millions from its people. Many who pay for religion are much poorer than the people who watch those programmes."

Helen just nodded. Then she hugged herself with her arms, rocked backwards and forwards on her chair.

"I wonder what's going to happen?" she asked. "Did Wilson say anything to you last night?"

Julius shook his head slowly. "I do not know. He said a few things. I rather think he has some plans for us. We will hear them soon enough."

Four hours later

Ed's Bar, downtown Dallas
November 10th 2003

David sat on a bar stool, looking down at the collection of pistachio shells he'd made on the polished bar top. There were few people in at this hour. The TV was showing a football game. He looked up at it as he drained his glass.

"Can I get you a refill?" said the barman, facing him on the other side, half talking to David and half watching the screen.

"Yes, why not," David said, with an air of resignation. The barman placed another beer in front of him, wrote on his tab ticket, and refreshed the small bowl of nuts.

David carefully manoeuvred his hand towards the glass, which, as it was his fifth one, was becoming increasingly difficult to manage gracefully. Lifting it precariously to his lips, he swallowed a large mouthful.

A woman in a business suit came into the bar. She appeared to be in her mid to late thirties, with elegantly styled auburn hair. She carried what was probably a laptop computer in her case.

"Hey, Penny," said the barman. "Beer?"

She nodded and sat at the bar, a few seats from David. She looked at him for several minutes, then turned and spoke, after he'd finished his beer in several swallows.

"Can't be that bad, can it?" she asked.

David shook his head, partly to respond to her question, and also to clear his head a little. He looked down at the bar.

"No...I s'pose not."

Penny looked at him with mild distaste. The barman met her glance and shrugged his shoulders. "You're a long way from home, buddy. England, yeah?" he said.

David nodded, in an exaggerated manner, like a small child.

"Where ya staying? Perhaps you need a cab?" the barman continued.

David's eyes went out of focus for a moment as he tried to recall. "Wilson Dall...Dallash Plaza. Top floor."

The barman shook his head. "Oh yeah. Come on pal. Time's up. I'll get you a cab myself. Unless..." he smiled sarcastically, "Mister Wilson's private helicopter is coming to collect you?"

David stood up, swaying. He looked puzzled for a moment. "No...we came in a plane. A little one. Not a helicopter. Little jet plane."

Penny held up a hand to stop the barman continuing.

"I'm sorry, I didn't catch your name?" she said.

"David. David Woodbridge."

She steadied him and sat him down. "Are you working for Myron Wilson, David?"

David half nodded and furrowed his eyebrows.

"Sort of," he said. "Special project."

"And you're staying in the top floor of his hotel?"

He nodded again. Still swaying on his seat. "The...presidential suite."

Penny thought for a minute. "Have you...had anything to eat, David?"

He shook his head. "Not today."

She took his arm, stood him up and guided him to the opposite side of the bar. There were several bays, with tables surrounded by upholstered chairs. She sat him down and called over to the barman.

"Ted, let's get some coffee over here. Bring the menu over too, will you."

Ted smiled knowingly to her and reached for the coffee pot. Penny reached into her jacket pocket. There was a faint click.

"Now David, you relax a while. What are you by the way? Engineer? Computer man?"

David struggled to pronounce his answer. "No. Archaeologist. Sort of, anyway."

Penny looked surprised for a few moments.

"Tell me David, what does Mister Wilson want with an archaeologist?"

"Helen's the archaeol...difficult to explain. Anyway, it's a bit of a secret."

Penny smiled. "Why don't you have some coffee David?"

"No. I want another drink. I want to forget about her."

"Who?"

"Helen of course! She hates me now."

"I'm sure she doesn't," said Penny. "Look er...where are you going to stay tonight?"

David looked up with a smile, then his face drooped again. "Dunno," he said.

"Why don't we go back to my apartment?" Penny continued. "You could tell me all about it. I've got a very comfortable sofa, you could sleep there. Yeah?"

"Do you have any whisky?"

"Whisky? Oh yeah," Penny said, smiling. "Of course I do, some real quality English stuff. I mean Scottish stuff! Smooth and warm."

The woman signalled to the barman and he came back to the table. Penny took forty dollars out of her bag and pressed it into his hand. "We have to go Ted. That's for your trouble. Keep it quiet for now, yeah?"

Ted smiled and nodded, tucked the money into his top pocket and helped Penny get David to his feet.

"OK, young man," she said, straining with the effort of lifting him. "Let's get us a cab!"

"Make sure he signs the contract!" Ted said, as he left them in the street.

Same day

Wilson Dallas Plaza Hotel
November 10th 2003

Keith Andrews looked around the huge marble lobby of the Plaza, as he waited in line at the reception desk. His battered briefcase and travel bag looked somewhat out of place in this expensive environment.

"Yes sir?" he was interrupted by the young Mexican clerk behind the desk.

"Ah...yes, I, er, wish to get in touch with some guests here. They're in the," he looked at the crumpled piece of paper in his hand. "The President's suite...I think."

The clerk raised his eyebrows. "Your name sir?"

"Oh yes. Andrews. Doctor Keith Andrews."

The clerk shook his head. "I'm afraid I haven't been informed of your name sir. The President's suite is..."

"Keith!" The clerk was interrupted by a booming voice from behind. Myron Wilson strode across the lobby, silhouetted by the sunlight at the entrance doors. Two of his black-suited minders flanked him. Another man in a light suit and an expensive looking briefcase followed behind. Wilson grabbed Andrews' hand and shook it vigorously.

"Keith, it's great to see you again! Hell, we came up trumps, didn't we?!"

Andrews smiled awkwardly.

"Boy!" Wilson shouted at the clerk.

"Yessir?" the clerk replied, like a soldier snapping to attention.

"This is a special guest of mine," Wilson said. "Get his luggage taken up to the Presidential suite. You come up there and do any registration you need to, OK? And you remember to get him anything he wants, anytime."

The clerk nodded briskly and snapped his fingers at the bellboys.

Wilson put his arm around Andrews and dragged him over to the lifts.

"You come along with me, Keith. You gotta meet my protégé! Oh by the way..." he turned to the man with the briefcase, who was following silently. "This is Fred Weinburger, my top lawyer. He's got some plans to talk about later."

Helen sat next to Julius, at one side of the giant boardroom table, in the conference room opposite the lounge. On the other side sat Andrews and Weinburger, the lawyer.

"Is your mother OK?" Helen whispered.

"She is in her room," Julius replied. "One of Wilson's people got her some Italian versions of old movies, on video. She is happy for now watching them."

"If I could begin?" Wilson boomed from the head of the table.

"Now, how are you all? Rested I hope. Where is David?"

Helen looked uncomfortable. Andrews looked at her, puzzled.

"He er, went out, this morning. I was expecting him back. I'm afraid I don't know where he went to," she said.

Wilson paused for a few moments, sighed, and then shrugged off any disappointment. "OK, no matter. I have been giving a great amount of consideration to the – how can I put it – wonderful surprise we have all had, and I have some proposals for..." he nodded to Julius, "...your future."

"Shouldn't Julius be able to decide for himself what he does?" Helen said.

Wilson smiled, then, hearing something, cocked his head to one side. There were sounds of many police sirens in the street below.

"Lewinski!" he shouted towards the lounge. "Find out what the hell is happening downstairs!"

Wilson smiled and continued.

"Let me just remind you of the situation here." He looked at Julius directly. "You have been created by a medical procedure which is illegal in the USA and most everywhere else in the civilised world. And if you start bragging about who you are, what do you think's gonna happen? Half the people will think you're crazy, and the other half will think you're the

Devil." He looked around at all of them. "Where are you gonna go? Back to the Abbey? How long do you think you can keep yourself a secret? You got just one sure-fire thing you can count on at the moment. I am your only friend here."

Julius and Helen were silent.

"Just what do you plan to do, Mister Wilson?" Andrews asked.

"Right now? You stay here. In the future?"

Wilson smiled again, and gestured to Weinburger, who was opening his briefcase and unfolding a large set of drawings.

"Here we are," said Weinburger. "Celestial City, Texas. At least that's what it'll look like in two years time."

Helen and Julius leaned forward, exchanging nervous glances with one another as they scanned the pictures of a huge monumental building, surrounded by other edifices.

"What is this?" asked Helen "A church of some kind?"

Wilson shook his head and scoffed at the suggestion.

"No, my dear. Not a church. A cathedral. The greatest in the world." Then he nodded to Julius. "It's yours. Your new home. You will preach there."

Lewinski entered the room, looking flustered, trying in vain to get some attention. Wilson's silenced him with a wave of his hand and continued.

"This is going to be the new world centre for the Christian Church. Millions will come here. The Catholic Church, the Orthodox people, and all the rest, they'll turn into sideshows!" he added with a flourish.

Helen and Andrews stood open-mouthed. Julius was impassive.

Wilson then turned with some irritation to Lewinski. "Now, what is going on?"

The man coughed slightly before replying. "Well sir, there are about a thousand journalists in the lobby. There are five TV trucks outside on the drive."

Wilson gestured to Weinburger, who jumped up and turned on the TV, flicking through channels until a news programme appeared.

"..and in case you haven't heard yet, an incredible story is breaking from Dallas, Texas. We advise you that some may find this item shocking, or disturbing." A picture of the Plaza Hotel appeared as the backdrop behind the newsreader. *"We have reports that an archaeological team have found the body of Jesus Christ in Palestine. There are unconfirmed reports that the body has actually been cloned and 'Jesus 2' is at this time in the President's suite in...."*

Another smart-suited man rushed in to the conference room, looking very flustered. Everyone looked up at him.

"Mister Wilson," he said, trying to catch his breath. "I have calls from the presidents of ABC, NBC and CNN holding for you. Also, I have a senior official at the State Department and someone from the White House. And the County Sheriff's office. What do you want me to do?"

Wilson thought for a few moments then spoke to the man, who was recovering his breath.

"OK, Pierce – go down and get the lobby cleared. Tell Police Captain Van Dyke you have my personal authority if you need to. Get back to all the callers and tell them I will speak to them all within half an hour. OK?"

The man rushed out. Wilson rubbed his hands together and his face once again broke into an enormous smile.

"It seems that our plans may have advanced a little, don't you think?"

One day later

US Catholic Church Central Ministry
New York City
November 11th 2003

"Your Grace?" O'Halloran's aide interrupted his paperwork, popping his head around the Cardinal's office door.

"What is it Charles?" he said, looking up from his desk. He was rather glad of the opportunity, as he hadn't been able to concentrate on any of his work since the crisis had broken.

"There's a visitor, your Grace, from the Vatican. He says he's on an urgent mission. Can you see him now?"

O'Halloran sighed and shook his head. Heaven knows what this visitor wanted. Probably just Vatican bureaucracy. He looked at his watch and shook his head.

"No, I have a meeting with an official from the State Department in half an hour. Can he wait?"

Bishop Charles Ford came further into the office and closed the door behind him.

"I think you may wish to see him. He is Cardinal Carlo Vanutti. He told me that he has met this 'man' in Italy."

"What?!" said O'Halloran, rising nervously from his chair. "Vanutti here in person? Good heavens, yes! Lord knows we need some information about all this. Send him in. Oh – call Francis and McQueen and any other senior staff that are around. Can you get Mrs Edwards to postpone the Government man by an hour? No, two hours."

Ford nodded and left. There was a small knock at the door and Mrs Edwards ushered in a dark haired man, dressed in a black business suit, with a Cardinal's tunic.

"Good morning, I am Carlo Vanutti."

"Welcome! Peter O'Halloran." The two men shook hands. "I am very pleased to see you!" said O'Halloran.

Vanutti nodded. "Primate of the US – your reputation as a man of wisdom and honour is well known to us."

O'Halloran brushed aside the compliment. "Ah, here are my aides." Three men came into the room and were introduced. "Monsignors Charles Ford, Devlin McQueen and Simon Francis. Shall we sit down gentlemen?"

The five sat around the office meeting table.

"Now, Carlo. I understand you have some knowledge of this man, whatever he is?"

Vanutti looked around at the four men, nodded gently and sighed.

"I have the unfortunate duty of telling you this news. I am afraid that almost everything the press are saying is indeed true. Julius is…authentic."

There were expressions of dismay around the table.

"You say you have met him? Such a thing can scarcely be believed. What can you tell us about him?" said McQueen.

"Despite the heresy of his creation, I wish I could say that he was a good man. But he seemed to me a dangerous radical. Subversive."

"But who on earth has done this...thing? How could it have happened?" said Francis.

Vanutti lowered his eyes for a moment, then spoke apologetically. "I have to tell you that it was a Vatican project."

There were gasps of disbelief. "Go on," said O'Halloran gravely.

"There was an archaeological discovery, twenty years ago. Christ's body. It was kept secret. Then, a misguided faction in the Vatican embarked on experiments without my knowledge. They brought in scientists under concealment. I do not know much more."

There was silence as the three Americans looked at each other, dumbfounded.

"We feel..." Vanutti continued, "that this event could have very serious consequences for our Church. Perhaps we are to blame as the...sponsors of this enterprise. But more than that it raises questions of faith and loyalty for Catholics, and all Christians worldwide."

O'Halloran nodded vigorously. "We have been besieged by our staff and even more from Catholics all over the US, seeking guidance. Heaven knows, we are only a minority religion in this country, what must it be like for the Anglicans?"

Francis spoke again. "Already the television preachers are saying that this Julius should be burned in public. Thousands of others are demanding that a new Church be formed with Julius as its Archbishop. It is crazy and dangerous."

Vanutti smiled gently and opened his hands.

"I foresaw all of this after I spoke with Julius at the Abbey in Italy. I wanted to solve the problem right then, but that crazy Texan spoiled my plans. Now I am here, among...friends to…"

The Americans sensed that Vanutti was looking for signs of trust. They smiled and nodded gravely for him to go on.

"Well," Vanutti said, "I wonder if it would be better for the problem to…go away?"

O'Halloran looked around at the others, none absolutely sure what Vanutti meant. He raised his chin slightly.

"Do you mean that he would not even get to speak in public?"

Vanutti shrugged. "If I can act in time. Perhaps he will be such a disappointment that his fame will evaporate. He will be ridiculed as an imposter. But who knows? I am not in my own country. I could make arrangements, but I may have some problems with access. Somebody with your knowledge and influence..?"

"What are you proposing to do?" asked Francis.

Vanutti held out his hands, palms down.

"Gentlemen, this problem was caused by the Vatican, and we are sorry that you have been so troubled by it. But perhaps it is best that we should take steps to remedy it ourselves, and not bother you with the details. I cannot pretend it will be easy, or comfortable. I am a man of peace, but this situation could be catastrophic to us and our community."

Vanutti's face darkened, with deadly intent. O'Halloran looked at the others, who were shrugging with resignation. After many moments of painful silence, he replied.

"I must agree with you, Carlo. Let us know how we can be of assistance to you. But let us pray, God willing, that this insanity subsides."

Wilson Dallas Plaza Hotel
November 11th 2003 10:30 a.m.

Joseph Steiner walked from the lift into the conference room. Julius, Helen and Andrews sat at the table. Wilson strode up and ushered the man into the room. He stood open-mouthed, looking at Julius. Then to Wilson, and back again. He was in his fifties, wearing designer glasses and the most expensive suit Helen had ever seen. It was obvious he was completely nonplussed, half laughing and shaking his head.

"I don't believe it. I don't know what to say! Sorry, believe me, I'm not normally lost for words! I'm very pleased to meet you – Julius, isn't it?"

Julius nodded, impassively.

Wilson gestured the man towards a seat.

"This is Joseph Steiner, the president of ABC television," said Wilson. "Joe is a friend of mine and I've asked him to give us a briefing on the media situation. Right Joe?"

Steiner suddenly snapped himself into attention.

"That's right Mister Wilson!" He relaxed and spread his hands.

"Look, let's get one thing straight now. This is not 'small' any more. It's huge. Football games are being de-scheduled so the news can run over. The country's going wild. You cannot stay locked up here forever. If the crowds don't break down the

door, sooner or later the government will take action.
That right?"

He glanced across to Wilson questioningly, who
nodded his agreement.

"Somehow," he looked at Julius, "we've got to get
you to speak to the people. Now, what I suggest is a
one-to-one in-depth interview, from here if you
like."

"No!" Helen said. "This is crazy! Don't any of you
realise that this is not what it's about? Cathedrals,
TV preaching? It's nothing like that."

"We're not talking about preaching here, Helen,"
Steiner said. "The public need to know what's
happening. There's panic out there."

"I know what you'll do," said Helen, sneering.
"You'll twist his message to suit your advertisers
and…"

Julius was holding his hand in the air. The
argument subsided. He waited until there was
silence, then spoke quietly.

"Mister Steiner. I agree with you."

"No Julius...don't..." Helen interrupted, but Julius
stilled her with a hand on her arm.

"I am responsible for the panic that you describe. I
can feel it in the atmosphere. People will be hurt if it
continues. I cannot hide. I will speak."

Wilson and Steiner smiled.

"Doctor Andrews," Julius continued. "I think you
are a man of wisdom and learning, and you know the

culture of this country. Please tell me what you would advise."

Andrews thought for a long while. Then, shaking his head, replied.

"I confess I don't know much about all of this," he gestured at Steiner. "I've only met you for the briefest time. If there's one thing I would advise? Speak live. In the open. In front of people."

Julius looked at Steiner. He was shrugging in agreement.

"No problem. We could fill a football stadium. We'd guarantee live coverage, full network."

Julius sat with his eyes closed for a short while. Then opened them. Everybody looked at him in silence. At last he gave a resigned nod of his head.

"I will do it," he said.

One day later

**Kennedy Boulevard, outside the Wilson
Dallas Plaza Hotel
November 12th 2003, 8 a.m.**

"Looks like this is as far as I can get you pal," said
the taxi driver. David looked out of the cab window
at the tree-lined entrance driveway, which forked off
the boulevard in front of the hotel. The whole drive
was thronged with people and vehicles. He looked to
the other side of the road. There were thousands
standing there. Police were trying to keep the traffic
moving along the boulevard.

David paid the driver and walked towards the
hotel, pressing his way through the hundreds of
reporters that hung around waiting. On all sides, TV
teams sat amongst their equipment. Reporters talked
to cameras in various languages. He made his way to
the hotel steps and threaded his way up to the glass
doors. A team of policemen blocked his path.

"Sorry Bud. The Lobby's now closed. If you have
belongings here you can leave a message," said one
of the officers, holding up both his hands.

"Er...I think you'll find that they'll let me in," said
David. The officer was shaking his head. "My
name's Woodbridge. David Woodbridge."

The policeman shrugged his shoulders and went in through the revolving door to check. A reporter came up the steps.

"Excuse me, did you say you're David Woodbridge? Can I ask you a couple of questions please sir?"

There was a buzz of activity in the crowd at the bottom of the steps as they homed in on David with tape recorders at the ready.

"Hey, Woodbridge is here!" "It's him – he's one of the team!" "Hey David! Is it true, have they got Jesus 2 in there?"

David was surrounded by reporters and photographers shouting questions at him. Microphones were thrust past through the forest of arms and into his face. Policemen grabbed his shoulders from behind, shouting at the reporters to move back. Several of them finally managed to create a space in front of the revolving doors and hauled David inside.

The House of Vincente Tardelli
New York City
November 12th 2003

Vanutti's car wound its way up the hillside. The long street was flanked by large plane trees, not quite full with leaves, but still concealing a clear view of the grand houses on either side. Here and there he saw a gap between them, glimpsing the Manhattan skyline in the distance. He stopped and squinted to try and make out a house number, peering through the swirling branches down the long driveway. He drove on up the hill. The very last house at the top was the one he was searching for. Large wrought-iron gates were closed in front of him. He stopped and pressed a button on the intercom.

"Yes?" said a voice.

"Hello this is Cardinal Vanutti. I have an appointment."

"Please proceed to the front door."

The electric gates hummed into life and opened onto a long sweeping gravel road leading up to a large mock Georgian mansion.

As his car passed inside the gate, Vanutti looked around at the sculpted gardens. Small trees interrupted wide expanses of immaculate lawn, with white stone statues nestling beneath them. He turned his head sharply as he saw a man in a black suit watching him, standing with his hand concealed inside his jacket.

Vanutti nodded but the man simply stared back without acknowledging.

The double front doors to the house opened as he stepped out of the car. Vanutti was met by two more men in dark suits and a younger man dressed casually, who stepped forward.

"Good morning, I am Franco Tardelli. Welcome. My father is expecting you."

The two suited men stepped forward and began frisking the Cardinal.

"Please, I am a man of the cloth. I do not carry any weapons," said Vanutti.

"Forgive us Father, this is routine," Franco said. "There are no exceptions." The young man nodded at the two guards as they finished searching, then ushered Vanutti inside.

"The Don will see you now."

They walked into the house through the lavish hallway. The floor was marble, with polished antique furniture and a huge, ornate staircase curving off to the right. Overhead bright chandeliers sparkled in rows. They stopped outside a mahogany door and Franco knocked gently.

Glancing to his left, Vanutti studied a large painting hanging on the wall. It was an impressionist scene of trees and water. A Cezanne. He smiled wryly. Many art experts throughout the world knew this picture, though not where it was located.

The door opened suddenly and Vincente Tardelli strode out. He took Vanutti's hand and shook it vigorously. He glanced around to the painting with a knowing smile.

"Ah. Of course, Father, you are the Vatican's master of antiquities. Did you wonder where this masterpiece had gone?"

"Indeed," said Vanutti. "This is the original?"

Tardelli nodded. "It certainly is. You know I got it at a very reasonable price. How do the Americans say it? It fell off the back of a truck."

The Don and his son laughed loudly as they guided Vanutti into the room.

"Actually, I paid a very great deal of money for it. It was bought from Sotheby's in London three years ago. Anonymously of course. One of my few extravagances."

The three men sat down on a huge leather sofa and Franco poured coffee.

The Don was a small man, simply dressed in black cotton trousers and an open necked white shirt. He had short grey hair, immaculately cut. He sat very still, regarding Vanutti with piercing eyes and an unreadable smile.

"Now what brings such an important man of the Church to the house of Vincente Tardelli?" he said.

Vanutti glanced at Franco and then back to the Don.

"It is rather a delicate matter."

"Please," the older man made an open-handed gesture towards both of them. "My son is present at all of my business meetings. One day he will have to do this all by himself, huh Franco?"

His son shifted uncomfortably. "It will be a long time before that day comes, father."

The Don smiled and nodded.

"Yes, don't worry, I am still smart enough to stay one step ahead of my enemies. We have plenty of time yet."

The Don looked back to Vanutti. "I am sorry Father, continue."

Vanutti nodded. "You must have heard about this religious imposter on television who is claiming to be the Second Coming of Jesus Christ?"

Vincente sighed and shook his head. "It is a bad business. We are used to crazy things on the TV, but this? It is going too far. It is disrespectful. This man is a lunatic, isn't he?"

Vanutti pursed his lips and steeled himself to continue. "Certainly he is mad. But this man is rather more dangerous than he appears. We need to put a stop to his ravings."

Vanutti saw no visible reaction from Tardelli.

The Don finally spoke, menacingly, but still with a light smile on his face. "We, Father? Why do you come to me? What has this to do with us?"

Vanutti's face darkened. He dropped his gaze for a moment and then spoke hesitantly. "We know you have…helped the Catholic Church in the past. And

I'm afraid that the Vatican has had – how can I put it – some part in this man's upbringing."

Once again the Don sat looking at Vanutti in silence. The he nodded, knowingly. "Aha, and now you want to cover up your great mistake, and get us to do your dirty work for you."

Vanutti wondered how much Tardelli knew. There was no way to tell. He had to proceed.

"Exactly. Can you help me in this?"

Vincente paused for one second then smiled slightly.

"Yes we can. We agree with you. This man must be silenced as soon as possible."

Vanutti smiled and sighed with relief. But the Don was holding up his hand.

"But it will cost you three million dollars," he said.

"What?" shouted Vanutti getting to his feet. "You must be joking!"

But the two men remained seated looking at Vanutti.

Vincente's eyes narrowed slightly. He held up both his hands and shook his head.

"This man is now world famous. His demise would be spread across every newspaper printed. We are not talking about eliminating some anonymous drug dealer that has overstepped his territory. This will be as big as the assassination of President Kennedy." Vincente relaxed and half smiled again.

"It is a fair offer. The Vatican has billions of dollars in its accounts. Take it or leave it Father."

Vanutti paused and sat down again. "Very well. I will have to authorise this with the Vatican. But I will need to speak with the man who is to do this. This has to take place in Dallas when Julius speaks at the football stadium."

"The man I have in mind is a true professional. The best. However he is rather a bitter man at the moment. Paulo has suffered some personal tragedy recently. My own limousine was taking his wife and son home. Some criminal scum had got to my car. There was an explosion in my own driveway. I lost a driver. Paulo lost his family. I think he will relish the chance for some...payback."

Vanutti nodded. "Very well. That will be an ideal solution. How can I get in touch with this man?"

The Don replied, "I think it is best that he will get in touch with you Father. Franco, see that we have the Cardinal's contact details before he leaves."

He put an arm around Vanutti's shoulder as they walked towards the door.

"Father, next weekend is the christening of one of my grandchildren. A beautiful little girl. I would be pleased if you could attend? It would be an honour to have such an important religious guest as yourself present."

"I am afraid that I will be in Dallas. Although thank you for the invitation," said Vanutti.

Vincente stopped at the door and opened it for the Cardinal.

"Oh it's not an invitation. I will see you there Father."

The front door closed loudly. Vanutti looked around at the calm gardens, trees waving quietly in the breeze, and at the two black suited men who flanked the porch. He stepped quickly back into his car.

Wilson Dallas Plaza Hotel
Same day

David stepped out of the lift into the quiet, carpeted atmosphere of the hotel penthouse. He saw Helen across the corridor. She was facing one of the huge plate glass windows on the west side, looking downcast as she pressed her forehead against the glass. She paid little attention to the crowd scenes far below.

"Er…hi." He coughed nervously.

She turned around slowly, a look of anger on her face.

"It was you, wasn't it?"

David didn't reply, just flicked his eyes downwards.

"You know," she said, "I thought I could trust you. Why did you do it?"

David could sense that she didn't really want to hear an answer. But he spoke up anyway.

"It wasn't like that. Anyway, it would have broken sooner or later."

"You befriended him with me. You helped to rescue him. If only we could have relied on you we might have had a little more time, before all this…" she waved in irritation at the window "…madness began."

"It's 'we' now is it?" David said, a little dismissively.

She was silent for some moments.

"Are you saying that you still can't feel anything?" she asked. "This is the most important thing that's ever happened. I'm trying to help, to protect him if I can. Why don't you help, instead of talking to those…journalist parasites?"

David shrugged and shook his head. "I don't think I can."

"Look, why don't you talk to him? Relax, give him a chance."

"There's nothing magical about him. He says clever things," David replied. "He's just a man, like me. Before him I had something wonderful and now it's gone."

"That's what this is about, isn't it?" Helen sneered. "Your self-pity. If you can't put that aside for a while, when something so wonderful is happening, you might as well leave."

David looked at her cold expression for a few seconds.

"Yes. Why don't I do that? I'll get my things," David replied, with anger in his voice. He turned and walked away towards his room.

Helen found Julius in an office room at the far end of the floor. He was sitting at a desk, looking at a computer screen.

"Hello," he said, without turning his head. "I am looking at the Internet. I seem to have stirred up a lot of argument." He spun around on the rotating executive chair to face her, with the ever-impassive smile.

She looked away, one of her hands resting against her teeth.

"It's crazy. How could you have agreed to this?" She was on the verge of shouting at him. He didn't reply for some moments. Then spoke calmly.

"You spend quite a lot of your life being angry, do you not?" said Julius.

She looked directly at him, accusingly, and then looked down, unable to confront him directly. Yet she knew what he was referring to.

"Let's just forget David, shall we?" she said, irritated.

Julius leaned forward. "Why don't you let go of your anger? Forgive him."

She shook her head. "He betrayed you. How can you pretend that it didn't happen?"

"Do you think he really wants to hurt me, or you?" Julius asked. "He made an unwise judgement. But have you never done that? I certainly have."

She crossed her arms. "I suppose you can understand Wilson? Or that TV mogul? Or even an evil bastard like Vanutti?" she said sarcastically.

"Helen, please sit down. Let me try to explain something to you."

She sat opposite him, frowning.

"You may think it's strange that I keep trying to talk to you about David. I don't do it because of him. I'm just trying to help you understand. Do you remember I said to you that you have a place inside you that's underneath all that anger. Your soul, if you like?"

She looked down at the carpet, quiet for several moments. "Yeah," she said, quietly, but still upset.

"Well so does everyone. If you go to that inner part of yourself, you will find peace and happiness. But you will also find answers to your questions. Have you ever thought of why that happens? It's because your soul is also a connector. A link to the souls of everyone else, including David, Doctor Andrews, like a vast network. But the trouble is…"

Helen sat, still brooding a little. "What?"

"Well," Julius replied. "On the way down to that place, you pass through your primitive mind, where your raw instincts are, like the greed, anger and violence that your conscience keeps in check. If you get trapped by that place, it will stop you and push you back up. It cuts you off, and when you search your 'self' for guidance, you only hear its terrible preaching rather than the voices from your soul. You asked about Wilson, or Vanutti? They are individual. They have lost their connections. They revel in power over others. Yet they are not evil. They still have that path, down inside, if only they could find it."

Helen looked at her feet. She had tears in her eyes. Julius touched her chin with his hand and lifted her head.

"Helen, if I can't explain it to you, what chance do I have? Yet I have to try. Believe me, I'm not going to go along with any of Myron Wilson's great schemes. I never had any intention of doing so. I'm not going to say what he wants me to. I will say my own words. That's all I can do. I know that many people will reject them, or will try to hurt me in any way they can. Do you still want to help?"

Helen pulled out a tissue and dried her eyes.

"Yes I do," she nodded and the smile returned to her face.

Wilson Dallas Plaza Hotel

November 13th 2003 – 2 a.m.

Julius looked across at the clock on his bedside cabinet and sighed. He could not sleep.

The room was dark and quiet. The only sounds he could hear were the clock ticking; the faint whine of some air-conditioning unit somewhere in the vicinity; a police car siren far below fading into the distance.

He switched on his small bedside lamp and got dressed.

Helen was sleeping on the other side of the room on a sofa, and Julius walked over to her. In the soft light he could see her eyes moving under her lids, she was in a deep sleep.

For a moment he closed his own eyes, smiled and breathed deeply. He gently brushed her hair back away from her face.

The bright lights of the city far below caught his eye and he gazed out through the window down to the streets. Even at this late hour there were thousands of cars, bustling activity and life. He yearned to go out and mingle with it. He was protected and cushioned in this glass tower. But all of his life he had been free to walk under the stars, to explore where he wished. He had no idea about the city below, or its people. He got dressed quickly and quietly slipped out of the room, making for the fire escape stairs. From what he'd heard about journalists (although he'd never met one) and the crowd of them supposedly camped in reception, he thought it wise to avoid the lifts.

The stairwell was dark and cool, almost cold. He did his best to avoid noisy footsteps on the metal staircase, but as he wound down floor after floor, he became less careful. At the bottom of the stairs he saw the door that entered into the reception area. He opened it a crack and peeked through. There were indeed hundreds of people, many sat in groups on the floor. TV camera equipment was dotted around; cigarette smoke hung in the air and used coffee cups stood everywhere. There was one further flight of stairs going down to the garage basement. He went down, pushed the bar on the fire door that opened to the car park at the rear of the hotel, and walked out into the rumble of the city. Reporters stood around in groups here and there, but in the darkness Julius managed to walk unnoticed to the road. A cold breeze blew in between the ranks of TV trucks and cars that were parked in every available space.

Julius pulled his coat closed and started walking.

Away from the hotel, there was nobody on the streets. He wandered along the wide boulevard for a few blocks. The pavement was still wet after a recent shower of rain and reflected the lights of a thousand neon signs advertising bars and cafés. Cars whooshed by anonymously. He smiled a little at the 'Don't Walk' signs that flashed at the junctions, even when there was nothing around. Then he turned off to walk down a smaller street, looking at the brightly lit shop windows. After fifteen minutes or so, all of the buildings around him were smaller and more plainly built than the skyscrapers downtown.

Across the road he saw a construction site, blocked off with a corrugated iron fence. There was a gap in it, just over a foot wide at one end, and he crossed to look. Inside he could see a fire burning, the other side of a mass of rubble and broken steel. He squeezed through the gap and picked his way over the debris towards its warmth.

Two men were sitting in the firelight, leaning against a wall of concrete, the flames lighting up their gaunt faces. They had dishevelled hair and matted beards, streaked with grey. They wore a ragged selection of clothes, including several overcoats on top of one another, all with torn patches. One held a bottle, the other an old beer can. They were both dragging the maximum amount of smoke they could from tiny hand-rolled cigarette stubs. They looked up and grinned at Julius as he approached.

"Hey, buddy," said one of the men.

Julius sat down with them. "May I join you?"

"Only if you got something to share," said the other.

Julius smiled at them. "I have lots to share with you," he said.

The two chuckled to each other, showing gaps in their brown decayed teeth.

"What are your names?" asked Julius.

One of the men thought for a minute, furrowing his brows, swaying a little, then spoke slowly and deliberately. "I am Patrick and this is my wife Charles." The man roared with drunken laughter as Charles pushed him in the chest.

"Don't you take any notice of him sir. Charlie McGrath at your service." He moved his head closer to Julius. His breath stank of industrial spirit.

"Do you have a drop of whisky on your person, or perhaps a cigarette or two?"

"I'm sorry I don't have anything like that," said Julius, "but I would like to talk to you for a while."

Patrick threw away the burning remains of his cigarette stub in disgust. "Talk? What are you, a goddam social worker? Why don't you just butt out, pal," he shouted.

Charles flinched at the sound of Patrick's voice.

"Keep it down." He looked around into the darkness and made an exaggerated calming gesture with his hands. We don't want old Jimbo coming around."

"Who is that?" asked Julius.

Charles shook his head vigorously and pretended to shiver. "Oh you don't wanna be interested in Jimmy," he said. "We don't trouble him none, but then we ain't much use to him. You're a pretty young feller, nice clothes. You got a credit card in your pocket? You don't want to see him."

"Whoever he is, I am not afraid of him," said Julius. "I have come to offer you help," Julius said.

"Help? Hah! We don't need help," shouted Patrick. "You got no booze, then go try your 'help' on Billy over there. Boy, he needs it." Patrick pointed to what Julius had thought was a bundle of rags on the floor, just out of the firelight.

Charles spoke more quietly. "Bill was a pretty boy like you. Jimmy gives him drugs, 'long as he...works, you know?"

Julius stood and walked across to the figure.

Patrick called after him. "If Billy don't last the night there might be a place for you here – on Jimboy's payroll, if you know what I mean!" The two sat back against the cold concrete and went back to their drinks, chuckling to each other.

Julius pulled back the blanket from the man's head and studied the haunted face under him. It was dirty and covered with matted hair. He was perhaps only eighteen or so. Blood stained his chin and the front of his ragged sweater.

"Billy?" said Julius quietly. At first he appeared to be dead. Then his eyelids fluttered and he strained to breathe. His pupils flicked around, as if unsure where he was.

"No...get your hands off...." he said, before his body shuddered with a fit of coughing. There was blood trickling from the corner of his mouth as Julius lifted his head to cradle him in his arms.

Billy screwed up his eyes to try and focus. He saw Julius' face, smiling down at him. Flecks of firelight danced in his crystal blue eyes. "Am I in the hospital?" he whispered. "Are you a doctor?"

"I am a friend," said Julius. "I'm here to take away some of your pain. "

"I'm real sick…" Billy whispered. "Am I gonna die?"

Julius stroked hair away from the man's forehead. "I don't know, Billy. But I won't leave you."

Billy's eyes were dreamy. His frown softened into a small smile of remembering.

"My mom used to take care of me, when I was sick," he croaked. "Just before she died she said that God would always look after me."

"Can you see her now, Billy, in your mind?"

The young man closed his eyes for a moment, then his face hardened into a miserable frown. He opened his eyes again, which seemed distant and full of fear, and shook his head a little.

"My mom's gone. She wouldn't wanna know about me no more. I done so many bad things."

His eyes closed again. The wracked expression faded from his face for a while and his body relaxed into unconsciousness. Then after a few moments his eyes flicked open again. He coughed and sprayed more blood from his mouth. Julius laid his hand across Billy's forehead. "Come with me," he said, his lips mouthing the words almost soundlessly. As Julius' eyes closed, so did Billy's. Julius drew in a large breath and tightened his other arm underneath Billy's shoulders.

"What can you see Billy?"

Billy was silent for a while, then he moaned. A tear ran from one eye.

"Dark rooms," he said, in a frightened whisper. "Shadows of bad people. Things like black spirits, only heavy. Holding me down."

Julius shook his head. "Don't be scared, Billy. Look around. Look up and down. What else do you see?"

Billy's voice suddenly jumped, "There's a light. But it's real far away. Like it's the end of a tunnel maybe."

Julius smiled. "Relax. You're holding on to those bad spirits, don't you see? Let them go. Walk to that light. That's where your mama went!"

Billy's body jerked in panic. "No! I can't see my mom! She won't like me now!" He coughed again, fighting for breath. Julius pulled Billy closer towards him.

"I'll help you Billy! Lean on me," Julius said. "Let me hold those bad spirits for a while. There! Run! It doesn't matter if you've been a bad boy. Your mom won't mind. Don't be afraid of that light. You can go to it if you want."

Julius pressed his eyes more tightly closed, then gritted his teeth, suddenly shivering. He shook his head and moaned as if in pain. Billy's body fought to shake and move as Julius held him. But after a while the movements gradually slowed, then stopped. Billy made no more sound and his limp body slumped in Julius' arms. He laid Billy's head onto the ground. The boy's face was calm and still, with a tiny smile. Julius sat back down on the ground exhausted, his eyes still closed. He hugged himself with his arms, shaking. Gradually he relaxed, taking shivering breaths, until finally he looked up and opened his eyes.

Patrick and Charles edged closer to see.

"Billy?" said Charles stooping down to look, "Has he gone?"

"Yes," said Julius. "He's dead."

"Damn waste," said Patrick, shaking his head. "Poor little guy."

Julius looked bleakly at the other two, as if something had just been wrenched away from his grasp.

"Yes, his life was wasted," Julius said. "He felt so bad. All he ever did was cover his bad feelings, he could never let go of them. I took the weight of his fear for a few moments, a great burden of guilt and shame." Then Julius swept his hands gently away from his body, as if clearing some imaginary objects away from himself. His expression began to change, as if some pain was slowly being relieved, and fading. His calm smile returned. "But he broke free. His spirit let go of all his pain. Like a convict being released and walking in the sunshine. He found his path to God, at last."

The two men both looked at Julius, open-mouthed. "Who are you?"

A loud voice shattered the night. Patrick and Charles both jumped in fright.

"Yeah, Bud, who the hell are you?"

Into the light of the fire stepped a large man, his head shaved except for a small ponytail at the back. He wore a sleeveless denim jacket. His arms were covered in tattoos.

Patrick and Charles retreated into the shadows.

The man strode over to Julius and rolled over Billy's body with his foot.

"Useless piece of scum!" he shouted and kicked the lifeless body. "He owed me!"

The man looked at Julius and took a step closer.

"I said who are you?" His right arm flashed upwards and he held a knife an inch from Julius' throat. Julius said nothing.

"OK buddy," the man said, "let's play it polite. My name is James. You tell me who you are in five seconds or I'll kill you."

Julius looked calmly and steadily into his eyes.

"My name is Julius."

James' knife hand drew away, rotating slowly, but still pointing the blade end at Julius. "Fancy name," he said. "And just what is a nice boy like you doing hanging with this lowlife?" He gestured towards where Patrick and Charles stood, without shifting his stare.

Julius ignored James' reference to the two vagrants. "I'm a friend. I've come to help you."

James looked around to one side, then the other, in a mocking gesture. "Oh really? Seems the main guy that needs help around here right now, is you. What makes you think I need help, pretty boy?"

Julius stood impassively, not moving, looking at James with a gentle smile.

"You prey on the weaknesses of others. You hide your own fear and you make them fear you."

James laughed loudly and then stopped, his face changing into a threatening glare.

"Well," he said, cocking his head to one side, feigning some confusion. "Haven't we got a strange one here?" He straightened his head again, curled his lip and snarled in reply. "I have no idea what sort of college bullshit you're talking, my friend. But I do know that I sure as hell don't like you!"

Julius' face still showed no reaction. "And yet you dislike your own self even more than me. Is that not so?" he said, quietly.

James showed his teeth, almost growling. He stepped backwards and stiffened into an attacking pose, pointing with the blade. "You think I'm scared of you, boy? This is my territory. I run things around here!"

Julius held up his palms in a peaceful gesture. He continued to smile gently, but the steady, serious gaze from his eyes did not waver, even though his head almost imperceptibly shook from side to side. "I do not wish to take anything from you. I have something to give. Why not sit down and talk with me?"

James stared motionless at Julius for several seconds. His right hand, with the knife, instinctively moved up to touch his ear, then back to point at Julius. It was shaking and he clamped his left hand over his wrist.

"What are you?" James shouted.

Julius seemed to think for a minute. Then he said, calmly, "I am a light that is shining inside you, if only you will reach down and look."

"Get out of my head you son of a bitch!" he shouted, then lunged forward, hitting Julius' chest with his right elbow. Julius fell backwards as James stumbled past, tripping over bricks, and shouting in pain as he lurched through the fire.

"I'll kill you, you bastard! I'll kill you!" he shouted as he ran off into the darkness.

As the sounds of James's flight faded into the night, Patrick and Charles scrambled over to Julius and helped him sit up.

"You hurt buddy?" asked Charles.

Julius massaged his ribs, wincing a little as he touched the spot where James had hit him.

"A little," he replied, but took a careful, deep breath and smiled up at the two men. "But not badly. I will be OK."

Patrick was shaking his head in disbelief. "How did you scare Jim like that?" he asked, "I never saw him like that before."

"I did not scare him," said Julius, smiling ruefully. "People scare themselves, when they confront the things they have done. James fights his fear and hate with violence and greed." Julius closed his eyes and hung his head. "He is lost in his darkness. I don't know if he will ever find any peace."

Patrick backed off, sitting miserably on a pile of broken concrete, his head dropping onto his hunched-up knees, shaking from the fear of the encounter with James. "We're all damn well lost," said Patrick despairingly.

Julius opened his eyes, stood up, went over to Patrick and lifted his head. He smiled gently. "No, my friend. You're not so lost. Don't you dream of..." Julius stopped for a moment, just as if he was reading. "...a place where the sun shines, crops and fruit trees grow, and where no one wants more than their little share?"

Patrick looked intently at Julius. "How do you know that?" Then he sighed and looked back down. "Anyway, it's just a dream. Dreams don't get you anything."

Julius was smiling and shaking his head. "How do I know? It's because I have the same dream. Many good things start with a dream. You just have to believe that at least a little part of it could come true."

He looked up at the sky as the first glimmer of dawn appeared in the East.

"I have to go now," Julius said.

"Where are you going?" asked Charles.

Julius stood silent in thought for a few moments. His eyes looked into space for a while, as if he was asking himself the same question. He smiled and shrugged his shoulders.

"I am not absolutely sure," he said. "But I do have to go. There are some important things I need to do."

Julius looked towards the exit in the corrugated iron fence. Patrick was gathering up the few plastic bags that held his belongings. "We're coming with you!" he said.

Julius shook his head.

"Where I have to go, they will not allow you in." He thought for a while and then took off his jacket. "Here, take this. Tomorrow, go to the Dallas Plaza Hotel. I will leave a message for you at the reception desk. This jacket will identify you. You will be able to go to a suite for a while, perhaps a few days. Have some warm showers. Order what you wish to eat."

He looked over at Billy's crumpled body. "Can you see that Billy's body is taken care of?"

"Sure, we'll take care of him," Charles nodded. "Come on Pat," he pulled at the other man's arm.

When they turned back, from straightening Billy's tangled limbs, Julius had gone.

CrossKeys Motel, Dallas
November 13th 2003

Sitting on his bed, Paulo Barelli leaned back against his headboard watching TV. He dialled a number on the telephone, then picked up the remote control, switching from channel to channel.

"...Church leaders have again denied that they have any knowledge of this individual. They say that it is impossible that he could be the reincarnation of..."

"...The Reverend Miller said this afternoon that this was an evil trick and real Christians should not be panicked into..."

"...Coming up in five minutes, we speak to USC professor of genetics, Doctor Harvey Fontaine, who maintains that such a breakthrough would be very unlikely at this time..."

"...TV shows are being cancelled across the US, as coverage switches to the events in Dallas. This afternoon, mystery shrouds 'Jesus 2', as he has been nicknamed, and Myron Wilson, the Texas billionare who is reported to have..."

"Carlo Vanutti? My name is Paulo Barelli. I understand that the transaction has been made to my boss's company. He has asked me to carry out your request. I will meet you at the venue? OK. One hour before. The entrance may be a little difficult."

He listened for a few moments.

"Ah, you have made arrangements then? That is good. I will see you then. Goodbye."

Paulo put down the telephone and continued idly switching channels, showing no interest in any of them. He took another large swallow from a bottle of vodka."

Next Day

Texas Stadium, Dallas
November 14th 2003

Carlo Vanutti stood by the east entrance to the stadium, watching an endless throng of people file in. Everywhere stood people with placards, either condemning or supporting Julius. Small knots of people gathered around preachers, stood on boxes. The setting sun behind the giant stadium complex cast a vast evening shadow over the scene.

He turned as someone tapped on his arm. Paulo was immaculately dressed in a designer suit with dark sunglasses. He wore an unchanging, flat expression.

"Paulo Barelli?" Vanutti asked.

The man simply nodded.

Vanutti smiled weakly at him. "Please accept my deepest sorrow at your loss…"

The man removed his sunglasses and stared, as unemotionally as a shark, into Vanutti's eyes. "Do not even offer, Man of God! I have been to church every Sunday of my life. I encouraged my family to worship God. And this is how He repays me? Explain that to me priest." Paulo almost spat the words at Vanutti.

"I cannot, my son. As you know, we cannot presume to understand why God acts the way he does…"

"Spare me the sermon. I am no longer concerned with God. If this is truly His son, He will find out how it feels having your only child taken away from you."

"Very well," said Vanutti. "You have perhaps forty minutes to be in position. However, you will only shoot if I give you the sign. I will wait for this man to perform some kind of miracle. He deserves one chance. In that case I will give you the signal not to shoot. However, I think that scenario is highly unlikely. I think you will have to kill him."

Paulo stood up to leave. "That will not be a problem."

Vanutti continued. "You must watch for me. I will be at the front of the stadium, down to the left of the stage area. I will give you a sign." He drew his fingers across his neck. "If you see this, you kill him. But if I do this…" he raised his hands, palms flat outwards, "you will not. Do you understand?"

Paulo nodded.

"Very well. I have made arrangements so that you can enter the stadium with your… equipment."

Vanutti looked down at the small holdall that Paulo carried. "Let us go around to the special guests' entrance. We have only thirty minutes."

The roar from the huge crowd at the front was growing louder. Julius sat in a waiting area to the side of the specially built stage, his eyes fixed ahead, silent and still.

"Even now you can stop this, you know," said Helen.

Julius turned his head slowly and smiled at her. "Every strand of fear inside of me is saying the same thing. Right now I wish I were back in my village, laughing in the bar with my old friends. But you know I must do this, don't you? Perhaps never again will I have the ears of the whole world at one time. I cannot pass this opportunity by."

Helen tried to smile, but her eyes flicked back and forth to the stage entrance. She listened to the huge noise from the stadium crowd. She felt sick. "I know. But most of them will expect to see miracles or something extraordinary to be convinced."

Julius sighed. "Then I will show them how to find miracles themselves, how to achieve all that they want, and how to open their own door to God."

Myron Wilson walked over to them.

"It's nearly time," he said. "Helen, do you mind? I'd like to have a few words alone with Julius."

She glared at Wilson, resolutely standing behind Julius with a hand on his shoulder.

But he gently guided her away and spoke quietly to her.

"Don't worry. I will be OK."

Wilson pulled up a chair and spoke, almost in a whisper.

"I...just had some news, from the hospital. The latest tests, they don't look good. I'm asking you...if there's anything you can do. I've not had much time for faith healers, but you, well..."

Julius gripped Wilson firmly on both shoulders, looking him directly in the eyes. He moved his head close and to one side, his mouth within inches of Wilson's ear.

"I cannot cure your disease. If your doctors say you are going to die, then you probably will. I am not your faith healer. You are. Heal yourself! I can feel your soul underneath your fear. It is calling to you – go and meet with it and your fear will fade away."

Julius moved back to look at Wilson's face, open-mouthed, eyes staring.

Julius left Wilson, his head in his hands, and walked towards the stage. The waiting area was dark. A gap in the canvas hangings formed the stage entrance and was illuminated by the brilliant stage spotlights.

Helen came up to Julius' side and took his arm. "I am ready," he said.

Suddenly, just to the right of the entrance, from the shadows, they saw the dark figure of a man, waiting, staring.

Helen started, stifling a scream.

"So. The hour has come," said Carlo Vanutti, menace and threat in his voice.

"Can you prove to these people that you are the reincarnation of Christ?" he spat.

Julius put out an arm, protecting Helen. "We are all a part of God. I am no different to any of the people out there. Why do you seek to harm me?"

"I created you. You are my project. I would stop it like any other that failed." Vanutti's words were venomous.

"You created me to increase your own power, your Church's dominance over its people. You control by fear. You think that if you stop frightening people they will stop giving you their money."

Vanutti's face was becoming red with anger. "If you go out there you will... suffer the consequences."

Julius took hold of both of Vanutti's hands. "I will help them to find for themselves what they are searching for. I could also help *you* to find the truth. Why are you so consumed with bitterness and revenge? Is it a refuge where you run in terror to avoid facing what you have become?"

He gazed deeply into Vanutti's eyes. The Cardinal stared back, the blood draining from his face. He felt as though a flash of light had suddenly appeared and raced through his mind. His heavy eyebrows furrowed as he tried to understand it. He felt warmth spreading through his body.

"I don't believe it!" he muttered to himself. "He *is* the Saviour."

Julius let go of the stunned Cardinal and walked through the entrance. The stadium crowd erupted with a deafening roar.

People surged forward, desperate for a closer view. A man at the front threw down his crutches and jumped in the air. "I can walk!" he shouted. "It's a miracle!"

All around the stadium people called out for cures, for help, for Jesus.

Julius stood alone on the stage in front of a single microphone and raised his hands into the air, palms outstretched.

Gradually the noise subsided, until there was a ghostly silence all around the stadium.

"*I stand before you as a simple human being. As you know, I am a biological copy of the man known as Jesus Christ…*"

Ripples of noise raced around the crowd.

Helen looked around at Vanutti, who was still shaking his head and lost in his thoughts. He too looked up and stared out onto the stage, listening to Julius' words.

"*But I have a new message. Not one that contradicts the principles of forgiveness, charity and faith, but one that only now, after two thousand years of experience, will enable us all to move on and heal the divisions on this planet. Look!*"

He pointed, straight up into the sky. A hundred thousand heads looked to see.

"There are the stars, and planets, and galaxies, the universe... But that is not where you will find God ..."

A wave of panic crossed Vanutti's face. He craned his head around to look up towards the crowds at the back of the stadium.

"No," he whispered to himself. "Not now. This mustn't be stopped."

Helen jabbed at Vanutti's arm. "What?! What are you saying? What have you done?"

"We do not exist because of God! God did not create us. God IS you and I. God exists because of us, as a combination of our souls. A tiny part of God is inside every single person and inside every other living thing on the earth."

"NO!" A sudden cry from Vanutti stunned Helen as he charged forward onto the stage. His eyes sought out the distant position of the gunman, far away at the back of the stadium. Frantically he held his up his hands, palms outward.

Paulo had completed the building of his weapon and raised it in the air.

Vanutti was by now right at the side of Julius. He continued to hold up his hands, slapping his palms back and forward in the air, as if he were beating at a door.

"No! No! Do not fire! Stop!"

At the back of the stadium Paulo fixed the crosshairs of his telescopic sight on the chest of Julius, ignoring the frantic signs from Vanutti.

"For you, Claudia and Gino!" he said and squeezed the trigger.

Vanutti leapt in front of Julius. The high velocity bullet ripped through his chest as the crowd screamed in shock. Vanutti stumbled and clutched at his heart, blood pumping through his fingers. He fell to his knees and turned to face Julius.

"Please forgive me. For all my sins."

Julius looked down at the stricken Cardinal, sunk to his knees and caressed the man's head, smiling. He spoke, his voice hoarse and faltering.

"Have no fear to die. You are leaving the darkness behind you!"

Julius coughed violently. He struggled to continue.

"Together…we will go to God's house."

Vanutti's life was ebbing away. He looked up puzzled at Julius. "Together?"

Vanutti followed his eyes as Julius looked down at his white shirt. A large red stain was growing bigger every second from the bullet that had passed straight through Vanutti.

The Cardinal slipped to the ground, his head coming to rest between the knees of Julius.

Vanutti looked up through eyes full of tears. "What have we done?" he whispered as he took his last breath.

The crowd suddenly went hysterical. Some trying to run away, others trying to get to the stage in panic. Officials shouted at each other from the shelter of the wings of the stage.

High in the arena, people drew away in terror from Paulo, who threw down the rifle and pulled a pistol from his jacket.

"Damn you all!" he shouted.

He drew the gun up to his temple, fired a single shot, and collapsed onto the concrete steps.

Helen ran towards Julius and Vanutti. She got to her knees and cradled the head of Julius in her arms. "What am I to do now?" she said through heavy sobs. Julius made a last effort to turn his head and looked at Helen, forcing words from his mouth.

"You know already."

His eyes began to glaze.

"Mother. Where are you mother?" he said.

Overhead, sudden clouds blocked the stars. As Julius' life ended, a loud thunderbolt erupted, adding to the chaos. People cried in fear, shouting that God was about to take His revenge. Helen blinked away tears that fell onto the brow of Julius, and noticed more drops appearing on his head. A soft gentle rain was falling. Lights appeared in the sky, and moved across the width of the stadium. More ripples of sound flashed around the crowd as many pointed upwards, listening to the buzzing noise getting ever louder. After a few moments it was clearly visible. A medical helicopter was descending into the stadium.

Helen walked away from the west entrance, her hair dripping around her ears, her clothes soaked with water and blood. As if sleepwalking, she passed through the crowds of people, some distraught, some arguing. Sobbing children were being comforted by parents who looked at each other with disbelief and fear.

She carried on through the huge car park towards the picnic areas at the edge of the stadium complex, dark trees standing tall along the border, waving in the wind.

"Helen." A gentle voice called her from ten yards to her right.

She stopped, still staring straight ahead.

David walked slowly up to her, took off his coat and placed it around her shoulders.

She lowered her head without looking at him.

"I thought you'd gone," she said in a flat voice.

"I was in the crowd," he said. "I...well somehow I had to see it."

She stood still, arms at her sides, defeated.

"Well it's all over. You saw what happened. It's finished," she said.

"Why?" David asked quietly.

Helen raised her head and looked at him.

"Why what?"

"Well," said David. "I...sort of liked what he said. Somehow it all seemed to make sense. Don't you remember, he said he was just a simple human being? Couldn't any simple humans spread the same message?"

Helen crossed her arms and shivered.

"David, I don't think I would have the strength."

He touched her arm, very lightly. "You have more strength than anyone I know. I...I can feel it." He smiled gently. She looked at him, puzzled, waiting.

"You absorbed Julius' message more naturally than anyone. You can't ignore it," he said. "Somehow you have to pass it on. And I know I don't really deserve to be your friend anymore, but I thought...if you needed some help?"

Helen's eyes pressed tight shut. She began to cry. Her head fell against David's shoulder. She sobbed for a minute then gradually raised her head, wiping tears away with her wet hands.

"What should we do? How do we start?" she asked, smiling gently for the first time.

"Dry clothes, I think," said David, smiling broadly too.

She took his arm and together they walked into the dark canopy under the trees.

Three months later

Ohio State University, USA
February 22nd 2004

Helen slept fitfully alone in her bed. She tossed and turned, unable to fall completely asleep, events of the day playing on her mind.

She had attended the funeral of Myron Wilson, whose cancer had finally won the war against his body, despite the battle he fought so ferociously to delay the inevitable.

Her mood had slipped back to despair, the sombre proceedings reminding her of the events of three months ago. Only her determined work with David to further the beliefs of Julius had kept her depression at bay.

She stirred and realised that she was awake again. Something made her open her eyes wide – a sense that she was being watched. The room was dark but she looked around with eyes wide. There was a figure standing at the foot of her bed, gazing at her face.

She caught her breath. Sat upright in bed.

"Julius?" she whispered, trying to make sense of the vision before her.

The unshaven face of Julius became clearer as she stared.

"Julius please!" she whimpered and outstretched an arm towards him.

The shape looking at her very slowly began to dissipate, fading to grey and dissolving in front of her eyes.

"No please wait!" she cried but he had gone. She started looking around frantically, waiting for another sign, but it was hopeless. The room remained quiet and empty.

Hours later she was still sobbing onto her soaked pillow, Julius's face still clear in her mind. There was a slight fluttering sensation in her tummy. She reached down and gently stroked the skin.

"There, there," she cooed at the unborn child inside her.